I0551677

To Toni Rakestraw of the editorial service, Rakestraw Book Design, for the work and patience she has demonstrated editing my stories. If you find any errors, the fault lies with the author.

To my fellow scribes at the Bucks County PA Writers Group and the Writer's Coffeehouse for the support they've given me putting together this anthology.

To Teresa Tunaley for her work on the cover.

To Michael, as always, with love.

City of Brotherly Death

Vampires, Revenants, and Zombies from Philadelphia

Barbara Custer

Night to Dawn Magazine & Books

ISBN: 978-1-937769-15-4
Cover Illustration: Teresa Tunaley
Illustrations on pages 96 and 110: Teresa Tunaley
Other interior art: Dreamstime
Editor for "The Lowly Workers": Scribendi
Editor for "A Lesson on Suffering": Ginger Johnson
Editor for remaining tales: Toni Rakestraw
All rights reserved.

Night to Dawn Magazine & Books
P. O. Box 643
Abington, PA 19001
www.bloodredshadow.com

First Edition, printed in the United States of America

Contents

Introduction

The train has arrived, and we're boarding. Destination: City of Brotherly Death. Here's hoping you brought your gun, and that you can execute a head shot. You'll be meeting a lot of revenants and zombies, and only a shot to the head will stop them. If you don't know weapons, you might have to get creative the way the characters in the upcoming stories have had to do to survive. Even vampires fear them, and Philadelphia is a popular city for the undead among the tourists.

"Sunset Kill" is the name Cathy gives a nursing home where the mistreatment of residents leaves many of them dead. The dead residents return to complete unfinished business with the nursing home staff, ugly business that involves bloodshed. To survive, Cathy brokers a deal with them.

People starve to death on Philadelphia's streets in "One Last Favor" because of overpopulation. Angry with a government that withheld medical treatment and benefits, the revenants—reanimated corpses who come back to harm the living—rise up to go after the ones they blame for their problems. The leader Kraven captures Tara, a nurse, and she is forced to trade sex with him for her life (the "one last favor" he requests). While the undead society grows and turns humans, using an ancient spell, Tara has his baby. Her child is kidnapped, and years later returns as a monster to confront her mother.

Frank Mazer, a crotchety manager, terrorizes his department, "the lowly workers," with his rules. His staff, through contact with a god, acquires the ability to change into walking mummified corpses at will. Mazer becomes their first victim.

All of the stories involve people who return from the dead to terrorize their abusers, but in "The Lowly Workers," Mazer's employees do not actually die. They go through a change. In these stories and others, the dead have the mission of terrorizing humans. The revenants and zombies of

1

"One Last Favor" whittle down the population, resulting in a zombie Apocalypse. The "Sunset Kill" dead consider Cathy their "friend" and try to avoid harming innocents. That doesn't make them any less hungry or dangerous. The monsters "the lowly workers" become destroy Mazer with psychological torture.

My introduction to people who don't stay dead happened when I was ten. My mother and I were walking the Boardwalk in Atlantic City. She'd stopped in a store while I checked out the amusements. A sign to this effect caught my eye: "1,000-year-old woman perfectly preserved." Curious kid that I was, I followed the crowd to a platform surrounded by black curtains. I expected to see a well-nourished but aged woman. Instead, a skeletal figure, dead for centuries, lay in a stone tub (I later learned that it was a sarcophagus). As I looked, the woman sat up and extended her skeleton hand toward the crowd. Screaming, I barreled into my mother's arms. Part of me realizes that some electrical gadget caused the woman to move, but another part of me isn't so sure. Hence, my interest in mummies, zombies, and other undead.

The train has stopped; we've arrived at the City of Brotherly Death. Take my hand, and I shall lead you on the tour.

Alexis

1820. When I think of time, I shudder at the agony each eternal second holds for me. Years ago, when my quest for love led me to Undeath, I learned that loneliness can have wretched consequences. This last year served as a forceful reminder. I once fantasized about immortal bliss; but now, only bittersweet memories remain to remind me of a happiness that I will never know again. I dare not attempt self-destruction because the fire of Hell awaits me.

Each night, as I prowl the streets for nourishment, I wonder how things went so wrong. How and why I came to feel what I did for Alexis I will not attempt to explain. I will say that when I assumed guardianship of Alexis, I had the noblest intentions.

I first met Alexis eight years ago when I was riding through the glens. I found her sprawled, unconscious, in the grass. One bound, and I stood at her feet. She stirred at my touch and thick curls the color of rose madder fell from her parchment face. Her blue eyes, glazed with tears, looked up at mine.

People like me can read humans, and her thoughts gave me the biography of a ten-year-old who lived with her father. Her mother died of consumption three years ago. Her father doled out whippings at the slightest provocation, and his recent ministrations left broken ribs. Her heart beckoned to me, stirring my thirst, but I ignored its call. Looking at Alexis reminded me of my own father, whose wooden rod had left bruises and scars.

"You needn't be afraid," I said, touching her cheek. "Where does it hurt?"

Alexis let out fright-filled sobs. With trembling hands, she gestured toward her bare feet.

I gingerly lifted her coat dress and petticoat, raising a curtain from the blisters and sores that exuded a virulent odor. "Alexis, I'm taking you to a hospital," I said quietly.

"How do you know my name? Am I going to die?"

"The doctors there will notify your father," I said, evading her questions. "Where do you live?"

Alexis shook her head, sobbing. "My mother said I should never trust strangers. Why are you doing this?"

"Because I, too, was afraid of my father. I can read your fear by the look on your face." I smiled a tight-lipped smile. "If you let me help you, I'll take you to my own doctor. He knows how to keep secrets."

Alexis looked up at me intently, rubbing her arms and shivering. "Please do," she said. "Thank you, Mr..."

"Edric." I smiled again. "No need for formalities."

At first, incipient infection and fevers rendered Alexis' nights uneasy. In her disturbed state, she rambled about her mother's death and her father's disciplinary measures. She said that the Amontillado her father drank brought out his dark and evil moods. He'd never hurt anyone again, though. I had insured this by draining him dry and burying his remains in the catacombs adjacent to my cellar. His drunken outbursts had not endeared him to his neighbors, so no one questioned his whereabouts.

Least of all, Alexis.

After Alexis recovered, I assumed guardianship through my lawyer. The adoption process moved swiftly since Alexis had no living relatives. Though nightmares about her father continued to haunt Alexis, caring for her was a joy I would have never willingly relinquished. I hired a tutor to look after her during the day while I slept. When Alexis ask me why I only kept night hours, I explained that I had a skin disease which made me sensitive to sunlight.

At night, Alexis and I spent hours in the study. She posed on the settee while I, with brush and oils, sought to recreate her beauty in every detail. I loved Alexis more than any guardian could—*or should*. As time ushered Alexis into her teenage years, my affinities for her only grew.

My father—God rest his miserable soul—left behind an endowment which provided enough money to pay Alexis' tutors and other expenses. Our three-story flagstone house boasted twenty rooms, each furnished with embroidered chairs, gold-weave carpets, and silver candelabra. My heart saddened when I realized that one day, Alexis would age and die like all humans. At first, I attempted to immortalize her on canvas. It's difficult to explain, but Alexis commanded, as no other human, the power to reach into my soul. Her beauty glowed like an invisible, but inextinguishable, flame. I worked each night, trying to capture this essence in my portraits until my parlor became a virtual gallery.

Her nightmares persisted, defying the knowledge of our most learned physicians. Her tutor suggested that outings with companions her age would remedy the situation. Unfortunately, my estate was surrounded by an expanse of unexplored trees and valleys. I decided to compensate by showering her with love and attention.

Our nearest neighbor, Stephen, in Marsh, lived a league distant. Sometimes, I would see him at the town market. He seemed agreeable, soft-spoken, though nondescript in appearance. Therefore, I was surprised when Alexis burst into my study one evening to describe her chance meeting with him. She talked about him at length, raving about his looks and demeanor. She even suggested that she and Stephen might become friends. This sudden infatuation struck me as odd, but I assumed that the novelty would fade. Even when he began visiting two, three, and sometimes four times a week, I saw no reason for concern.

The disquiet I felt turned to anger when I overheard their voices in the study. Given my keen senses, I could hear distant conversations as if they were taking place in my middle ear.

"Edric doesn't seem to like me," Stephen said. "He barely acknowledges my greetings."

"Maybe he's not feeling well," Alexis said.

"He looks like a ghost. Why does he sleep all day?"

"He's got a disease which makes his skin so fragile that sunlight causes blisters."

"I see." A profound silence followed, and then he asked, "When does he eat? He never joins us at dinner."

Dark tumors of rage threatened to choke me. How dare Stephen question my personal habits? Somewhere amid the red haze of fury, I heard Alexis' muffled voice say she didn't know.

"Maybe he suffers from vampirism," Steven said gravely. "At the village market, I've heard some bone-chilling recitals of mysterious deaths in your woods. Last week, the constable found two bruised, bloodied corpses."

Alexis gasped. "Do you think Edric killed those people?"

"Maybe wolves attacked them." Stephen sighed. "Their throats had teeth marks. Be careful, Alexis."

There was another remarkable silence, followed by gentle footfalls. "Edric's behavior seems odd," she allowed, "but I can't imagine him feeding on people."

"Even monsters can dress as lambs," Stephen said. "Did you know that vampires use hypnosis to conceal their ghastly habits? After feeding, they hypnotize their victims into forgetting."

"But Edric never..."

In a frenzy of wrath, I slammed open the door and stormed into the study, shuddering at the sudden craving. "You miserable cur!" I shouted, waving my fists. "You know nothing about me to make such accusations."

I expected Stephen to quake in his boots and faint. Instead, he turned toward me, brandishing a wooden crucifix.

"Oh, indeed," he said coolly.

"Indeed, yes." I yanked the crucifix from his hand and hurled it into the fireplace.

Stephen let out a long, loud scream. He didn't know that the tale about vampires and religious objects was a superstition. His self-assured pomposity fled, replaced by a deadly pallor.

"You've misjudged me, Stephen." My eyes bore into his like heated coals. "I suggest you leave now."

A blank look stole upon his face. "I suppose I will," he said meekly. "Alexis, I will see you tomorrow."

After Stephen quit the study, Alexis stood facing me. Her red eyes glittered with unbridled fury. "Why did you send him away? Stephen loves me. He's worried about me."

"Worried?" I grimaced. "He's spreading lies about me."

"Your moodiness gave him a bad impression," she said hotly.

"But I saved you." My voice hitched as I fought a sudden onslaught of tears. "I love you, Alexis."

Alexis lowered her head. "I know you do," she conceded, her voice softening. "I will always be grateful for you rescuing me from my father. But I must move on."

"Not with Stephen," I said in a measured, quiet voice. "I forbid you to see him."

"Just answer me this. Why do you fear sunlight? We both know you don't have any skin disease."

In the eight years I'd lived with Alexis, I never raised my hand or voice against her. But that night, I slapped her hard across her face. Tears flowed from her puzzled eyes. Sobbing, she raced to her room and bolted the door behind her.

I stood outside her room for several hours, knocking on her door and pleading with her to talk to me. Contrary to popular belief, vampires

6

cannot walk through walls. My tears and words had no effect. She threatened to destroy me.

My bloodlust soon got the better of me, and I went outside to hunt. That night, I killed relentlessly, but nothing could assuage my thirst. I thought of hypnotizing Alexis into submission, but I wanted her to love me, *willingly*.

When the rosy fingers of dawn streaked the sky, I hurried to my secret room in the wine cellar. I kept thinking about the sudden antipathy that Alexis seemed to feel toward me. I told myself that childhood memories still troubled her, but we'd never argued until she met Stephen. Stephen, whom I'd once considered *agreeable*, ruined our relationship.

A phantom voice whispered that Stephen was a pestilence, a disease that had invaded the haven I'd work so hard to achieve. I licked my lips, trying to ease the burning thirst. The shadowy voice urged me to feed on Stephen, imparting a taste of the pain that he'd brought me. I would have done so, if day sleep hadn't overtaken me.

I remember little about the weeks following that first set-to; only the bloodlust and loneliness that became my sole intimates. My relationship with Alexis deteriorated beyond repair. Our nights together in the study had become distant memories. She openly defied me, coming and going at will, never speaking unless I approached her first.

I rarely had cause to approach her; my admonitions, after all, would fall on deaf ears. Rather, I sought to allay my grief on the warm, sweet sensation of *fresh blood*. The catacombs that adjoined my cellar soon filled with scores of kills. The hours blurred into nights, and the nights into weeks. My better mind tried to warn me of the self-destructive path I had taken.

If only I had listened.

The night Alexis died began as any other. Though I had just fed, my throat burned with a piercing intensity. I sat by the fireplace, staring at my unread book. Alexis stepped into the parlor, wearing her blue coat dress. She was carrying a matching parasol and her leather purse. Despite my thirst, I managed to collect my thoughts. "Where are you going?" I asked, forcing calmness into my voice.

Alexis stopped by the fireplace, a fist pressed against her trembling lips. "I'm leaving, Edric. I was going to wait until noon, and leave you a note, but I decided it best if I go now."

"Go? Where?" Hugging my cloak around me, I started toward Alexis.

"Stephen has proposed to me, and I've accepted," she said quietly. "His uncle owns a steak house in Philadelphia. We will leave tomorrow. I will send for my belongings after we settle."

I thought that nothing could surprise me, but Alexis' words left me speechless. I stood there, stunned silent, shivering like a condemned man. "You can't leave me," I managed to say, my voice quaking. "How will I live without you?"

"You're not living now, Edric. Your human side has died, leaving only a husk." Her voice wavered, and her eyes brightened ominously. "We should go our separate ways. I have my own life to live, my dreams..."

"The hell with your dreams!" Overcome with dark throes of hate, I hurled my book into the fire. "What about my dreams? Do you even care?"

Alexis' cheeks reddened, and her eyes flashed with that same anger I'd seen these last weeks. "I am not your property. You don't love me, Edric. You're not even capable of loving. At least Stephen loves me."

She turned and started toward the door.

"So he really cares about you," I said softly.

Alexis sighed. "I didn't make my decision lightly."

"Of course, you didn't." I smiled sardonically. "Let's see if he still loves you at sunset."

Having forgotten the love which had hitherto stayed my bloodlust, I seized Alexis, thrashing and kicking, and sank my teeth into her throat. Her warmth blossomed inside my stomach. When her struggles ceased, I tore a gash into my right arm. Left hand grabbing her hair, I press my wounded arm against her lips and forced her to drink.

I then scooped Alexis into my arms and proceeded to her bedroom. She did not stir, even when I laid her on the bed. "There," I said, smiling. "You'll never leave me now."

No matter what humanity thinks, people like me have a code of honor. Years ago, when a love interest led me to Undeath, I promised to follow civilization's mores to the extent that my needs would permit me. Alas, the bloodlust provides little freedom. Sometimes, it roars like a dragon, destroying everyone in its wake, including the one person who'd ever loved me.

I retrieved Alexis' parasol and bag, and laid them on her bureau. After I sealed her windows, I shuffled to my chamber, head lowered and shoulders drooping. Before settling into my day sleep, I lay in bed, peering at the darkness, shuddering at the shadows alive with every specter.

When I woke at sunset, I recalled the previous night's events with a hellish clarity. Two overturned chairs and the carpet, now speckled with her blood, served as painful reminders. The despair weighed on me so that I barely made it up the stairs.

After stumbling to Alexis' room, I knocked on the door and called her name. She did not answer. Thinking that she might have already awakened and fled, disoriented, to the woods, I rushed into her room.

No words could describe the horror I felt when I gazed at Alexis. She lay on the floor, facing the door, impaled on her parasol's silver tip. One arm folded over her chest, fingers curled around the parasol. The other rested in a pool of blood. Most vampires initially experience vertigo and confusion after the change, and I believe such was the case with Alexis. I imagined Alexis in her agitated state, lurching to the door with her parasol and stumbling. The sight of her body, mottled and purple, would haunt me forever. Screaming, I ran down the stairs, fully intending to leave the house, when forceful knocking sounded at the front door.

"Alexis?" called Stephen's voice.

I sagged against the wall, shaking uncontrollably. Skeletal fingers of terror clutched my spine, twisting until I thought I'd scream.

"Alexis?" Stephen called again, this time more urgently. "Are you all right?"

What should I do? If Stephen saw the blood on the carpet, he'd suspect foul play. I'd have to hypnotize him into forgetting, maybe even kill him. Could I do it?

With a deep sigh of relief, I decided that I could. I'd start by faking horror over Alexis' disappearance, and...

The knocking faded, replaced by the thudding of boots against dirt. When I peeked between the drapes, I saw Stephen running toward his horse. "Wait!" I called, bursting outside.

Stephen whirled, facing me. "Where's Alexis?"

"She left hours ago," I said, feigning surprise. "She said that you were going to marry and move to Philadelphia."

"That was the plan." His voice softened, but he gave me a wary look. Understanding dawned when I probed his thoughts. He had planned to meet Alexis at the town market, but she'd never showed.

"That's right." I stared intently into his eyes. "She's taken her horse..."

"She shouldn't have gone anywhere alone!" Stephen cried, waving his fists. His eyes focused on the bloodstained carpet without seeing it. "Maybe some bandit kidnapped her."

"You don't know that," I said. "Let me pour you some Amontillado. A drink will clear your head."

"No!" Stephen recoiled several paces. "The longer we wait, the more likely harm will befall her."

9

"I must insist." I gazed into his eyes, using my left arm to steer him toward the wine cellar.

"The Amontillado." He wagged his head feebly. "Why are we going to your cellar? We should look for Alexis."

"We will," I said, ushering him down the moldy steps. "It's cold outside. We should warm ourselves before searching."

At the landing, Stephen stepped unsteadily forward, while I followed at his heels. After shoving him against the granite wall, I tore into his throat. He was too astounded to resist. I licked and swallowed, savoring the sweet taste that blossomed warm inside me. After he collapsed to the floor, I stepped away from the wall.

"I enjoyed my drink," I said, licking my lips. "Maybe you can help me find Alexis. No? Then I must leave you. But first, I will render you all the little attentions at my disposal."

Stephen did not answer. He was unconscious.

After hauling Stephen over my shoulders, I proceeded to the most remote end of the catacombs. The crypt there was filled with decomposing leftovers from previous dinners. The foul stench brought tears to my eyes. At my left, the skeletons lay upon the earth, forming a mound six feet high. I laid Stephen beside the skeletons, and then sealed the crypt with mortar and sand.

Knowing that the police would question Stephen's disappearance, I composed a letter to his uncle, forging Alexis' handwriting, saying that the couple planned to travel for a year before settling in Philadelphia. To back up my story, I led their horses, fully saddled, deep into the woods and freed them to roam at will.

Finally, Alexis' burial. I did not consider the catacombs worthy of Alexis. Instead, I procured a wooden coffin and buried her in our rose garden. Despite the liquid fear cruising through my veins, I found this task so loathsome that I could not get through it without feeding on wildlife. I finished my work before sunrise.

The next evening, knocking sounded at the door again. This time, the constable greeted me.

He seemed rather shocked by the genial way I answered his questions. I offered him tea cakes and Amontillado. After producing the letter, I explained that Alexis and Stephen had planned to travel west. He read the letter thoughtfully, thanked me for my time, and then hurried outside to his carriage.

A search revealed the horses, but no bodies. The officers presumed that the couple was shot by bandits, and they closed the case.

No doubt, you will fancy me a monster—you, who sit smugly wrapped in your invisible blankets of hypocritical humanity. I daresay that any of you, had you experienced first-hand the craving, would have behaved in the same manner. I've always loved Alexis, and I always will. *But I was terrified*—not only of the police, but of the toll that dwelling on her death would take on me. I took no pleasure in burning her paintings and other personal possessions. To assuage my guilt, I had to destroy everything that reminded me of her death.

As the night passed, a strange sense of serenity came over me. When I wasn't hunting, I sat in my study, reposing before a fire and reading my favorite books. The events of the last few weeks took on a dream-like quality. I started to believe my lies. The house lay quiet, except for the crackling flames and the occasional hoot of an owl. The dark moods that plagued me had vanished, and I thought that this new peace might last forever.

Certainly longer than a fortnight.

Two weeks after the police concluded their investigation, I found Alexis' portrait, the one with the wooden frame, hanging in my study over the fireplace mantle. How did it get there, I wondered? While searching the room, I noticed that my easel cast a shadow in relation to the room's only window, adequate enough to conceal the portrait. Perhaps in my haste to dispose of her belongings, I'd passed that one by. While the shadow explained the portrait's presence, unease coated my stomach. I couldn't help noticing how life-like her features looked, especially her blue eyes. *How then, could I have forgotten it?*

With a deep sigh, I tossed it into the fire.

I'd all but forgotten about the portrait until the next evening, when I found another hanging from the same wall. This time, utter terror speared me, causing me to shake.

I stared at it for a long time, frozen, my mouth opening and closing. When I'd gotten hold of myself, I unhinged the painting for a closer look. It amused me to think how the first portrait had startled me. In this one, blood was dripping down her face and onto the wooden frame. Screaming, I flung the portrait against the wall. Blood splattered across the carpet. Using a towel, I grabbed the portrait and threw it into the fire.

Despite a craving for blood-induced peace, I resisted, knowing that I'd need a clear head to solve this mystery. I couldn't assume that I'd overlooked these two portraits. One, perhaps, but not two. How did they come to exist? How did I find them in my study?

Maybe Stephen had warned the townsfolk about me. Maybe one of his kinsmen had ridden to my house the night Alexis died and heard her screams. Maybe I didn't want to know the origin of those two portraits. The wary look in the constable's eyes warned that he held me suspect.

But none of those theories made sense. If the constable and townsfolk knew about my Undeath, why didn't they stake me and be done with it? Perhaps they considered death too kind and decided to drive me insane instead? Face it, dear reader; Stephen despised me from the beginning. His friends considered my kind loathsome. Upon hearing about Stephen's disappearance, they would exact their own brand of punishment.

It did not surprise me to find a third painting awaiting me the following evening—any more than it did to find a fourth, a fifth... and a sixth. I always thought I'd catch the miscreant, but each time my eyes discovered a newer, more grisly portrait, my hope waned. I reveled in the thrill of the kill, though I knew that indiscreet hunting would invite discovery. I kept pacing at night until my legs collapsed. I bought combination locks for all the doors, set traps by the door to my chamber, and prayed that I would one day confront my assailant.

No one could understand the dread I felt when the shadows grew long, and my throat grew dry, and I quivered with the thought of the forthcoming nightmares my mind would accrue from the sight of another portrait.

Only this time, nothing hung over the fireplace mantle.

A breeze wafted through the room, chill and strong with the smell of rotting tomatoes. The candles which had earlier illuminated the room were no longer burning, but my senses enabled me to see as if it were daylight. No portrait hung over the mantle. I let out a deep sigh, feeling relieved that I hadn't found anything, and alarmed because I suspected that I'd gotten to the fireplace before my enemy could strike.

Then a chilling draft caressed my cheek. Turning toward the window, I found it open, the biting wind slapping against the drapes. As I peered outside, I noticed the lattice which extended from the house's foundation to the window. *The lattice!* Why hadn't I noticed it before? The perpetrator of these crimes against me had used the lattice to gain entry to my study and deposit the portraits.

Grabbing my cloak, I bolted to the garden behind the house. The moon cast ghostly shadows on footprints in the moist soil. I found mud on the lattice—brown stains left by his hands and feet, which covered the white wood to my window ledge.

I gazed toward the surrounding woods, but I only made out gnarled trees and moonlit sky. The howling wind blustered through the trees, causing them to scrape against the house. Perhaps my assailant had forgotten something and had gone to retrieve it. In case he returned, I planned to be ready for him. My mouth salivated at the prospect of fresh blood. I proceeded toward the stable, which would give me a clear view of the house and gardens. Then...

In the few minutes that I'd left my study, clouds swept across the sky, blanketing the moon, and shrouding me in darkness. I crept toward the stable—little more than a shadow, black as tar against the bruise-colored sky.

The sky grew pitch black as I approached. The temperature seemed to drop, its chill sending shivers up my spine. A foul odor reeking of things long dead crept down my lungs like smoke. It took all the willpower I could muster to concentrate on the matter at hand, but I couldn't shake this sudden feeling of doom. Though I only saw rose bushes, trees, and sky, I felt eyes, icy and penetrating, drill into the back of my neck. My thoughts ran wild; my imagination burned like a raging fire.

Screaming, I dashed to the stable, but I didn't quite make it.

Three steps, and then I tumbled into a deep pit.

Though I know now that greater horrors exist, nothing could have convinced me as I lay sprawled in an open casket, worms crawling over my hands and face. Screams came and died in my throat. The smell of putrefaction was unbearable. If I were human, I would have died of fright.

My hand brushed against the casket's upturned lid, and I felt long, irregular grooves etched into the wood. At the moment, this didn't seem important; only getting out intact mattered. After scrambling to the surface, I calmed myself. For the first time, I noticed the full moon and the golden shadows it cast throughout the gardens.

I'd dug that grave myself. The marks in the wood were not imperfections; Alexis had made them when she regained consciousness and clawed her way to the surface.

In my panic, I'd buried my beloved alive. Or perhaps undead.

Finding Alexis' grave defiled did not horrify or even surprise me. The discovery of her portraits had prepared me for this event. But tonight, I expect to find something far more ghastly in my house.

I wasn't disappointed.

In my study, I gagged on the stench of flyblown meat. There, in the gloom, I paused by the door, hand reaching for a candle. I felt those eyes on me again. Terror speared me, urging me to run, but something about those eyes compelled me to stay.

After I lit the candles, I turned toward the fireplace and there beheld the truest and final portrait of Alexis.

Alexis herself.

In the midst of all my theorizing, I never accused the one with the greatest motive and ability to hurt me. Alexis knew best how to bring my fears to the surface. She knew me better than I knew myself.

Consider me mad, but Alexis did not truly die. Though her body has putrefied, her spirit, her individuality—whatever power makes us all so different and distinct—survives. I can feel her spirit reaching out to me, probing the dim recesses of my mind. I cannot help but laugh bitterly when I think of the way I'd tried to make her undead. Alexis will live forever after all, and she has chosen to share her immortality with me.

She is calling me now, and I must answer. If only someone could hear as I hear her voice that chills my senses and makes my blood run cold. I have not rested easy since Alexis returned, and I don't believe I'll ever rest easy again. Even my vampire day sleep eludes me while I lie with her in my chamber, staring into her eyes, and knowing that she, through moldering eye sockets, is staring back.

Darkness Rising

With trembling fingers, Brianna Sandor wedged four Mylar balloons around her pillow, determined to obliterate the image of the blackened skull that haunted her. For a week now, in her dreams, she saw herself tied to a burning tree, flesh falling away from her face in charcoal tufts. In the distance, a milk-pale young man in gray watched her from the shadows.

Since her brother, Alec, had gone on a business trip, Brianna faced her nightmares alone. Though she couldn't see the glittering designs, she hoped that the feel of the balloons on her face and their soft shushing sounds would offer a refuge.

As Brianna eased into bed, the balloons rubbed against her head. Their swishing sounded like ocean waves. From the depths of that sound, Brianna heard a man's silvery voice.

"Brianna." The voice brought her to slow consciousness. "Brianna, my love. Brianna."

The shushing sounds faded, and Brianna found herself in a hall lit by torches. Their hissing sounded like helium escaping from the balloons. A portrait hung before her—her portrait, she noted with surprise. Curly blond hair, caught in a bow, and chestnut eyes. In the painting, she wore a gray homespun overdress and cream under-tunic that complemented her smooth complexion.

At the end of the stone hall, the torches revealed two open caskets. A blond man lay inside one, appearing to be asleep. In the other, she saw herself prone, face covered with blood. Brianna screamed until shrill ringing cut into her cries. The images evaporated, leaving behind her familiar bedroom furniture. Her lamp reflected the bright balloons bobbing around her.

The harsh ringing came from her bedside phone. With shaking hands, she snatched up the receiver.

"Brianna Sandor?" questioned a female voice. "Your brother, Alec, gave me this number in case of an emergency..."

"Was he in an accident?" Brianna cut in, her fingers digging into the receiver. "Who's this?"

"Dr. Schneider of Philadelphia Memorial Hospital. Your brother came to the emergency room because he had trouble breathing."

"Oh, no!" Her voice quivered. Alec, her twenty-three year-old brother, had fought cystic fibrosis since he was a child. One day, she feared, he and his disease would have a show down. "Every time he travels, he gets careless with his therapy and winds up in the hospital."

"He's stable now," Schneider said. "Alec mentioned that you're a respiratory therapist, so I wanted you to know that we've ruled out pneumonia. He'll go to a regular patient floor soon."

"Thank you for letting me know," Brianna said in a broken voice. "Please call me if anything changes."

Mylar balloons or not, Brianna would sleep no more tonight. Even their soft, shushing sounds brought no comfort. What caused her nightmares? Alec's illness? No, she'd lived with his condition since she was a child. Work? Maybe. While staring at the ceiling, Brianna contemplated her nightmares and the reality behind them.

When Brianna worked in the intensive care last Monday on a code call, trying to revive a patient, someone had tapped on the glass doors. Despite the code team's best efforts, her patient's heart monitor showed a flat line.

The tapping escalated to urgent knocking. Still feeding her patient oxygen, Brianna glanced at the door. A stranger dressed in navy beckoned to her. Short-cropped blond hair surrounded his angular face. His emaciated appearance and parchment skin made him look older, but the smooth skin around his eyes and mouth said that he was still in his twenties. For some reason, Brianna thought he looked familiar.

"What are you doing here?" a nurse demanded. "You'll have to leave."

The stranger backed toward the hall. Brianna felt his intent gaze on her, but she continued to pump oxygen into her patient. The patient's heart remained still as death.

"We're not getting anywhere," her boss, Dr. Dorfman, said, referring to the monitors. "Let's call it. Time of death: 2045. Thanks, everyone."

The code team's chatter trickled back from the hall while the doctor made notes on his clipboard. Brianna headed to a sink.

"Not so fast, young lady," Dorfman snapped.

Brianna glanced at her watch and sighed. It was almost 9 o'clock, two hours from her end of shift, and she hadn't yet begun charting. "What's wrong?"

"Your attitude, for starters. I won't have you mooning over your boyfriend while my patient fights for his life."

"What boyfriend?" Brianna arched her brows. "I thought another patient needed me."

"Cardiac arrests get top priority," Dorfman said harshly. "If you don't know how to prioritize, then learn."

"I hear what you're saying." Brianna sighed again, hurrying to the nurses' station. "You don't have to yell."

"I'll talk to you any way I want." Dorfman kept at her heels. "Perhaps you'd prefer a written warning."

"Excuse me," floated a silvery voice out of the dimly lit corridor. "Is there a problem?"

Brianna whirled around. The voice belonged to the stranger. He seemed to materialize from nowhere.

"Thank you," she said, "but I can handle this."

Dorfman's face reddened; his eyes narrowed. "Visiting hours ended long ago, young man," he said, pointing to the clock. "I'm calling Security."

"That won't be necessary," Brianna told him. "I'll escort him outside myself."

"I'd better not see him here again," Dorfman grunted before storming off.

"I've caused trouble between you and your superior," the young man said sadly. "I'm sorry, Brianna."

God, he knows my name. An image flashed before her—Brianna in an ankle-length dress, the dried yellow grass tickling her bare feet, carrying a small iron pot with a ladle, passing rows of pale, distended bodies. She grimaced at the stench of her fellow villagers' decaying flesh. The image only lasted a second, but that second sent frissons of dread shivering through her spine. "Don't worry about Dorfman," she said after a pause. "He's a pompous ass."

"My name is Marek," he said abruptly.

"Marek, you look like you need a doctor." Brianna studied her visitor. His eyes shone like sapphires, but his pale-as-paper skin and rancid odor warned he was harboring some rare disease. She then glanced toward the nurses' desk, where she'd laid a bouquet of Mylar balloons. The shiny balloons reflected her face, but not Marek's. She had to be imagining things.

"No doctor. No emergency room." Marek walked over to the desk. He ran his fingers through the balloons, the maze of reds, pinks, and blues. "Very nice."

"I bought them for the patients." Brianna swallowed hard, glancing toward the exit. "Please go. Dorfman will return any minute."

"I should have known," Marek murmured, ignoring her request. "You always tried to make the sick comfortable."

"Tried?" Brianna looked at him. "I'm still trying."

Gently, she caressed a red heart-shaped balloon. Instead of plastic, she saw herself lying on a tier of fire, her flesh burning and dropping in charcoal crumbs.

Jerking away, she blotted the sweat dripping from her blond curls. What was wrong with her? It was only a balloon.

Hands feeling like satiny ice caressed her cheeks. "Easy, Brianna," Marek said. "Romanian history can explain your dreams."

I shouldn't let him touch me. Brianna rubbed her elbows. But her visitor's rich, musky voice seduced her, causing her body to tingle. She sensed a mutual attraction and hoped that they would become friends. "How can Romanian history explain my dreams?"

"Later." Marek's lips curled into a tight smile. "We'll talk after you finish your watch."

"All right." Brianna managed to smile back. "Maybe you can give me a history lesson tonight."

After finishing her shift, Brianna found Marek waiting for her in the lobby. He walked her through the gardens surrounding the hospital, describing Vlad Tepes, the medieval prince of Wallachia. When he wasn't discussing Romanian princes, Brianna found herself telling him about her childhood, her brother's illness, and her job at Philadelphia Memorial Hospital. She hoped their talk might ease her nightmares. Instead, when she went to sleep, her big dreams escalated into horrific visions, worse than anything she had ever seen.

The blond man in the coffin was Marek.

After work the next afternoon, Brianna visited her brother. A Mylar balloon bobbed from behind his intravenous pump. Alec lay in bed, his face pale as chalk. Nasal prongs provided supplemental oxygen, and the two needles in his arms fed him fluids and antibiotics.

"You look awfully tired," Alec said after they exchanged greetings. "I gave you quite a scare, didn't I?"

"Yes, you have." Brianna nodded, studying his flow sheets. She noted his vital signs and prescribed medicines. "Dr. Schneider said that you'll be okay. You'd better watch yourself when you travel."

"I'm doing better than you appear to be. Is that guy keeping you awake?"

"What?" Brianna looked up from the sheet and started.

"The one who follows you like a puppy." Alec smiled a crooked grin. "My nurse said that you caught hell from Dorfman because of him."

Brianna averted her eyes. She felt her face flush. "His name is Marek. I don't like people talking behind my back."

"Hey, relax. She thought it was funny."

"Dorfman didn't find Marek's attention to me so amusing." Without thinking, Brianna traced her hand across the drawing on the balloon, a picture of a soldier riding on horseback. While she looked, blood oozed from the soldier's cheek, coloring the balloon scarlet.

"No!" She slapped at the balloon.

Alec's brown eyes widened. "Brianna, what's gotten into you?"

"Nothing." Brianna stepped away and looked again at the balloon. Its face showed only a soldier and his horse. No blood. "I haven't been sleeping well, that's all."

"Go out with Marek. Maybe he can help you relax. I sure hope so."

Brianna was sipping a Coke when Marek's cool hand brushed her shoulder. The full moon illuminated his bone china face, dark shirt with Roman collar, and matching overcoat.

"Interesting shirt," she said, fingering his collar. "It makes you look like a priest."

"It's interesting that you mentioned priests," Marek said. "One of Vlad's sons was a monk."

"I find that hard to believe." Smiling, she offered him her can. "Would you like some Coke?"

"I don't drink... soda."

What a strange man. But the gentle way Marek spoke invited friendship. He draped his arms across her shoulder, caressing her green scrub top with his fingertips.

"Most of Vlad's descendents loved to kill," he said, "but his youngest son joined a monastery. *His* downfall began when he fell in love."

"Why?" Brianna arched her eyebrows. "If he fell in love, he could leave the monastery."

"Not without serious repercussions. He had to settle for stolen moments. When he and his lover were alone, he'd take her in his arms and kiss her like this."

Marek pulled her close and pressed his lips against her cheek. She started to protest, but the feel of his arms around her sent waves of heat through her body. His tongue glided languidly over hers. Her lips could feel his teeth. They seemed unusually sharp.

"His lover could pass for your twin," he said.

Brianna felt her skin turn to gooseflesh. "Where do you get your information?"

"I've got a library filled with Romanian history. Textbooks, paintings, antiques. You should come to my house and see for yourself."

Brianna hugged herself to lessen her shivering and looked at Marek. His bisque complexion was almost transparent in the moonlight. His glowing eyes bored into her soul. "I'd like that," she heard her voice say. "If you don't mind the balloons in my backseat, we can take my car."

Brianna drove down Route 95 with her windows down, savoring the scents of wildflowers and grass. Their fragrances lingered during their ride down the expressway. In the backseat, her balloons made soft shushing sounds.

At Marek's prompting, she doglegged off an exit that led to Route 66, an s-shaped road winding through woods. Moments later, he guided her up a gravel driveway. A three-story flagstone with stained-glass windows loomed ahead like a shiny mass in the sky.

Brianna parked in the driveway and followed Marek to the front door. He lit two candles and handed one to her. Inside, the candlelight cast eerie shadows on embroidered furniture and hardwood floors.

"No electricity?" Brianna cast her gaze toward the slate fireplace. "You must have the eyes of a cat."

"The fifteenth-century people lived by candlelight," Marek said. "They had no choice. You'd be surprised at what the body can do when necessary."

"I believe it." Brianna traced her fingers along the wall portraits. "You've got some beautiful paintings, and... hey!" Her gaze settled on a rat-bitten, dog-eared canvas, the one bearing her features, right down to the dimples on her cheeks. "Where did you get this?"

"An antique shop in Romania." Marek took her elbow. "Come, let me show you upstairs."

He walked her up a winding staircase. At the landing, he stopped and kissed her again. His lips brushed along her cheeks and glided their way down her chin.

Mesmerized by his touch, Brianna withdrew gently and began removing her clothes. As her scrubs fell away, so did her nightmares. Nothing mattered now except the two of them and the passion that overwhelmed her.

Marek scooped her into his arms and carried her into a bedroom. He arranged her in the center of the bed and then lay beside her, caressing her and murmuring soft words that made her want to love him. Moments later, he mounted her, and what was this? Sharp pain flashed through her throat; he was biting her, licking and swallowing.

"Stop!" Brianna shouted, thrashing against his grip. "Let go, you bastard!"

Her clawing fingers reached for a candlestick. Breath coming out in ragged screams, she held the light to his face.

Marek leaped away, shielding his eyes. His cheeks flushed scarlet. Blood dripping from his mouth stained his silk sheets.

Brianna threw the sheet around her shoulders and bolted to the stairs. Her car keys lay inside her purse which she had hung on the bottom stair post. Close enough to see, but too far to reach safely.

"No!" Marek grabbed her shoulders. "You can't run from your past. Things are not as they seem."

Brianna scanned the walls for something that might work as a weapon. Candlesticks illuminated the hall, anchored in holders far beyond her reach. "Why don't you enlighten me?"

"I can't. You have to find out for yourself."

Brianna felt her teeth chatter. In her mind's eye, she saw a woman attacked by Marek, lying in a pool of blood. The vision passed.

"Why me?" She pleaded in a weepy voice. "My brother needs me alive. During his bad days, he needs me to do his chest therapy. Without aggressive treatment, he could get really sick. Do you even care?"

"Sure, I do," Marek said. "I only wanted to love you, but my bloodlust demands that I feed."

"You're crazy." Brianna tried to muster anger, but her voice sounded like the decree of a weak queen. "You can't—you aren't supposed to drink blood. It can give you a disease. If you take too much, you'll kill me."

"You won't die, Brianna," Marek said in a measured, quiet voice. "My kisses will enable you to live forever."

"No way!" Brianna's mind refused to process what she started to suspect was true.

Grabbing a candle, Marek walked her to a mirror by the closet. The mirror gave Brianna a wide view of the bedroom, but her eyes focused on the blood trickling from the two punctures under her chin. When she felt his hands on her shoulders, she realized that she could not see his reflection.

"Take a good look, Brianna," he said. "Then tell me whether Undeath is impossible."

Horrible waves of dizziness rolled through Brianna, causing her reflection in the mirror to blur. Moments later, she felt herself drift through a pearly mist. Scenes flashed out of that mist like those from a fast-forwarding movie.

When the mist parted, a dirt road littered with bloated bodies stretched ahead of her. The plague had turned the bodies purplish black. Two figures emerged, both wearing full-length dresses. Brianna saw herself walking barefoot in the yellow grass.

Nodding stoically, the woman beside her pointed to a dark gray stone building. "This is our last refuge," she said. "The Church of Lost Souls."

With shaky hands, Brianna tugged the bell rope. Silence followed a moment, and then a silver-haired monk opened the door.

"Could you spare us some bread?" she begged in a tearful voice. "We haven't eaten for three days."

The monk disappeared a moment, and then he returned with three loaves of bread. Another monk, a young blonde man, emerged from the hall. "Food comes from God," he said. "He must feed His children so that they don't starve."

"The plague has taken most of my village," Brianna told him. "Too many for the monks to bury."

The younger monk brought her a basket of potatoes and greens. "Please come here when you need food," he said, staring at her. "We've got plenty in the catacombs."

"You're truly a man of God." Brianna smiled. "I'll never forget this, Brother..."

"Marek," he supplied. "I'll do what I can to help."

This scene faded, and another took its place. Brianna was standing by a river. Her face had reddened with sunburn and sweat drenched her clothes, but her eyes focused on a familiar figure in the water.

Marek was swimming nude in the river.

Without thinking, Brianna stripped off her clothes and dove into the river. She swam into Marek's arms. They made love in the water and on the surrounding rocks. Afterwards, they lay in the grass, nesting in each other's arms.

"We can't continue this, Marek," she said after a pause. "One day we're going to be found out."

"I don't care," Marek said. "I have to keep seeing you."

"Why did you decide to become a monk?"

"My father sent me to the monastery when I was very young," Marek said. "I know no other way."

Footfalls sounded from the shadows, and the silver-haired monk stepped into the clearing. His dark eyes flashed with indignation. His gnarled hand brandished a knotted leather whip.

"You know better than to submit to temptation," the older monk shouted, rushing at Marek. Yanking Marek by the arm, he shoved him toward a tree. Down the whip went, cutting into Marek's shoulders. Marek's eyes brightened ominously, but he did not cry or flinch.

"You must return for evening prayers and cleanse the transgression from your soul."

"No, Father Sebastian, I love her," Marek said.

"If you keep this up, you'll never be ordained. The burden of holiness is never easy. You must atone for the sins of your father." Turning to Brianna, Father Sebastian smiled sardonically. "Vlad, the Impaler."

The whip swung again, crackling across Marek's back.

"Your father's evil still lives in you," Father Sebastian cried. "He continues to walk as undead, feeding on the blood of the living. Is this what you want?"

Turning around slowly, Marek looked at Father Sebastian, his eyes darkening with hatred. "I am not my father."

"You can't do this to him!" Brianna cried, flinging herself before Marek. "I love him. I want to marry him."

"If you pursue this relationship," the old monk said in a pained voice, "you'll only get hurt. Do you understand the crimes against life that his father has committed?"

Brianna nodded.

"Church of Lost Souls has a violent history. Twenty years ago, we got overzealous with our preaching and opposed Prince Vlad. Vlad retaliated by beheading most of my brothers. He placed their heads on stakes surrounding the monastery for show. He later asked us to raise his son. Some people say that Vlad offered Marek to the monastery to pray for his soul."

Brianna leaned back and shivered. "Vlad's dead, right?"

"Gone, but not dead," Sebastian said somberly. "You cannot marry Marek because he has promised his life to God. If you continue seeing him, you'll burn for witchcraft."

The grayness set in again. "Listen to your visions," she heard Marek's distant voice whisper. "See how my memories have merged with yours. Maybe then you can understand what I've done."

The mist parted again, and Brianna saw a throng of people, led by Father Sebastian, rushing up the hill toward her, bearing lit torches. "There she is!" The old monk pointed toward Brianna. "She is a witch."

"Witch!" the mob shouted. "Witch!"

"She started the plague."

"Stop!" Brianna heard herself cry. "I am not a witch."

The crowd converged on Brianna, dragging her to a wooden stake. Unseen hands yanked her arms around a pole. Corded rope cut into her sunburned wrists and ankles. Someone tossed branches under her feet. Father Sebastian threw a lit torch onto the pile.

Bright tendrils of flame ignited the woodchips. Sparks landed on her skirt, catching fire. Brianna screamed as the flames muttered up her calves. Through the conflagration, her body burned cherry red, and then black. Crumbs of baked flesh fell like grisly rain, leaving behind a skeleton and ashes.

Marek burst through the crowd moments later. He rushed toward the flames, but Father Sebastian grabbed his arms. "You've committed grave sins with this woman," the older monk said. "Her wicked ways are no loss to you."

The flames died, leaving behind ashes and splintered bones. After the crowd dispersed, Marek stripped off his stole and tossed it on the rubble. Then he trudged further up the mountain, where he happened upon a battered castle. His father's palace.

He crept through the vestibule. Light exploded by an open window. Brianna saw herself in that light, surrounded by flames. She heard her cries of mad fear and agony.

"Brianna!" Marek rushed toward the flames.

The image faded, and Marek slammed into a cold stone wall.

"Brianna!" he cried again, bursting into the parlor. The lit torches cast ghostly shapes on the furniture and marble floor.

"You fool," a deep voice thundered from the shadows. "No matter where you go, I can read you like an open book."

"Father?" Marek's eyes darted around the room.

A broad-shouldered man stepped into the parlor, fists clenched, staring at Marek with ice-green eyes. "I sent you to the monastery to pray for my soul," he cried. "Instead, you betrayed me with a young woman."

"No, Father, I fell in love." Marek met his father's gaze, eyes resolute as steel. "Are you going to impale me like you did the other monks?"

His father frowned. His face turned gray as the stones lining the hearth. "Who told you that?"

"Father Sebastian. Those stories never die."

"That's because vampires don't die," his father said steadily. The angry look on his face evaporated, and a crafty gleam in his eyes took its place. A crooked sneer surfaced on his lips. "I'm not going to impale you, Marek, because you might still be of some use to me. If you do as I say, Brianna's soul will return one day, and she'll come back to you."

"I would wait an eternity for Brianna," Marek told him.

"I can spare you grief if you follow me." His father smiled, showing his pointed teeth. "It's your decision."

And if you refuse, his smile said with curled lips, *I'll make sure you don't live to grieve anything.*

"Follow me and turn from the light. Serve me, and you'll live forever. Challenge me and you'll die; you'll never see Brianna again."

Laying his hands on Marek's shoulders, Prince Vlad turned him around. Slowly, almost reluctantly, Marek pulled his shirt away, exposing his neck. Vlad tore a gash in his left wrist. Mouth gaping and eyes rolled back, he then bit into Marek's throat. His left wrist covered Marek's mouth, and Brianna cringed at the soft sucking sounds.

The images faded into blackness. When Brianna opened her eyes, she was alone in bed, surrounded by lit candles. Her clothes lay over a chair. Something sticky trickled down her neck. Dried blood coated her tongue. She understood now they shared a past life that had somehow carried over to the present.

Feeling terrified and yet intrigued, Brianna slipped into her clothes and crept through a gloomy hall to look for Marek. The candle played ghostly shadows on two other bedrooms and a stairwell that led to the living room and kitchen. The rooms were furnished with embroidered chairs, expensive looking paintings, and more stained-glass windows, but she saw no sign of Marek.

Past the kitchen, she found the library. A six-tiered bookcase faced the door with crystal candlesticks poking from its sides. "Marek," she called, "where are you?"

Silence.

Her candle illuminated a myriad of titles—*Wallachia, Prince Vlad,* and other books related to Vlad the Impaler. The older books, bound with ragged parchment, were a maze of dog-eared yellowed pages. Standing on tiptoe, she grabbed a candlestick.

The candlestick shifted. The bookcase swung sideways, revealing cement stairs that led to a cellar. An acrid stench blasted in her direction, the smell of things long dead, exploding on the gas of their own decay.

"No, no, I can't look," Brianna cried, shuddering. But she forced one foot before the other into a passageway lit by torches. Their glow illuminated mildewed brick walls, ceiling cobwebs, and rust puddles that had congealed. A damp breeze from an underground current blew wisps of hair into her eyes.

As she continued walking, her foot stumbled into a human skull. A trail of broken bones stretched ahead, piling against the rear wall. Tufts of debris coated the bones. The rancid stench caused Brianna to gag and vomit. A scream came and died in her throat.

Breath hitching, she bolted to the library. She shot a glance across the hall. No sign of Marek. At the living room, she sprinted out the front door.

Outside, the full moon illuminated her car, waiting for her. After plopping behind the wheel, Brianna jarred the engine into a harsh roar, and sped toward Route 95 in a cloud of blue smoke.

The balloons bobbed and wobbled in her rear seat. Her knuckles turned white as she clenched the steering wheel. Her car skirted the white line as she rounded the curves.

Moments later, something flashed white, and then a tractor-trailer truck barreled toward her. At the curve, the truck jackknifed, blocking the road. Its pistons hissed like angry dragons. Screaming, Brianna slammed on the brakes. Her car screeched, and then skated toward the guardrail.

Hood bobbing, her car flip-flopped down a ravine. The shrubbery flew by until her car slammed into a tree. The agony of pointed knives tore through her chest. Loud popping sounded behind her, even as she sank into the darkness.

The stink of smoke, fumes, and gasoline assaulted Brianna's nostrils, and searing hot flames crackled around her. Melted Mylar plastic film from her balloons hit her face, burning her skin. Her chest ached terribly, her burns worse, and each intake of breath became a struggle. *So this is what it's like to die,* she thought.

Instead, strong hands lifted her from the wreck and carried her up the slope. A gentle breeze caressed her cheek. She coughed up thick wads of blood. As her head cleared, she looked into Marek's eyes.

"I know about you," she managed between gasps. "Now I'm going to die."

"Why did you run away?" Marek asked.

"Because I saw those skulls. You are death, Marek."

"No, I'm Undeath," Marek said, stroking her cheek. "I'll take you with me."

"No, no, no!" Brianna groaned at the tentacles of pain clutching at her chest.

"We should have never separated." Marek sighed. "Do you understand why I chose Undeath?"

Brianna nodded, coughing again.

"Your nightmares were recollections from your past," Marek said. "While you were sleeping, I exchanged my blood with yours. By the next sunset, you'll have immortality."

Brianna shook her head. "I can't love someone who kills."

"How can you say that? I love you."

"Not really, Marek." Brianna looked at him with sad eyes. "If you loved me, you would have left me alone."

"I killed out of loneliness." Marek cradled her cheeks in his hands. "If I let you die, the grief will aggravate my bloodlust."

Another explosive cough. Already, the numbness worked its way up her legs. "Please don't make me responsible for your casualties," she begged in a faint voice.

"Then let me bring you home." Marek brushed his lips over her forehead. "You yourself said that your brother needs you alive. Only by loving each other will we have peace."

Tears rolled Brianna's face, tears of understanding that she couldn't run from her fate. "You're right about my brother," she conceded at last. "I can still help him. Maybe I can even minimize your casualties. But I'll never have peace."

Brianna wrapped her bruised arms around his shoulders, and her shadow was like a ghost on the moonlit grass. Marek was her heartbeat; fear was her voice. The scattering bones, the cold breath, all around her was the darkness rising.

Lorraine's Life Preserver

A full moon illuminated the woods where Lorraine hunched over a tree stump, shivering and struggling to breathe. The howling November wind blew her copper hair and nipped her cheeks. She'd heard terrifying stories about these woods, ramblings about night creatures that attacked, leaving battered, lifeless bodies strewn among the trees. Every time she tried to move, she wheezed audibly with gasping respirations.

"Face it, Lorraine," she whispered. "You're lost, and you're going to die."

Determined to conserve her oxygen, Lorraine pursed her lips and took slow, deep breaths. She contemplated on what happened before she got lost. Her capital mistake, she concluded, was underestimating her niece, Terri.

Her sister, Janet, and her sixteen-year-old daughter, Terri, had arrived from Buffalo three days ago. Janet, a CEO at Atomic Manufacturing, had acquired an ego to match her income and Terri followed her example. Lorraine dreaded the shrill criticisms that accompanied their visits. They chorused her father's scathing accusations – even in his frail condition. Shortly after their arrival, her asthma started as a whisper, and built in crescendo to a bull roar.

In anticipation.

This time, Terri kept to herself, except for an occasional "hi" and "bye." She looked pale and gaunt. Dark circles surrounded her blue eyes, and what looked like bruises peppered her arms. Janet murmured something about Terri "not feeling well." Lorraine didn't care, so long as they left her alone.

But sometimes, Terri stared at Lorraine with her dilated pupils, as if trying to see something. "Auntie, you're wheezing," she observed during supper. "My mom and I make you nervous, don't we?"

"Sometimes you do," Lorraine said, meeting her gaze.

"I feel bad, seeing how awful you look," she said in a syrupy voice. "Why don't you lie down?"

Lorraine shook her head. *Girl, the only time you felt bad was when Mommy Dearest overran her credit limit and couldn't buy you a fancy toy.* "I can't. Your mother won't be home until late, and my dad's nurse called out sick."

"I'll look after Poppop." Terri prodded Lorraine toward the stairs. "Now go on. Get to bed."

Sometime after she laid down, a creaking door and whispering footsteps woke Lorraine. Moonlight filtered through the window blinds, throwing ribbed shadows on her walls, bureau, and her niece's Jefferson High School sweatshirt and dungarees.

"Terri," Lorraine whispered, fighting the haze of sleepiness engulfing her.

In the next instant, Terri's sneaker-clad foot shot out. Stabbing pain flared through Lorraine's right knee. Her unstable knee, which had suffered a torn ligament and three surgeries, casualties of her father's temper.

Screaming, Lorraine clutched her leg. "Terri, what are you *doing?*" The wheezing started again, causing her to explode with a spate of coughing.

Hands gripping Lorraine's foot, Terri yanked her sore leg. Biting pain exploded around the kneecap. Lorraine jumped and tumbled out of bed.

"You monster!" she croaked. Thrashing with her good leg, she rammed her foot into Terri's stomach.

"Ow-ow-ow!" Terri cried, releasing her grip. She dropped to the floor, hugging her stomach.

Lorraine's wheezing drowned out the sound of Terri's groans. Her breath came out in short gasps.

The Proventil, she thought, struggling to her feet. *That's the ticket.* She kept Proventil inhalers in her purse and by her bed. What felt like rusty nails corkscrewed through her knee, but she needed the Proventil to open her chest. Right now.

Her drawers were empty. All of them. Snapping on a light, she grabbed her leather purse from the dresser. She dumped its contents on the bed. No Proventil.

Terri snickered. "What's the matter, Auntie? You lost something?"

Lorraine turned around slowly.

Terri sat cross-legged on the floor, lazily twirling her tangled blonde hair. Her eyes glittered like blue ice chips surrounding her dilated pupils.

"What have you done with my inhalers?" Lorraine asked in a hoarse whisper.

Terri's full lips curled into a smirk. "That's for me to know and you to find out."

"Damn you!" Lorraine coughed and gasped for air. "You don't fool with someone's medicine."

"Who said I was fooling?" Terri asked. "Considering what will happen if you don't get your inhalers."

"You won't get away with this. Not if your mother finds out." But Janet wasn't home, and when the cat's away, the mice will play. "Never mind. I'm calling 9-1-1." She reached for her telephone.

Lunging forward, Terri snatched the phone from Lorraine's stubby finger and hurled it out of reach. She sat in front of the door and cradled the phone in her elbow. "Gee, I think I mislaid your inhalers." Her voice oozed oily sweetness. "By gosh, the phone is out of order, too. I'll have to stay here and watch you suffocate."

Lorraine hugged herself, shivering. Though she had three inches and forty pounds over Terri, she couldn't expect to match Terri's drug-crazed strength, especially when she was fighting for every breath. "Why? What have I done to you?"

Terri burst into a gale of laughter. "Come on, Auntie. It's nothing personal. It's about timing and circumstances."

Lorraine shook her head, panting between pursed lips. "I ... don't understand."

"Poppop's had two bouts of pneumonia since last August, and he hasn't left his wheelchair in months. He'll croak by the end of winter, don't you think?"

Lorraine nodded, knowing that a stroke two years ago left her father prone to pneumonia, especially during cold weather. Of course, this winter could be his last.

"I've got some expensive habits that need financing," Terri continued. "Mom said that Poppop's worth a million dollars, and that he's leaving you and her fifty percent each. More important, if you die, I get your share." She grinned. "Enough cash to keep me happy a long time."

"Don't ... don't bet on it." Lorraine gasped, her teeth chattering. "Your mom's talking about putting him in a nursing home. An *expensive* home, where he may surprise you and live another five years. His money will go fast."

"It won't," Terri said, smiling, "because sickly people like him often have accidents. *Fatal* accidents."

31

And if he doesn't, her smile said, *I will arrange one.* Her message came through loud and clear with the curl of two lips.

"Mom stopped respecting you after you flunked out of nursing school. She and Poppop always complain about the sloppy way you keep his house and bankbook. They won't miss you."

You're mad, Lorraine longed to shout, but her tightening chest discouraged her from provoking her niece. "Your mother values appearances and academic success, but she'd never justify murder."

"Who will tell her? I can forge your voluminous handwriting and write a convincing suicide note. Mom will buy it because she thinks you're unstable." She glanced at her watch. "My mother won't be home for a *long* time. You look bad, Auntie. You'd better shut up and say your last prayers."

A door downstairs slammed. Unintelligible voices. Seconds later, footsteps clattered up the stairs. The doorknob twisted, followed by sharp rapping. "Open up," came Janet's boardroom voice.

Still smiling, Terri unlocked the door and snapped on the light.

Janet marched into the room, clad in a navy suit and pumps with heels the size of a dime. Short, blonde hair surrounded her square, ruddy face. Her thin lips twisted into a scowl, and her ice-blue eyes darted around the room.

"What a pigsty." She sniffed.

"Mom, why are you home so early?" Terri asked.

"Migraines." Janet massaged her temples. "Dad said he heard noises up here. I can't go anywhere without ... hey!" Her gaze dropped toward Lorraine's hunched over body. "What's going on here?"

"I can't ... breathe," Lorraine whispered between gasps. "Terri ... stole ... my inhalers."

"Auntie fell out of bed," Terri said quickly. "I kept her inhalers because I know how she loses things."

"Well, don't just stand there!" Janet shouted. "Get her medicine."

Her tented, manicured fingers caressed Lorraine's cheek. "Oh, my God, you're turning blue! You belong in a hospital. Why didn't ..."

The door opened behind her, and Terri returned with the inhalers. She laid them on the floor besides Lorraine.

Still purse-lipped breathing, Lorraine took several drags on her Proventil. As the moments ticked by, she listened to her shallow breaths, waiting for relief. Finally, she hawked up a ball of thick, green phlegm.

Janet began to fidget. "I should call 9-1-1."

Lorraine hesitated. Her gasping eased, but the tightness and wheezing persisted, warning that she'd need much more than an inhaler to get through this flare-up. Definitely antibiotics for a brewing infection, steroids, and maybe someone to check out her knee.

But bad as things were, the future could not be forgotten. Janet would make a family show out of her asthma attack. She'd urge Terri to visit and bring food, setting the stage for a fatal accident. Her death was guaranteed unless she drove to the hospital herself and used a Jane Doe name.

"No hospital." Lorraine managed a weak smile. "I'll make an appointment with my doctor tomorrow morning."

"Are you sure?" Janet asked, her blue eyes widening.

"Very sure. But watch Terri's temper. She kicked me and damn near broke my kneecap. She withheld my inhalers on purpose."

"Stop it right there." Janet's eyes blazed like burning embers.

"Why? I'm telling the truth." Lorraine hiked up her flannel gown. "Look at the swelling."

"You must have hurt your knee when you fell." Janet folded her slender arms across her chest. "My Terri wouldn't harm anyone. She does volunteer work at our hospital. She gets straight A's in school and spoils Dad during our visits. Granted, she mouths off when she shouldn't. And she used poor judgment with your medicine. I'll speak to her about it."

Yeah, right, Lorraine thought. "When you do, take a good look at her arms and her eyes. Even in the light, her pupils are dilated. She could be taking …"

"That's enough!" Janet snapped. "Before you castigate Terri, you'd better clean up your own mess."

Jabbing her right forefinger against each finger on her left hand, she roll-called Lorraine's offenses. "Flunking out of nursing school, wasting the taxpayers' hard-earned money by welshing off of disability. Avoiding Dad. Doing only what's absolutely necessary. Thanks to your lax housekeeping, our Meadowood home looks like Ghettowood."

Lorraine's chest tightened. Another puff on the Proventil followed.

"You want to talk about drugs?" Janet continued in a shrill voice. "You constantly overdose on your inhalers."

"Janet, you're not a doctor." Lorraine got up and donned her pearl gray velour robe and slippers. "Try getting by with a chronic illness, and see how you feel. I'm allergic to dust, but Dad refuses to pay for hired help. No matter what I do, it's never enough." She sighed. "Why are you so angry? When Dad goes, you and I will be the only family left."

"You trash my daughter, then call me angry?" Janet shook her head disgustedly. "I'm getting sick and tired of your whining and lies. You ought to be grateful to live so cheaply in a nice home, with a sizeable inheritance forthcoming. But you crumble when trivial things go wrong."

She paced around the room, stopping to pick up knickknacks that had fallen on the floor. "I should have never moved to Buffalo. Dad will want me here every weekend."

"I suppose you're right." Understanding dawned, and Lorraine knew that her father respected Janet's academic intellect and successes. She gathered her purse and medications. "So enjoy your visit. I will come home Sunday after you leave."

"Where are you going?" Janet demanded.

"What do you care?" Lorraine scurried downstairs, ignoring the cutting pain in her knee and whistling in her chest. Grabbing her woolen coat, she bolted to the garage.

Jackson Hospital. There's no getting around it. She scrambled into her Ford, a dilapidated white sedan. Driving at a steady pace, she took Sycamore Street, an S-shaped road surrounded by woods.

Her engine made a sputtering noise. Seconds later, her car drifted to a stop, even as she tramped on the gas pedal. Lorraine turned off the ignition. "Shit!" she hollered.

Think, she told herself, wiping the sweat from her forehead. *Conserve your oxygen.* It didn't work. Her poverty of breath made thinking impossible. She tried again and again to start her car without success.

Grabbing a flashlight, Lorraine stepped out of her car and took in her surroundings. No restaurants, homes, or gas stations within sight. But she spotted a dirt path which led into the woods, and which would eventually lead to a gas station. She'd walked it before during the day after mishaps with her car. Her knee ached. Her leg wobbled with each step; but if she took her time, she'd make it.

Darkness shrouded the trees. The moon cast ghostly shapes on the piles of fallen leaves and the trees' skeletal branches. What if the "night creature" she'd heard about existed?

She sighed and hobbled up the path. By now, Terri and Janet would be looking for her. Better to take her chances in the woods than risk another go-round with Terri.

The path narrowed in spots, and the low tree branches made it barely passable. Brambles scratched her face and hands, and tore her coat. She stumbled on fallen trees and hidden potholes, jarring her knee. A cloudburst of pain surrounded her leg. *Where was the gas station,* she wondered, casting her light. Things looked so different at night.

The grove of trees seemed endless. The damp cold seeped through her blue overcoat, chilling her bones. Her heaving chest sounded like a pipe organ. Shivering, Lorraine flopped on a tree stump and felt through her pockets for her Proventil.

Her pockets were empty. Ditto for her purse.

"Damn it!" She burst into tears. She was going to die after all. Right here in these woods.

Moments later, the rustling of branches and snapping of twigs impinged on her thoughts. "You dropped something, Miss," came a husky, masculine voice.

Lorraine's flashlight cast bright circles on his black cloak and maroon shirt. Coarse jet hair surrounded his bone china angular features. Staring with obsidian eyes, he handed her the Proventil inhaler.

"Thank you," she said, gasping. She followed up with three deep drags on the inhaler.

"Something – or someone – has hurt you," he observed. "Perhaps you could use a friend."

"Friend." Lorraine nodded, mesmerized by his gaze.

Gliding forward, he cupped her face in his hands. "Look at you. Scratches on your pretty face. And your leg's swollen. You don't deserve this."

His tapered hands felt like cool satin. His gentle voice made her think everything would turn out all right.

"You were made to be loved," he added, flashing his teeth. Two of them, pointed, glistened in the moonlight.

A night creature! She jerked away. "My God! Who are you?"

"Brandon. Some people might consider me loathsome. But you needn't be afraid. You remind me of someone I loved a long time ago. Her family treated her poorly and she died after a brutal beating. If only she had let me, I could've saved her."

Lorraine's hazel eyes widened. Those ancient stories had described his kind as repulsive. Yet his voice lacked the sharp edge she had come to fear over the years. He had come to her rescue. His thin lips curved into a smile, inviting her confidence.

"I'm having an asthma attack," she told him. "It's serious. Can you take me to the hospital?"

"I can't do that, Lorraine," Brandon said, stroking her cheek. "If I take you to the hospital, your would-be killer will find you."

Lorraine gasped. "How did you know my name, let alone …"

"I can read people's lives by looking into their eyes," he told her. "Your niece dipped into a powder which affected her mind and made her want to kill you. Instead of listening to you, her mother considers you the villain. You've spent the last five years looking after your father and putting up with his vicious lies. This," he concluded, caressing her throbbing knee, "was the thanks you got."

Lorraine coughed again, yielding another mucus sample into her hanky. "You've got it right," she admitted after catching her breath, "but my asthma ..."

"Know why you can't breathe?" His eyes burned into her like fiery embers. "The heartache authored by your family is choking you."

Lorraine tried to speak. Instead, she burst into tears.

Brendon cradled her in his arms, running his slender fingers through her wavy hair, warding off the cold with his cloak. "You've put your own needs aside to look after your father. Begged for love that should have been unconditional."

Hands on her cheeks, he turned her face toward his. "I can see you drowning, so I'm throwing you a life preserver."

"Life preserver?" Lorraine echoed feebly.

"I'm offering you life, something I reserve for a chosen few," he said quietly. "Not life as most people know it. But you will heal and grow strong from the life forces of mortals. In time, you'll want other things. Fulfillment of your secret desires. Immortality."

"I could never," Lorraine began, and then she paused to think about what his offer really meant. What if Brandon offered a refuge from her pain and nightmares? What if, by joining him, she could shed the bodily frailties that left her so vulnerable to her family's attacks? Terri's assault on her life aside, she'd taken constant battering from her relatives since her mother's death. Soon, they would break her spirit, or destroy her altogether, unless she sought shelter.

"What I mean," she said after a long pause, "is that I want to be with you."

"Let's go to my cabin." Brandon scooped Lorraine in his arms. Gliding deeper into the woods, he passed a lake, where Lorraine could see her reflection in the water, but not his. He carried her to a plywood cabin with sparse furnishings: three wooden chairs, a sawed-off table, and a fireplace. The cabin's warmth and his soothing voice eased her chest tightness.

Sitting in a chair, Brandon eased Lorraine onto his lap, with her legs straddling his hips. His satiny-smooth fingers caressed her cheeks, and his thin lips brushed her lips and eyebrows. A twinge of pleasure ran through Lorraine's spine as his muscular body pressed against hers.

Only dimly aware of the pin pricks at her neck, Lorraine listened to her heart beat in her ears, savored the feel of his cool skin. Her body started to tingle and grow numb. Moments later, she fell limp against him, and her surroundings faded into darkness.

When Lorraine came to, she lay sprawled across her front car seat, still wearing her blue coat. No sign of Brandon. But the dampness around her collar told her that their encounter had been real. She glanced at her watch. It was two a.m.

Struggling sleepily to a sitting position, Lorraine noticed that blood had dribbled over the seat and pooled on the mat. The swelling and pain in her leg had gone away. Her chest no longer whistled, but her throat felt bone dry, as if someone had stuffed it with cotton.

Of course, Brandon would figure out that her car had broken down. But why had he brought her there? "Life preserver," she murmured. "He said …"

A blaring horn interrupted her speculations. Janet's Cadillac wove unsteadily down Sycamore Street with Terri's gaunt face at the wheel, illuminated by the full moon. Terri pulled up behind the Ford and bumped into it. Lorraine guessed that Terri's expensive habits had affected her driving.

The passenger door creaked open, showing Terri's grinning face. A knife dangled from her fist, its blade shimmering in the moonlight.

Lorraine met Terri's gaze, no longer feeling intimidated. "Let me guess," she said ponderously. "Mom's asleep, and you borrowed her car. Without asking."

Terri nodded and burst into a fit of giggles. "Mom thought you went to the hospital. But I fixed this piece of junk so you would get stranded. Like car, like owner, right?"

Lorraine shrugged without answering, while staring at the curve of Terri's slender neck.

"Looks like someone mangled you." Brandishing her knife, Terri swung open the Ford's door and plopped into the seat beside her. "Makes my job easier."

You will heal and grow strong from the life forces of mortals. With one swift movement, Lorraine's fists locked Terri's wrists in a steel grip.

Terri's knife clattered on the floor. "What the …"

"Just a matter of timing and circumstances," Lorraine whispered. "I've got a present for you."

Hands pinning her niece's shoulders, mouth gaping, Lorraine fed on Terri's life force ... and savored the healing process.

A Lesson on Suffering

The fever came over Viola Gaunt again, causing her to shiver as her ice-black eyes examined her client: an elderly, diabetic male sprawled in his chair, chest heaving, and face turning the color of cement. Gasps issued from his pale lips. Though neighbors called him her patient, most home health aides like herself preferred the term *client*. Her trembling fingers tugged at the blood-red scrub pants that hugged her big-boned hips.

The shivering did not come from fear for her client's life. Though Viola had just turned fifty, she hadn't felt anything resembling fear since her attack five years ago at Silver Slipper Nursing Center, the one which left her with three prolapsed disks and her subsequent firing. A certified nursing assistant, she used health care to bleed her clients' savings with her exorbitant fees for fictional services, reimbursements for imaginary house expenses, and money lifted from her clients' secret caches. Typical hiding places ranged from old socks to metal safes; she knew them all. Getting caught meant prison time, but fear of the consequences did not motivate her shivering either.

It came from the thrill of deciding whether her client lived or died.

A crooked, hungry smile surfaced on Viola's lips. With her furrowed cheeks, pearly teeth, and deep-set eyes, her face looked like a grinning skull. Her gaze settled on her client, Ernest Morton, who was clutching his chest. Fearful gray eyes stared from his milk-pale face, a map of wrinkles surrounded by wisps of white hair. Panting gasps escaped his lips. His bifocals slid off his sweat-drenched nose and plopped on the olive green carpet.

The other day, he'd called his son, complaining about Viola's mood swings, spotty attendance, and disappearing cash—his last complaint, she decided. She insured his silence by substituting placebos for his insulin and heart pills, and letting nature do the rest. Looking at Morton's emaciated form, she thought about the technique a certain Silver Slipper client had used to retool her spine and the way Dr. Walters had let her suffer. Her shivering grew more intense, almost orgasmic.

The clock overhead struck eleven. Voices filtered through the open window. Viola glanced through the blinds at her red Toyota, parked on the narrow street. A couple that lived in a row house across the street sat on the stoop talking. Sometimes they stopped by to chat. No problem. The next time, she'd tell them that Morton wasn't feeling up to company.

Viola turned, facing the brass-framed mirror over the sofa. Her eyes opened wide as soup plates.

"What the hell?" She stared at the mirror again, but only saw her shocked reflection. Forcing a lopsided smile, she shook her head. For a moment, she thought she spotted a woman wearing green. She looked like Morton's friend and neighbor, Anne Kruise.

Anne's visits began with friendly what's-new chats. Sometimes she told Morton jokes. The questions and observations came next, the pointed ones directed at Viola. *Morton's ankles look swollen. Why is he losing weight?* Though Anne's voice remained cheerful, her intent stare coated Viola's stomach with unease, a sense of things gone eight miles from right.

Anne did not cast a shadow when she walked.

Something soft brushed Viola's shoulder, jarring her to the present. Morton was lurching to his telephone in a sidestroke motion. One hand grabbed the receiver; the other braced him against the coffee table. Viola wrenched the phone from his grasp. "Relax, Mr. Morton," she said, smiling. "I'll give you something to make you feel better."

Morton's lips opened and closed, letting out unintelligible syllables. He doubled over again, hand gripping his chest. His face dripped with sweat. His breath came out in shallow grunts. Viola stood watching, smile tucked in place, holding the phone out of his reach. Morton's chest heaved; he sank to the floor. Tears rolled down his cheeks, eyes pleading. Viola liked that look. With tentative fingers, she felt his pulse. Fast and thready.

More tears slid down the creases in Morton's cheeks. "Please call an ambulance," he begged in a papery voice.

"You complained about me to your son." Her death's head grin widened. "Capital mistake, Mr. Morton."

Morton jerked upright, his panting lips seeking air and finding none. Viola glanced at the mirror again and bit back a scream. Instead of Morton's familiar living room furniture, the mirror reflected her attacker and herself in his bedroom at Silver Slipper. She watched him pound her back with his cane; she listened to her plaintive cries. She even gagged on the odor of the room's sickeningly strong disinfectant.

"No more." Viola turned toward Morton again, giving him a snake-advancing-on-a- mouse smile. "Go lie on the sofa."

Morton's face was turning blue, but he complied.

Viola leaned over the old man, hands pressed against the sofa cushions. His breath exuded a fruity odor. Diabetic acidosis, courtesy of the fake insulin injections. Her nail-bitten fingers stroked his cheeks. She felt him stiffen at her touch. Croaking sobs wracked his body. Viola giggled.

"You look bad," she said, licking her lips. "I'll make this easy."

Leaning closer, she grabbed a pillow. Morton let out a shrill scream, a scream cut short by the pillow squashed against his face. His fists struck at her unyielding arms, weak blows that felt like love taps.

Moments later, his fists fell away, and his gasping ebbed to a stop. His head rolled back, eyes fixed and dilated. Viola glanced at the clock again, prepared to wait at least fifteen minutes before calling 911. The longer she waited, the poorer his chances for revival.

Viola ran to the dining room and rooted through the sideboard, where Morton kept his bank books. She found a cigar box crammed with wads of twenties and two diamond rings with a matching necklace, leavings from a fifty-year marriage. By the time she finished her search, fifteen minutes passed. After calling 911, she stuffed the box into her tote bag and rushed to the living room. She sneaked another peek at the mirror; but this time, her eyes saw nothing unusual.

Viola stumbled. The room spun around her, red and white wallpaper streaking. A kaleidoscope of glittering pinks, reds, blues, and lavender flashed before her eyes. The spinning slammed to a stop.

Body trembling like a wire, Viola struggled to her feet. She wobbled through the living room, regarding the sofa fixedly. Fright drifted through the hollow places of her body, turning her skin to gooseflesh.

"Dammit!" she cried, eyes bulging.

Morton's body was gone. Any second, she expected to hear wailing sirens, but the air remained quiet as death. Movement at her hand speared her attention to her tote bag. The cigar box, which previously held money and jewelry, crawled with cockroaches.

Cursing to herself, Viola flung the bag across the room. Cockroaches skittered across the carpet, running over her sneakers. She inched backward, spit running down her chin, and then broke into a staggering run. The cockroaches fled to the sofa and chair. What happened to Morton? He couldn't have escaped. The arthritis in his legs made it hard for him to walk, let alone run, even in ideal circumstances.

At the front door, Viola whipped a penknife from her pants pocket. She'd learned to use a knife after her combat at Silver Slipper. Thrills forgotten, she rushed outside to the sidewalk. Bright moonlight stung her eyes. Shielding her eyes with her left hand, she gazed across the street, heart hammering in her chest.

The moon splashed silver shadows on the pavement and cars. She made out a spattering of stars surrounded by pitch black sky, too black to be real. The moon shone too bright, a ball of fire peeping between the rooftops that arched eerily toward her.

The hell with it. Viola scrambled across the street, shaking more than she cared to admit, only making a few feet before slamming to a stop.

Her Toyota... what happened to her Toyota?

Viola scanned the moonlit street, but her car was gone. She had no time to wonder who'd stolen her car because an emaciated figure in white emerged from the shadows, a man with blood drooling down his lips and chin.

His name tag read "Chuck Walters, M.D." Cold blue eyes stared at Viola from behind his wire-rimmed glasses. When he and Viola made eye contact, his face broke into a grin, revealing his teeth. Two of them, pointed, glistened in the moonlight.

Viola... His voice, low and gravelly, issued from behind bloodstained lips.

"No!" Tension edged into Viola's voice. "This can't be happening."

Closer and closer he advanced, crepe soles whispering on the pavement. Heart thudding in her chest, Viola searched Morton's porch for a makeshift weapon. Grabbing a rock, she hurled it at her visitor. It smacked his head, gouging his left temple. The doctor trembled, but he kept coming. The head laceration healed without leaving a scar.

Viola...

Screaming, Viola spun left. Her sneakers thudded down the street, dull thumps that became squashy and liquid. Looking down, she saw the reason why. Fresh blood rippled down the pavement and the black-topped street. Another scream came and died in her throat.

Damn it all, you're a fighter, Viola, a phantom voice inside her screamed. *Act like one.*

Viola sprinted down the street, her lungs screaming for air, and bolted into an alley. She slowed, gasping.

"What's wrong with you?" she chided herself. "People say you're crazy. Next, you'll see bugs on the wall, and..."

A door whispered inward. Viola stared at it, door attached to a run-down row house. Its former inhabitants had abandoned it long ago, but something about its dusky interior compelled her to explore.

Viola...

The undead doctor's voice echoed from somewhere behind her. Viola rushed into the house and slammed the door shut. She sagged against it, ear leaning against the wood, eyes surveying the battered windows. Hugging herself and shivering, she listened for sounds beyond the door.

"Hello, Viola."

Viola whirled around, brandishing her knife. Morton's friend, Anne, dressed in a beaded green shirt and matching pants, stood near the opposite window. She stared at Viola, one hand fingering her shirt, the other cradling a red heart-shaped balloon against her lips. She was *kissing* the balloon, wet, slippery kisses.

Now, who's the crazy one?

The silvery moonlight spilling through the windows illuminated Viola's shadow, but not Anne's. The fear, which draped over Viola's shoulders like a mantle turned her skin to gooseflesh. *"You're a fighter,"* the shadowy voice said again.

"What do you want?" she shouted.

Anne smiled her tight-lipped grin, twirling the balloon's ribbon around her fingers. Red dye from the balloon streaked her chin. "I look out for Morton. Don't you get that?"

"Yeah, right." Viola swallowed hard. "Pigs like you hang around Morton, hoping he'll leave you his dough."

"That's rich," Anne chuckled. "Considering that you bled his checking account dry."

"Stop playing with me." Viola waved her knife within inches from Anne's face. Anne did not flinch. "Just tell me what's going on."

"You have a choice," Anne said.

"Damn straight, I do." Viola managed to keep her voice calm, though her knuckles turned white. "Now quit milking it and answer me before I rearrange your face."

Anne's head lifted, her flame curls bobbing with the movement. "When I worked at the sweater mill, three thugs jumped me. By the time paramedics arrived... let's put it this way. I never appreciated life until I almost lost mine. Do you understand me?"

Viola sighed. "Get to the point."

"The blows to my head destroyed my medulla, the part of the brain which controls respirations." Anne rubbed the balloon against her lips again and looked at Viola. "Dr. Walters gave me his serum..."

"What?" Chills wreaked Viola's body.

"Do you remember him?"

With a deep sigh, Viola thought about Silver Slipper's resident assailant and the blows he'd inflicted while she cringed against the wall. The screaming sirens and ride to the hospital. Walters, a world-renowned trauma surgeon, seemed oh-so-concerned when he examined her in the emergency room. In a voice reeking with sincerity, he promised that treatment would ensure a complete recovery.

Instead, the agony burned through Viola like a poison sun, despite bed rest and cortisone injections. Surgery never helped. She became worse. Silver Slipper paid workmen's compensation, but the money offered small comfort, given the agony that whispered rumors of permanent disability.

Viola made it back to work a year later, pain notwithstanding. Her flaring temper or "mental status change," as her supervisor put it, began with snapping at coworkers, and built in crescendo to cursing out and hitting clients who so much as looked at her crooked. Each day,

Viola received another tongue-lashing regarding her inappropriate behavior. "This is the second time you've assaulted a client," her boss said during their last disciplinary conference. "I find your behavior appalling."

"Mrs. Hill tried to punch me when I gave her a bath," Viola told her. "That woman needs restraints."

"Well, your fists left bruises and a torn shoulder," her boss said. "Clean out your locker and leave before I call Security."

That weekend, Viola went home to visit her parents. She felt her dad's censuring glare when she stepped out of her car. More warmth issued from the trees lining the street than from his shadowed features.

"I heard Silver Slipper fired you," he said in a disgusted voice. "You tried using your back injury to avoid honest work. When that failed, you started beating up on sick people."

Viola cowered against her car, spine pressed against the door jam, fists burrowed in her scrub pockets. "Daddy, I..."

"Shut up! Thelma and I taught you better. You have disgraced this family."

"That woman almost gave me a busted lip," Viola cried, tears running down her cheeks. "She reminded me of the creep who tried to maim me with his cane."

"Then find a different line of work. Better yet, sue Silver Slipper. I can't excuse violence." Her father heaved a weary sigh. "Since you still have your CNA license, maybe Care Unlimited will hire you. Those agencies take help that no one else wants."

A week later, Care Unlimited hired Viola. The agency paid its workers under the table, albeit a lower wage. According to management, this enabled the agency to charge its clients lower fees. Most people who worked for Care Unlimited worked full-time at other jobs. It didn't matter so long as it kept Viola off the street.

Six months after Viola's hire, Care Unlimited took on Florence Walters, Dr. Walters' mother. Pneumonia and a stroke consigned Florence to a ventilator and feeding tube. Florence needed a CNA, and Viola volunteered for the job.

At first, Viola made a show of caring. She fluffed Florence's pillows, turned her every two hours, and dressed her in her favorite clothes. She administered Florence's medicine at the precise dose and time. When Dr. Walters called or visited, it crossed her mind to even the score against Walters through his mother, but she was waiting for the right moment.

While gazing at Florence's pale slip of a face one night, Viola snapped off her ventilator. Florence thrashed in bed, gasping for air. The ventilator tubing popped off the old woman's tracheotomy tube, and her hissing breath sounded like air escaping from a tire with a big nail in it. Florence's eyes rolled in their sockets, much like those of a fear maddened horse.

Viola pinched her tracheotomy tube shut. The average person can last nine to twelve minutes without permanent brain damage if his air is cut off, and he lies still. Of course, struggling, terror, and disease cuts into that survival time a great deal. Florence struggled for forty seconds until her efforts to get air flagged. Her mouth drooled. Her wrinkled face turned blue. Her eyes glazed over and became fixed in their sockets. Viola remembered her own fruitless struggles against her attacker, a geriatric version of Mike Tyson, who swung his cane like a hammer. The compassion she'd felt drained out of her, leaving her with a dead feeling. The fever took control that first night, when she gazed at Florence's lifeless eyes, followed by many others.

"Yes, I remember," she said at last.

"Dr. Walters tried to help you, but you abused the painkillers and refused to cooperate with your physical therapist." Anne's pale lips barely moved, but her voice came through loud and clear. "He values human life, unlike you and your friends." A thin smile played on her lips. "Your friends

Carmela and Danielle died of drug overdoses, I hear. That leaves you, Viola Gaunt."

"Walters ignored my complaints." Viola shuddered at the familiar dark tremors of rage. "He never answered my questions until I threatened to sue him. Then he got me fired."

"No, Viola, you got yourself fired," Anne said. "Walters brought a psychiatrist on board, but you refused his help. Instead, you took your anger out on frail people."

"Yeah, right." Viola shook her head. "Why do you care about Walters? He's nothing to you."

"While I lay in a coma, Walters gave me a serum to promote cell regeneration. The next day, I regained consciousness and weaned off the ventilator. This medicine, or whatever it was, healed my injuries within days." She nodded, confirming this to herself. "I owe him my life."

"You can't help Walters now," Viola said. "According to Care Unlimited's rumor mill, he's dead."

"Wrong, Viola." Anne tilted her head. "He's a vampire and vampires never die."

"What are you saying?" Viola burst into gales of laughter. "Vampires don't exist."

"His kind does. The serum changed his basic cell structure, making his body immune to disease. Cuts heal within seconds. Of course, this affected his dietary requirements." Her smile widened and became horribly predatory. "He knows you killed his mother."

"You're crazy, Anne." Viola forced another laugh, this one sounding like rattling bones. "I kept his old lady clean and comfortable. The house looked spotless during his visits. He doesn't suspect a thing."

"That's what you think." A defiant gleam rose in Anne's eyes. "Dr. Walters knows what you did because he read your thoughts. This serum brings out one's paranormal abilities."

"You're lying." Viola tried another laugh, and instead let out a choked snarl. "If this serum works so well, why didn't he give it to his mother?"

"She refused, saying that she wanted to die when her time came. He planned to teach you a lesson, but his lessons work best when his pupils get careless. So he waited. At the moment, he's preparing your lesson at his mausoleum on Widow's Hill. If you apologize and mean it, he might spare you."

"No way! I'll be damned if I apologize to that monster."

"Better yet, check yourself into a psych hospital." Anne's eyes darkened and she became thoughtful, moody, and introspective. "You used to have nothing but compassion for people, but Silver Slipper's client drowned that woman in a sea of hate. You're sick, just like someone with diabetes or cancer, but the right medicine and therapy will save you."

Grabbing Anne by the hair, Viola shoved her against the wall. Her head slammed against the plaster. Her foot caught in a gnarled floorboard, and she stumbled and fell. The balloon floated from Anne's outstretched fingers, snagged itself on a jagged piece of glass, and then exploded with a bang. To Viola's astonishment, warm ruby-red liquid splashed all over herself and Anne, their clothes, and the floor. A coppery stench filled her nostrils.

But she was too busy having fun to give the matter much thought. Left arm pinning Anne to the floor, Viola held her knife against her throat. Anne did not kick or thrash. Her eyes held no fear, only knowing mixed with contempt.

"What's the matter?" Viola taunted her. "Afraid to fight? No strength? So much for Doc Walters' famous serum."

Anne's shiny green eyes drilled into Viola's. "Whatever you say."

"I'll see you rot in hell, that's what."

"It's your call."

"You've got that right." Viola drew the blade across Anne's throat and watched the blood gush from her wound. Anne did not scream or try to fight. One hand moved toward her throat as if to stop the bleeding, and then dropped to the floor.

Viola grinned, shivering with the fever, reveling in her fantasies about the dancing shadows around her. During her childhood, those shadows gave her nightmares. Sometimes she woke up screaming. When she did, her father slapped her on the head and told her to go back to bed.

Now, a surge of power rushed through Viola, the same power she felt when she smothered Florence Walters. She laughed, giddy with the sensation.

Her laughter stopped when she glanced toward the floor. Anne still lay in a pool of blood, but her neck wound fused together without scarring. Blood splattered everywhere, even in the corners away from Anne. It leaked from the tatters of red plastic still hanging on the jagged windowpane. Viola turned her attention back to Anne again, and as she watched, Anne's body grew faint, taking on a ghostly appearance, and then... disappeared.

Viola scanned the house, but she only saw the blood, her knife, and the dripping remains of the balloon. Anne had vanished before her eyes.

Another wave of dizziness rolled through Viola. Her surroundings blurred and glittering colors spun around her. She opened her mouth to scream.

The dizziness stopped.

When her head cleared, Viola found herself at Widow's Hill, a cemetery and cliff that looked down toward a river. The moon illuminated a marble structure the size of a large garden shed. She strained her eyes and read out names on the side facing her: Charles Walters – born 1910, died 1990; Florence Walters – born 1912, died 1996; Chuck Walters, MD – born 1950. She told herself that she was in the psych ward having the granddaddy of hallucinations, but her better mind knew this wasn't true. How did she get here? What happened to Anne?

As she looked, the marble wall swung open, releasing the stench of things long dead and exploded by the gases of their decay. Walters stepped through the aperture, dressed in a businessman's suit and white lab coat. The moon illuminated his milk-pale complexion, bloodstained lips, and jagged teeth.

Screaming, Viola skittered sideways. Her sneakers caught on a rock, sending her into a sprawl. Razor blades of pain muttered through her spine as she slammed into a tombstone.

Rumbling echoed from the surrounding graves. The decayed leaves on the ground quivered and churned as something swelled beneath them. Fissures zipped through the soil. Dirt sprayed around Viola, and mud-crusted cobwebs of fingers clawed through the earth, groping and seeking purchase. Viola lay frozen to the ground, eyes on the two figures climbing from their graves.

Walters stood before Viola. His lab coat, soaked with blood and pink gristle, flowed comber-like around his husky body. An expensive looking stethoscope draped over his broad shoulders. Flecks of pink and dried blood stuck to his hands and chin. He had not aged since her treatment for the back injury. Not even one wrinkle.

Two other figures in tattered robes unearthed themselves. Pink gristle bearded their lips with rivulets of blood flowing down the chins, leftovers from previous feedings. She recognized them as former patients; but their waxy complexions appeared intact despite the ravages of the grave. A rancid odor overwhelmed Viola's senses. The stink of flyblown meat. A horrible understanding dawned, and Viola realized that Walters and his companions staged this reunion and none of it friendly.

"What are you people?" she croaked in a whisper. "What do you want with me?"

Walters met her gaze with steely eyes. "Anne already explained, Viola," he replied in a voice sounding like tearing papyrus.

"Anne doesn't know squat."

"Then how did you get here?"

"I don't know."

"At one time, I had nothing but high praise for your technique and bedside manner toward the sick, but you let one attack by a client make you bitter. I'll never forget your olive oil voice when you pretended to grieve over my mother only hours after you suffocated her. Don't look at me like that. I can read a person from miles away."

Walters glanced toward his companions. "Know what makes this so sad? You took your pain out on sickly people. I'm partially to blame because I saw the signs of your illness and failed to intervene. I kept hoping that you would get treatment. It's time I set things right. It's only fair, Viola."

Viola's hand grabbed a rock. Mustering as much force as she could, she hurled it at Walters. It hit his shoulders and ricocheted along the mausoleum wall before plopping to the ground.

Walters did not stumble or flinch. Viola screamed and screamed. Her eyes moved from side to side, searching for escape, but they saw nothing.

Hands with skin the consistency of cool marble yanked her wrists, snapping her bones like twigs. Agony blared through her arms in a golden shriek of trumpets. Walters thrust her to the grass and straddled her hips, face only inches from hers. He stared at her with a dark intensity.

"You complained about your suffering, but you never needed a ventilator, feeding tube, or other assistive device." Walters paused, as if to let his message sink in. "Maybe you never understood the meaning of suffering. You'll have to find out the hard way."

Eyes rolled back, teeth gaping, Walters tore into her throat. His lips formed a vacuum around her wound, licking and swallowing. Viola bucked and writhed under his weight. Her heels drummed a muffled retreat, chased by the clutch of chilly hands. She used her elbows to beat against Walters' shoulders and only managed to jar her shattered wrists.

Something sharp sliced through her thighs. Walters' companions were kneeling over her legs, guzzling the blood that rushed in an angry gush from her wounds. Her breath came out in pants. Shrieks lodged in her aching throat. The stabbing burned through her legs and back. Had the clients she'd eliminated felt the same agony? When did she get so mean?

Only dimly aware of their hushed voices, Viola watched the three figures rise to their feet. Her blood infused a pink glow to their cheeks. Walters adjusted his stethoscope and gave Viola a cold smile.

A smoky wisp issued from the mausoleum panel. Anne materialized from the smoke, still wearing her green outfit. Blood coated her lips and dripped on her beaded shirt. She carried another heart-shaped Mylar balloon.

Numbness worked its way up Viola's legs. Grayness waded in around her. Blood bubbled from her mouth and gashes.

"That was a tough job, faking my death," she heard Anne say. "Viola bought my act."

"You performed well," Walters said, smiling. "Feeling thirsty?"

"I'm always thirsty, but I've got my stash." Anne tilted her head back, held the balloon over her open mouth, and squeezed. Ruby fluid oozed from the bottom seam of the balloon and poured in a steady stream down her throat.

"That's very clever, Anne," Walters said, laughing. "Let's see about getting you some real nourishment."

The grayness washed over Viola's eyes. She had a fleeting glimpse of fading figures and the short-lived lesson on suffering that would remain for her forever.

Sunset Kill

"Cathy, I've gotten complaints about the dirty linen and trash littering your floor again." Linda Freeman folded her plaid-sleeved arms across her chest. Her blue eyes narrowed into slits, glittering like ice chips. "I'll have to write you up."

Cathy Kirk was sipping a Pepsi when her boss, Freeman, called her into the office. Her shaking hands dropped the can, spraying soda on Freeman's desk and woolen suit.

"I don't believe this." Freeman wiped her clothes with a hanky. "Know what really upsets me? I heard these complaints from visitors. People judge our facility by what they see."

With a deep sigh, Cathy brushed the wisps of sandy hair from her eyes. Of course, cosmetic appearances mattered. Appearances meant that visiting relatives wouldn't notice the missed meals or spotty treatment regimens.

Hugging herself and shivering, she gazed toward the food cart parked by the nurses' desk. "I'm sorry about the mess," she said in a small voice, "but my peeps need help with their meals, especially Sarah. I had to spoon feed her breakfast."

Freeman arched her eyebrows. Her mouth tightened into a thin-lipped frown. "When you're busy, prioritize. Make sure everyone gets their medicines and dressing changes. If people need help with their meals, give your first consideration to residents with visitors." She exhaled deeply. "While you're at it, drop the slang."

"Right." With trembling fingers, Cathy wiped the sweat from her freckled forehead.

"Unless a resident has visiting relatives, don't give them so much attention. Take Sarah, for example. She's gone on Medicaid, and …"

"We're losing money every day she survives," Cathy said without thinking.

"What?" Freeman's voice sounded like a harsh whip cracking in a quiet room. "What did you say?"

Cathy swallowed hard. "Nothing."

"I'm paying your salary," Freeman warned. "If you want to continue working here, you'll follow my rules."

Cathy nodded, dragging a set of clammy fingers through her curly hair. More than anything, she wanted this lecture to end.

Freeman's frown evaporated. A cunning smirk took its place. "One other thing. Yesterday, someone caught you tampering with the attic lock. Did you know that's a firing offense?"

Cathy's hazel eyes widened like soup plates. She knew that some residents stored their off-season belongings and valuables in the attic. The padlocked door and the scratching she heard from the attic tempted her to explore, but not enough to jeopardize her job.

"Whoever told you has it wrong. I've steered clear of the attic."

Freeman paced around her office, staring at Cathy. "Considering my source of information, I doubt it. If the residents need anything from the attic, ask Security to get it."

Cathy averted her eyes, not caring to admit that the security guards shrugged off most requests. Her fists clenched inside her scrub pockets, fingernails digging into her palms. She would have given anything to quit Sunset Hill and spend time with her daughter, Jenny. Even in Freeman's closet-sized office, Cathy pictured her child's sad blue eyes and whimpering voice.

"Mommy, you're never around," she complained. "When you're around, you're not there. You talk like you've got your nose in a book."

"Jenny, I have to work because we can't live with Daddy."

"I know." Jenny's lower lip trembled. "Will Daddy come back, or maybe try to hurt us?"

"Only if we let him." Cathy fingered her scarred shoulders, leftovers from Daddy's whippings. She took Jenny into her arms. "I have to pay the bills. If I don't work, then I might have to ask Daddy for money. Can you understand that?"

"No, because…because your boss beats up people, too, only they're old." She shivered. "I heard you tell Gramma about it."

Out of the mouth of babes, Cathy remembered thinking. She'd tried to find other work, but with a struggling economy…

"Are you listening?" Freeman's harsh voice snapped her back to the present. "Keep your nose out of things that don't concern you." Standing

52

up stiffly, she marched to the door. "You may go, Cathy. We'd better not have this talk again."

"Right." Choking back sobs, Cathy rushed from her office and ducked inside the chapel. A silent prayer slipped from her lips. Pausing by a Gothic window, she gazed at the overcast sky. The courtyard's wrought iron fence, yellowed grass, and marble statues looked like a cemetery. "I should see a lawyer," she said, "or write to some government agency about good old Sunset Hill."

What makes you think anyone will listen? a voice whispered from the deep recesses of her mind. *Freeman could fire and blackball you.*

"Especially if I blab about the deaths." Nose pressed against the stained glass, she thought about the way previously healthy residents had keeled over and died. It happened more times than she cared to remember. *They should name this place Sunset Kill. After what...*

A shrill cry from Room 204 cut into her thoughts. Sarah Parker's quarters. "Stop!" she screamed. "You're hurting me."

"Shit!" Cathy sprinted to a semi-private room by the rear exit. The curtains were drawn, but she could hear Sarah's anguished cries, punctuated by *spla-splash-smack!*

An icy finger of terror crept up Cathy's spine as she peered between the drapes. Sarah lay in threadbare sheets, her gaunt body peppered with lacerations. Tiny ribbons of blood trickled from her cuts. Having read Sarah's chart, Cathy knew that years of steroid treatments had made her skin papery thin.

"Come on, I just gave you a love tap. What?" Sheri raised her manicured hand. Her lips curled into a smug grin. "You want more?"

Sheri's threats bumped Cathy back into her past, before she mustered the courage to get a divorce. Her husband had worn the same shit-eating grin that Sheri did. His eyes held a chilling reptilian watchfulness, especially before his "disciplinary" sessions. "*What?*" he'd asked after each blow. "*You want more?*"

Cathy was reliving it all again, only this time was worse because Sarah couldn't run or defend herself. Her memories and hurt feelings slithered like skeletons from their graves, causing her to break into a sweat.

"Sheri!" She yanked aside the curtain. "Stop!"

Sheri straightened up and favored Cathy with a pleased-with-herself smirk. "I was giving Sarah a bath. She got combative, so I reasoned with her. Right, Sarah?"

Sarah's head bobbed up and down. Her bony shoulders shook, and tears ran down her wrinkled cheeks. The fresh blood staining the sheets sent arrows through Cathy's heart.

"Combative, my ass!" Her voice cracked. "Lay off, Sheri, or I'll tell Ms. Freeman."

Sheri flipped back her dirty blonde hair and shot Cathy a defiant look. "I'd keep my eyes on Sarah if I were you. Otherwise, she might have an accident." She smiled.

If not, her smile said, *I'll arrange one.* The message came through loud and clear with the curl of two lips.

"You little…" Cathy's voice faded into a muffled gasp. She stared, mouth gaping, at Sheri's retreating figure.

After Sheri left, Sarah's weeping subsided. "I don't want to stay here," she whimpered, clutching Cathy's shoulder. "Take me home with you."

Blinking back tears, Cathy wiped Sarah's face. She'd have to call a doctor and make out an incident report, detailing Sarah's lacerations. Dare she tell the truth, or should she blame Sarah's injuries on the usual fall?

"Sarah, you can make the hurting stop," she said after a pause, "if you tell your doctor or the charge nurse."

"They won't listen because they think I'm crazy. I have no family to speak for me." Sarah's voice cracked. She huddled under the sheets, arm folded over her chest. "No one! Loneliness can kill you."

Cathy stroked Sarah's forehead. "I'll pretend I'm a relative," she offered. "Would that help?"

"Oh, yes!" Sarah's gnarled hands grabbed Cathy's. "I'd love having a daughter like you, but you've got a mother. Think I could be your aunt?"

"Maybe." Cathy made notes about Sarah's wounds. "Want to talk to my boss before I turn in my report?"

"Freeman can rot in hell! Walt will see to that." A steely glint crossed Sarah's gray eyes. "He hides upstairs in the attic. At night he visits me."

"Walt?" Cathy rolled her eyes. "I don't think I know—"

"Don't worry about old Walt." Sarah's hand patted Cathy's shoulder. "He only goes after the bad people."

Walt who? Cathy wondered as she finished her afternoon chores. *Friend? Relative? Another resident?* She didn't know any Walts except Walt McMahon, who died three months ago. He and Sarah used to sit on the porch every night before pneumonia had taken him.

According to the charts, Sarah had dementia, and hallucinations came with the territory. No doubt, births and deaths had become obscure memories. Most times, Sarah could not remember what she ate for

54

breakfast. Still, her reference to Walt had turned Cathy's skin to gooseflesh. A chill settled in her bones.

When Cathy showed up for work the following Monday, men in blue uniforms patrolled the parking lot. An officer asked to see her badge. More officers searched the halls, moving furniture, lifting drapes, working their way from room to room. Freeman paced around the desk, arms folded across her chest, eyes darting out the windows.

Cathy hugged her jacket around her, trying to ward off the shivers. Something had gone wrong. Dead wrong. It wasn't like Freeman to become rattled.

"Cathy." Freeman motioned her to the office. After closing the door behind them, she cleared her throat. "Sheri's not coming to work anymore. You'll have to take her assignment."

"No problem." Cathy covered her mouth, hiding a grin. Glancing at her census sheet, she noticed blank spaces by room 204. "What are the cops doing here?"

Freeman's eyes opened wide as soup plates, betraying utter terror. The circles underneath them slipped through her makeup, creating shadows. For the moment, Cathy forgot about her run-ins with Freeman. She forgot about everything except her boss's horrorstricken look.

"Was something stolen?" she asked quietly.

"I suppose you'll find out soon enough." Freeman sighed—a long skeletal sound, like wind rattling newspapers. "Sheri's mother called and said she never came home Friday. She simply disappeared. Her mother called the police."

"What?" Cathy gasped.

"Don't say anything to the residents." Freeman's voice grew shrill. "This isn't the first. Three others are missing. People who've worked here. No clues, no suspects." She paced around the office. "Hereafter, no one may leave the building unescorted."

Walt only goes after the bad people, Sarah had said, and her frosty eyes had not looked like dementia. Cathy averted her face, shuddering. "Where's Sarah?"

"Sarah went into cardiac arrest and died the other night." Freeman checked off room numbers on her census sheet. Her hands shook. She softened her tone, as if struck by an unspoken fear. "I'm sorry about the extra work, but I've got chaos this morning."

Cracking the door, Freeman glanced up the hall. "Have you seen anything strange around the attic door?"

He hides upstairs in the attic. At night, he visits me. Cathy rubbed her arms and stared out the window. "Why? Have the police—?"

"No, and don't give them any ideas!" Freeman snapped, back to her I'm-the-boss demeanor. "Keep your mouth shut. If I find any laundry on your floor, you'll hear about it."

After searching the resident floors, the uniformed men headed to their cars. Cathy gave out the morning medicines and fed the residents their lunches. During rounds, she caught a male aide shoving an elderly man, and she reamed him out for it. Business as usual.

After lunch, Cathy glanced at the grandfather clock, standing like a sentinel in the lobby. It was one o'clock. She seldom finished her chores so early. Usually, she'd see if one of the other nurses needed help, but today, she kept looking at the lobby's steel gray elevator.

With shaky hands, she pressed the button marked "three." The third floor, reserved for out-of-town visiting families. Cathy remembered this floor from her orientation: white plaster walls everywhere, velvet furniture, private bedrooms, and a staircase leading to the attic.

The furnishings hadn't changed, but a rancid, coppery smell lingered in the air. The padlock to the attic door was missing. She took two tentative steps toward the brass banister, noting the red poppy designs on the staircase runner. Those weren't there before either. At the sound of nails scraping the floor boards, she started.

Whirling, she threw her arms across her face and bit back a scream. A mouse scuttled from under the sofa. Only a mouse. Slowly she let out a deep breath.

Have you seen anything strange around the attic? Freeman had asked. Cathy's eyes shifted between the elevator and attic door. The police hadn't searched the third floor. She imagined Freeman trumping up excuses to keep the officers away from the attic. Perhaps Freeman wanted that floor left alone so that she and her favorite workers could help themselves to the valuables. Somehow that felt right.

At the stairway, the stench became nauseating. Cathy climbed the first step and slid on something wet. Clumps of stringy red material coated the poppy designs. Not poppies. Blood. Drying blood, big blotches of it, coated stair step and riser. Bile rose in her throat. She gulped, fighting the scream building in her throat. If Freeman heard her, she'd be in a world of shit.

That blood. All that blood.

Maybe Sheri had gotten into a nasty fight, her way of reasoning with people. Cathy didn't want to know the details. Any moment, the people involved would come back to clean up and dispose of any evidence. Cathy didn't want to be around when that happened.

"I've got no business snooping around here." She shuddered. "Jenny's counting on me. I'd better get back to work."

That's right, Cathy, her inner voice warned. *Run while you can.*

Instead, her legs developed minds of their own and walked her up the steps. She tried the doorknob. Locked. She contemplated the old folks laying for hours in excrement, the aides who manhandled them, and the way Freeman smiled, congratulating the aides for doing a great job. After darting a glance over her shoulder, Cathy fished through her pocket for a bobby pin.

A click sounding like grating bones followed. The door creaked inward. Cathy snapped open a light, illuminating a gloomy room. Inside, a woman wearing a pink robe sat on a torn leather couch. Tangled yellow hair surrounded her wrinkled face. Sarah's face, except ... Sarah was two days dead.

"Cathy, why are you staring?" the woman cackled. Her laugh sounded like a death rattle. "Aren't you glad to see me?"

"Sarah?" Cathy swallowed hard, her teeth chattering. "Ms. Freeman said you ... you ..."

"Don't be so frightened." Sarah licked her blood red lips. Hands cold as marble clasped Cathy's hands. "You treated me like family. I'd never hurt my flesh and blood."

Cathy's rasping breaths echoed through the room. With trembling fingers, she groped for Sarah's pulse.

There was none. Sarah's parchment skin felt cold as death.

Dizziness rolled through Cathy, blurring her surroundings. Seconds later, she plummeted into darkness.

When Cathy came to, she lay on the sofa, head cradled in Sarah's lap. A damp cloth lay over her forehead. Sarah's sickeningly strong smell caused her to gag.

"Feeling better?" Sarah smiled, her crooked, bloodstained teeth dangling from gray gums.

Cathy nodded, sitting up. She turned and faced Sarah. The attic's overhead light illuminated blisters the size of quarters on Sarah's arms. White patches streaked her cheeks. *Two days dead. Like zombies.* Cathy shivered. "How ... why?"

"My friends and I came here after we died to settle the score with Sunset," Sarah answered sadly. "Sealed coffins and locked doors couldn't stop us. I heard Miss Sheri and some of the others got you in trouble, but they won't bother you any more."

"They won't?" Cathy mopped the sweat from her forehead. The unreality and horror of the situation was sinking in. A grayness washing over her caused her to sway.

"Stop that." Sarah's bony hand braced her shoulder. "Fainting will not make this go away. The people who hurt us will pay."

Cathy pressed her fist against her mouth to stop the trembling. She told herself she'd handled worse during her marriage. *Is that so?* her inner voice whispered. *It sounds like your husband had provided a mere schoolroom for your present nightmare.*

"Maybe you should fear the living," Sarah added, as if reading her thoughts. "Your rotten husband left deep scars. The kind only the dead can see."

Cathy thought about Sunset's bullies and the way they terrified the residents by squeezing them too hard or withholding their food. "He did," she conceded at last. "The same way my coworkers scarred you. Maybe I can help you set things right."

"I knew you'd come through." Sarah hugged Cathy against her chest, almost crushing her. Her stench was like rotting tomatoes. "After we've taught them some lessons, then I'll rest."

A lump welled in Cathy's throat, partly from terror, partly from remorse. "I'm sorry for working with these monsters, but I just got divorced, and I need the money. I tried finding work somewhere else, but I couldn't because of the economy."

"You helped more than you realized. Your peer workers acted nice when you were around." Sarah lowered her voice to a whisper. "Freeman used her snake oil charm on us when we had the money. After our funds ran out, she made us miserable."

"If you want to hurt Freeman, there's a watchdog agency called Join Commission on Accreditation of Healthcare Organizations. JCAHO. Too many complaints, too many violations, and Ms. Freeman will have to close up shop." Cathy managed a weak smile, but it felt like a ghastly effort. "Shall we contact JCAHO?"

"No government agencies." Sarah's thin-lipped frown discouraged any argument. She met Cathy's gaze with eyes resolute as steel. "A life for a life, a limb for a limb."

"A limb for a limb?" Cathy echoed feebly, thinking about the disappearances again. Understanding dawned when she noticed flecks of maroon on Sarah's hands and fingernails, and bits of gristle coating her teeth. "Oh, my God!"

"God has nothing to do with this." Sarah ushered Cathy to her feet. "When you meet the others, you'll understand."

"Where are you—" The room spun around Cathy, causing her to lurch against Sarah's grip. She squeezed her eyes shut. Colors flowed in disgusting shapes under her lids. When she opened her eyes again, Sarah was ushering her into what looked like a day room.

Inside, skeletal figures wearing hospital gowns rose from their cushioned chairs. They stared at Cathy with eyes like bottomless pits. Chalky bones poked through their cracked, leathery skin. Insects buzzed around the room, forming dark clouds over her hosts. The room reeked of flyblown meat.

Cathy clutched her stomach, fighting waves of nausea. A scream lodged in her throat, but her tightening chest afforded a barely audible croak.

"Everyone, meet Cathy Kirk." Smiling, Sarah prodded Cathy toward the group. "Some of you may remember her from downstairs. She's our dear friend."

"Fr-fr-friend," Cathy managed between chattering teeth. Chills racked her body, drenching her with icy perspiration. Death had obliterated most of the figures' features, reducing them to mummified skeletons.

A man wearing a blue robe approached her, extending his skeletal hand. His wire-rimmed glasses and gold-studded teeth looked vaguely familiar. The gold caps might have looked interesting on a human, but nested in his death's head face, they made Cathy shiver.

"Welcome aboard, Cathy," he said in a gravelly voice. He shook her hand with skeletal fingers coated with greasy flesh. "After you finish your training, maybe you can join us on a permanent basis."

Walt McMahon had gold-capped teeth! The realization came like the snapping of brittle bones. Cathy's breathing came fast and hard. Her heart thudded. "What—what training?"

"The other nurses treated us like dirt," Walt said, "but you brought our meals on time."

"We never forgot your kindness," one of the others spoke up, "and the grief you took from Freeman on our behalf."

"I did what I thought was right." Cathy swallowed hard. "I tried to do my best for all of you."

"Don't sweat it." Walt's grip tightened. "Bring us our meat, and we'll be happy. That's what I meant by training."

Cathy turned her head, waving away the flies that circled Walt, but with careful movements. She would do well to avoid actions that projected hostility. "What kind of meat?"

"We want your workers," Walt said in a measured, quiet voice, releasing his grip. "The nasty folks who mistreated us. Take Miss Sheri, for instance. Last night, she made an excellent entrée."

"You had her for dinner." Cathy gasped. Her mind refused to process what she knew was true.

"Oh, yes, we had her for dinner." Sarah giggled. The others joined in until the laughter reached a crescendo.

"Oh, no!" Cathy covered her eyes. "My God, what are you asking me to do?"

No answer. The others continued staring at her with their sunken eyes. Maybe she should worry for her own life. "Look, I hate working at Sunset Kill—"

"Hey!" Walt flashed a toothy grin. "What an interesting Freudian slip!"

"I mean, Sunset Hill." Cathy kept her tone neutral. The difference between the right and almost right word could lead to a wrong, deadly wrong situation. "The aides, nurses … whoever mistreated you should go to jail. A word to the right people can make that happen."

She lifted her gaze, trying hard not to see their stick-like limbs, or gag on their fetid odor. "A prison for a prison. Right?"

"Wrong." Walt cradled her face in his greasy, bony hands. His flesh-crusted fingernails pressed into her cheeks. A twisted and rather menacing grin surfaced on his skull-caved face. "After those bastards finish doing time, they'll start over in another home."

"Besides, if your officials shut down this place, you won't have an income," Sarah told her. "You just said you couldn't find other work."

Cathy nodded, her face flushing. "That's right, I did."

"Look at this as an opportunity," Sarah said, her tone like a guidance counselor advising a student. "I promise we'll make it worth your while."

For some reason, Cathy looked at her hands. Bands of corded muscle ran from her palms to elbows, gotten from lifting patients. In a physical contest, she'd have no trouble overpowering people like Sheri and Freeman. As for these walking corpses … different story.

"Use a subtle approach," Sarah continued. "Take Ms. Freeman, for instance. Tell her you heard noises in the attic. She'll check. We'll dispose of her."

"We could hunt them out ourselves," Walt said, "but then we'd attract attention, and innocent people might get hurt. We want to wipe the slate clean."

Cathy blotted the salty sweat burning into her eyes. Right now, these people were capable of thinking. But she could tell by their wasted appearance, milk-pale skin, and foul odor that their decaying processes would continue. What remained of their brains would rot, and there was no telling where the crumbs would fall.

"What will happen if I refuse?"

"You might become the next entrée." Walt's fingers dug deeper into her cheeks. Cathy winced at the stinging pain, the blood trickling down her face. His sinister voice intimated that those fingers could dig into her brain.

"Walt, leave her alone!" Sarah grabbed his wrist. "Cathy needs time to get used to the idea, and your bullying her won't help." She shoved him into a chair. "Shut up and sit down."

"Yeah, yeah, yeah." Walt slumped in his chair, jutting out his bony chin. Under other circumstances, he'd remind Cathy of a little boy caught with his hand in the cookie jar.

Instead, she saw a monster. A grotesque monster. With her breath gulping with sobs, she sank to the floor, knees against her chest.

"Cathy?" Sarah's voice softened. Her cool fingers stroked Cathy's hair.

Cathy's shoulders shook with sobs. She cringed against the wall, covering her eyes, and braced herself for the inevitable agony. "Please don't hurt me. My daughter needs me—"

"No one's going to hurt you." Sarah pried Cathy's arms loose. "But you've got to listen."

"I already have." Cathy's voice came out in choked gasps. She had no weapons, and even if she did, there had to be twenty of those monsters surrounding her. "Either I kill or be killed. Why me? I did my best to help you. You don't know how often I cried myself to sleep over things that were done to you. Why don't you appreciate my efforts?"

"We appreciate everything you've done, but your coworkers have hurt us in ways you don't even know." Gnarled hand pointing to her companions, Sarah roll-called the abuses. "Walt caught pneumonia because his caregiver didn't bother to wash her hands. She never reported his cough. Joe choked to death after an aide gave him water, even though a doctor put up the 'no clear liquids' sign by his bed. Melanie died because no one took her chest pain seriously. Instead of checking vital signs, her aide copied the previous day's vital signs in her chart."

61

"The ones who took blood were no better," a withered woman in the rear spoke up. "One technician dug around my arm as if though he were prospecting for gold. He laughed about it."

"I believe it." Their pained voices and wasted appearances sank through Cathy's heart like jagged teeth. "Ms. Freeman majored in I Am God 101, and she hired—" She snapped her mouth shut, trembling. What was she saying? Commiserating implied a willingness to do what they asked.

"You say you care," Sarah said, "but if you don't help us, those animals will continue to make people suffer the way we did. Don't you wonder why some of us died so suddenly? Why so many people become catatonic after just a week at Sunset?"

"The staff broke our spirit," Walt jumped in. "They made their lethal errors after our money ran out."

"Lethal errors?" Cathy struggled to her feet, thinking about the incident reports detailing falls, ripped feeding tubes, et cetera. "I—I don't know what to tell you."

"Maybe now you understand what we're saying," Walt said with finality, "and what has to be done."

"It's not that simple," a woman next to him piped up. "Cathy has a little girl. What happens to the child if someone catches on to her?"

"Good question," Sarah said. "Cathy, you should go downstairs before someone misses you." After motioning the others to stay, she escorted Cathy to the door. "I want you to think about our talk, and ask yourself how you felt when your husband hit you. How you'd feel if your mother went into a home like Sunset."

A blush burned its way up Cathy's cheeks. "I should have seen everything that happened. I'm—I'm sorry, Sarah."

"No need to be." Sarah pressed her lips against Cathy's forehead. Her kiss felt like shards of glass. "I know you'll do the right thing."

"The right thing." Head lowered and shoulders sagging, Cathy shuffled down the steps. She stopped in a restroom to wash the smell of death from her arms and face. Moments later, she headed to the first floor, where the other nurses were giving their end-of-shift report. Freeman posted assignments on the bulletin board.

She then turned around and met Cathy's gaze. "What happened to you?" she asked in a voice oozing with concern. "Where did you get your bruises?"

"I'm all right." Cathy rubbed her cheek. "I tripped."

Titters rose from her coworkers. "Maybe next time, she'll break her leg," someone said.

"Connie, that wasn't nice," Freeman said, no longer edgy. She was smiling, the same kind of smile Cathy had seen in the bullying aides.

These animals will continue to make people suffer the way we did. Cathy squeezed her eyes shut, trying to blot out the echoes in her head. *The staff broke our spirit.*

Cathy opened her eyes again. Her coworkers were heading toward the time clock. "Damn it all," she whispered, rubbing her aching head. "I can't ignore these old folks."

More giggles erupted from the clock. "What did you say?" Freeman asked, an evil glint in her eyes.

Cathy ambled toward the bulletin board, eyes on Freeman. "I said I can't ignore these disappearances." She placed her lips close to Freeman's left ear. "I found Sheri."

Freeman's smile dropped off her face like fingerprints wiped with bleach. "Where?" she asked.

"Um … in the attic. I heard a scratching sound, and the door was unlocked. I went inside and, ah, tripped over her body."

"Call the police!" Freeman scooted around the desk. "Don't say anything to the others." She bolted to the elevator. The other workers clocked out and headed to the exit.

Cathy watched the elevator doors close behind Freeman while with one hand, she reached for the phone. She called her daughter's school, saying that she'd be late picking up Jenny. After that, she sat at the desk, elbows propped on the blotter, and stared at the clock. Ten minutes passed. Twenty minutes. When forty minutes went by, and Freeman hadn't returned, a sunken and rather horrible grin worked its way to her face.

Things were going to be different at Sunset Hill.

Very different.

Take the aides who roughed up the residents. Cathy supposed she'd have to watch herself around their friends. But when they were alone, she would lure them to the attic, where Sarah, Walt, and the others would be waiting…

Cathy laughed softly.

It was just another way to reason with people.

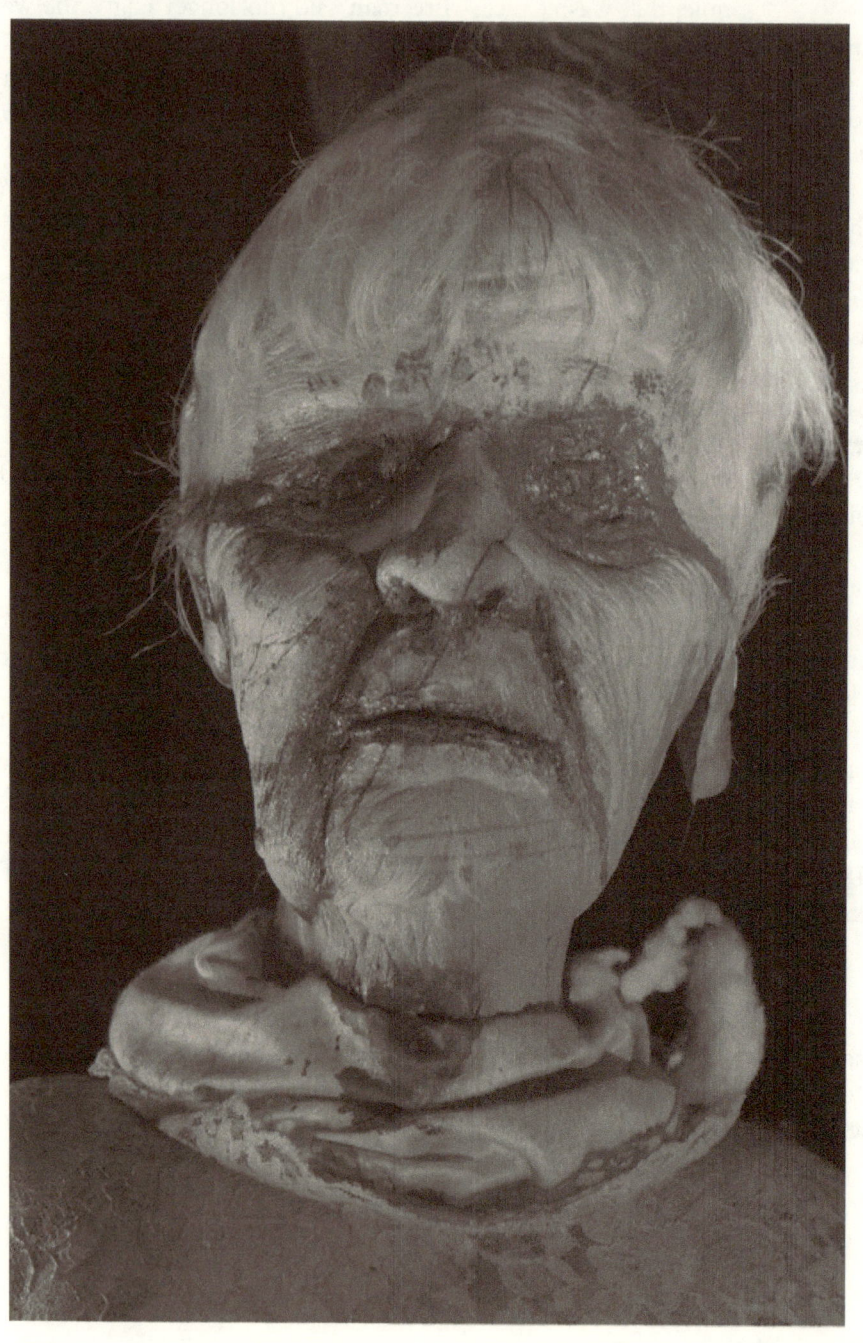

Death's Dividend

Leila's stethoscope, a 2035 Littman Model, refused to stay still. Every time she bent or reached for something, its ears inched up her lab coat pocket and snagged onto an intravenous pump or other equipment. Back stiffening, she glanced over her shoulder, thinking she heard footsteps. The hall appeared deserted, but she sensed that someone—or something—was watching her.

Patients on air mattresses lined the cold, white corridor behind the Intensive Care Unit, where Leila worked, obscured by the nurses' station. Their groans, sounding like rattling bones, reminded her that they were long overdue for pain medicine. She shuddered at the thought of even looking at them, let alone working in the ICU next door, especially when a patient's health insurance had expired.

"Leila!" boomed a voice belonging to a man in a three-piece suit. His name tag labeled him as Frank Mitchell, M.D., Respiratory Therapy.

With a startled gasp, Leila jumped sideways. The stethoscope popped loose and clattered on the floor.

"This morning, I saw you and your *friend* laughing like hyenas." Mitchell leaned against the doorway, gray-sleeved arms folded across his chest. His blue eyes glittered like ice chips. "Do you find medicine amusing?"

Leila glanced toward her patient, a young man covered head to toe with tubes. She scratched her head thoughtfully, thinking about her coworker's zombie sketch. "No, sir," she replied. "Harvey showed me a funny drawing."

"Is that right?" Mitchell advanced slowly toward the bed. His cologne's sickening sweet odor wafted through the room, causing Leila's eyes to water. "If you don't watch yourself, I'll wipe that smile off your face."

Leila nodded, blinking back tears. Her fists tightened inside her scrub pockets.

Reaching into his jacket, Mitchell slammed a folded paper on the side table. "Harvey went home sick," he said. "You think he's so funny, you can cover his assignment."

"Whatever you say," Leila heard her small voice whisper. She knew that Harvey's asthma flared if he inhaled any fragrant oils, like the kind Mitchell wore.

"This is the third time this year he's gone home sick," Mitchell said. "Next time, he's out the door. I'll be damned if I employ invalids in my department." He strode down the hallway, shaking his head.

With a deep sigh, Leila snatched up her stethoscope, cursing softly so that Mitchell wouldn't hear. Using an alcohol swab, she scrubbed its bell, as she always did between patients.

Arms hugging her assignment sheets, she headed to the cardiac ward adjoining ICU. She began doling out breathing treatments and other therapies. The nurses at the desk looked up and smiled as she shuffled by, *real* smiles instead of the condescending smirks given by Mitchell.

The other respiratory therapists had scattered like pigeons after morning report. Leila knew that treatment rounds kept them busy, even if they weren't seeing patients. Her friend, Charlotte, had explained that "treatment rounds" meant staying out of Mitchell's way.

For the Serenity Springs patients—the ones whose insurances and funds had run out—Mitchell's visit promised a death sentence. According to the Mason-Hoover Act passed in 2020, the one eliminating Medicaid benefits, patients without health insurance had to fork over cash payment, and Mitchell acted as chief enforcer. When their money ran out, Mitchell cut all treatments, from headache pills to antibiotics to life support equipment.

"Earth calling Leila! Earth calling Leila!" Mitchell's voice invaded her thoughts. He stood by the heart station, arms propped against the desk. With his dark mustache, granite eyes, and thin-lipped frown, he reminded Leila of Adolph Hitler.

Leila brushed moist wisps of chestnut hair from her eyes. "I'm sorry," she said, swallowing hard. "I didn't hear you."

"I suggest you pay attention." Mitchell's voice was edged with annoyance. "Professionals don't lurch like they're in a trance."

Leila glanced at her watch. It was almost twelve. She'd have to finish her treatments before the lunch trays arrived. "What did I do now?"

"Your shoes have to go." Mitchell folded his bulky arms across his chest, meeting her gaze with eyes cold as a wind in January. "Next time I see you wearing them, I'll have you suspended."

Hugging herself and shivering, Leila lowered her face. Her pink leather shoes showed no stains or scuff marks. She'd chosen the color to match her scrubs. "What's wrong with my shoes?"

"Pink looks unprofessional," Mitchell said coolly. "You look like you've stepped in strawberry tube feeding."

Several nurses lifted their heads from their charting. One of them gave Leila a subtle glance. "Don't let that bastard get to you," she whispered.

"Excuse me, Do-*lor*-es." Mitchell's ruddy face darkened like clouds before a storm. Leila thought that if his looks could kill, Dolores would drop dead. "You have something to say? You can tell me."

Delores leaned back in her chair, defiance rising in her green eyes. "One day, Mr. Mitchell, you'll lose all your best workers."

Leila stared at the linoleum floor, longing for a hole to open up and swallow her. She hated people fighting over her even more than she dreaded Mitchell's harassment.

"I suggest you mind your own business," Mitchell sneered softly. "Otherwise, I'll have to fire you."

"I'm sure you will, Doctor." Dolores rested her hands on her hips and glared at Mitchell. "Gets lonely at the top, doesn't it?"

Leila edged away from the desk, tracing her manicured finger along her scar, an incision hidden by her thick, chestnut curls. Dr. Keene, her neurologist, had implanted a microchip in her right temple to prevent epileptic seizures. Did Mitchell know? The idea of him finding out had repercussions she couldn't face. She bolted down the hall.

"Get back here, Leila!" Mitchell shouted. There was no mistaking the menace in his voice. "I'm not done with you yet."

"Guess not." Leila rubbed her bony arms, trying to soothe the goose bumps.

"I'm giving you fair warning. If you want to continue working here, you'll have to dress appropriately." After giving Leila a frosty stare, he strode toward the rear hall.

"Dr. Mitchell," a female voice called from the air mattresses. The plate above her head gave her age at thirty, but her voice sounded dim and ancient. "Would your doctors consider doing my liver transplant pro bono? I'll die without the surgery, and my two boys need me."

"I wish I could help you," Mitchell said in a smooth voice, the oily one he reserved for patients. "But if Serenity Springs Hospital treated everyone pro bono, it would go bankrupt."

"I understand." The woman's voice broke. Leila could see tears pooling in her eyes. "Could you make an exception just this once? Please?"

"No cash, no card, no care." This time, Mitchell's voice chilled like winter frost. He hurried his pace, keeping out of arm's reach from the patient's skeletal hands in case he'd catch their illnesses.

So much for poetic justice, Leila thought sadly.

Buzzing drowned his footsteps. The elevator's doors slid open, and Plexiglas robots rolled forth in large lazy lopes, delivering medicine trays.

"Damn you, Mitchell!" Leila clenched her fists. She told herself that she should count herself lucky to afford her medical care. The telling did not alleviate her shivering. After a moment of consideration, Leila concluded that Mitchell couldn't fire her for her condition if he didn't know about it. Heaving a deep sigh, she shuffled to a computer to begin her charting.

After what could have been moments or hours, a plump hand rubbed her shoulder. It belonged to her friend, Charlotte. She looked down at Leila with a mournful look.

"Hand me your beeper," she said, reaching for Leila's assignment sheets. "Go get your lunch. I'll cover your floors."

"Thanks." Leila glanced at the screen. "I'll go after I finish this last note."

"Serenity Springs Hospital is holding a virtual reality carnival this Saturday," Charlotte said, leaning against the desk. "Coming?"

"Not with Mitchell and his buddies breathing down my neck," Leila said. "I wouldn't go to any show hosted by this place."

Charlotte wiped the sweat dripping from her tanned face. "Why do you let that man get to you?"

Leila sighed—a long, skeletal sigh, sounding like a breeze blowing through window drapes. "Because I need a job."

"No job is worth making yourself sick." Charlotte hovered over Leila, eyes wide and frightened. "Didn't Chadwick warn that stress could cause another seizure?"

"Thank you for sharing," Leila said between clenched teeth as she typed furiously. "You want to talk about stress? Unemployment would make me really sick."

"Face it. You've got a bad job." Charlotte's voice softened, offering a reprieve. "The best thing about a bad job is that you'll never lose it."

"Don't bet on it." Leila leaned against her chair and looked at Charlotte. "Mitchell's had it in for me ever since that night with Anna. If he fires me, I won't have insurance or money to replace my microchip. Get my drift?"

Charlotte nodded somberly. "And so Mighty Mouth continues picking on you because he knows he can get away with it. He's a chicken-shit." Charlotte flapped her arms. "Buc-buc-buc!"

"You've got a point there." A weak giggle escaped Leila's pale lips. "All right, I'll go. I can use a break."

While Leila completed her progress notes, steel gray robots lumbered through ICU, moving beds and other equipment. The rear glass doors slid open, and a horrible stench wafted from the hall patients. Cries of mad fear and agony echoed through the ward. Most of the patients appeared near death. That didn't surprise Leila. Afterwards, these people would go to the cemetery behind the hospital, unless their families could afford a traditional burial or cremation. Most couldn't.

Everyone in town called these woods Serenity Springs Cemetery because its grounds adjoined the hospital. Rows of battered, unmarked graves ran several miles, where anyone on the run could hide. *And,* Leila pondered, *where a crooked administrator could dispose of his casualties.*

The thought sent shivers up her spine. Swallowing hard, she tiptoed through the crowded hallway and gazed at the patients. Bathed in sweat and urine, they had withered to skeletons. The chills settled around her neck.

Her friend, Anna Shuster, had died in that hall.

An elderly patient, Anna had spent her last years in and out of Serenity Springs, fighting emphysema and losing the battle an inch at a time. During the last six months, her name languished on a waiting list for a lung transplant, while a ventilator pumped air through her tracheotomy. Still, she kept her platinum wavy hair neatly groomed, and layers of blush hid her grayish complexion. "I have to look good," she'd told Leila, "in case I go to the operating room."

If Anna's insurance had lasted a few more months, Leila felt sure she would have gotten the lung. Anna had become her best friend—almost replacing her mother, who'd died years ago. Their friendship had blossomed the night Leila aspirated a mucus plug that had almost choked Anna. Anna wrote a note to Mitchell, swearing that Leila had saved her life.

Leila had never understood why Anna made so much fuss over someone who was just doing their job. But the gentle way that Anna spoke invited trust, and Leila began visiting her after work. During those times, she talked about her father, her experiences in school—whatever crossed her mind—and found herself laughing off the tensions at Serenity Springs.

At night, Leila researched Anna's medical history, hoping to find something that the doctors missed. She had to thank her father, a laboratory technologist, for explaining which test results excluded patients from insurance coverage, and how to doctor blood samples accordingly. Working shoulder-to-shoulder with trusted nurses, she fudged the numbers to keep

Mitchell and his watchdogs at bay.

But Mitchell always badgered his staff with why-wasn't-this-done questions, especially Leila. He went through every lab report with a magnifying glass. More than once, when Leila cut through the hospital's courtyard to run blood samples, she would hear whispering footsteps behind her. Mitchell's crepe soles. He said he was taking a walk, but his narrowed eyes and pleased-with-himself smirk warned that he was up to something.

It was less than a year ago when she'd visited Anna for the last time. Winter had announced its arrival with a blizzard and freezing temperatures, leaving the staff, including Leila, stranded at the hospital. A frosty wind howled, rattling the trees' skeletal branches.

Drafts seeping through the oblong windows caused Anna to shiver. Her lungs pooled with fluid, and Leila kept aspirating copious secretions from her tracheotomy. There would be no conversation tonight. Instead, Leila read Anna a magazine story. Moments later, she heard swishing steps.

The glass doors to Anna's cubicle slid open. Mitchell sauntered in, cradling his alligator briefcase, flanked by two security guards and a nurse administrator. All of them wore black suits. Always black or gray, Leila remembered thinking. Dressed for someone's funeral.

Pausing at Anna's bedside, Mitchell glanced at the wall clock, and then gave Leila a patronizing look. "It's getting late, Leila," he said in a voice reeking with cheer—the kind of cheer he used when he got high off of his own meanness. "Don't you think you should rest, in case they need you for a third shift?"

Liquid fear ran through Leila's heart. "I'm all right," she said, rubbing her arms, trying to soothe the goose bumps. "Anna said I could visit until someone needs me."

"Anna and I have some important matters to discuss." Mitchell grinned—a crooked and rather malignant grin. "*Very* important. Right, Anna?"

Anna nodded, but said nothing. Tears trickled down her wrinkled face, leaving pale smudges in her makeup. Her blue-veined hands shook, and her eyes opened wide as soup plates. *Please don't go,* her trembling lips begged silently. *That bastard's going to sign my death warrant.*

"Anna wants me to stay," Leila heard her small voice say.

"Suit yourself." Mitchell eased himself into a chair by the bed while the guards lingered by the door. "Ms. Shuster, your government insurance has expired. Do you have savings?"

More tears rolled down Anna's wrinkled cheeks. Her mouth hitched with hoarse sobs. Leila squeezed her hand and held a finger to her lips.

What made me think I could keep faking the test results? "Anna believes in saving for a rainy day," Leila said, mustering her best therapist's smile. She nudged Anna's shoulder. "I'll be glad to help her contact her bank."

"I hope her bank comes through," Mitchell chanted in a sing-song voice. "Because it's *ra-a-aining!*"

Anna's right hand tugged her white sheets, and the left clutched at her chest. The streaks under her makeup turned purple. Her chest gurgled, setting off a chorus of ventilator alarms as she struggled to mouth the words. "No money."

"No money?" Mitchell arched his thickset brows. "This poses a problem. Are you sure?"

With trembling fingers, Anna reached for a pen and note pad. She scribbled, "Money went to my retirement home."

"That's too bad. We'll have to withdraw your ventilator and other treatments."

Leila gulped, fighting an onslaught of tears. "She's got a grace period, though. Right?"

"Grace periods are nothing more than glorified charity." Mitchell turned toward the nurse administrator. "Ms. Shannon, I authorize you to shut down the ventilator."

The blonde woman nodded. With a grim look and steely eyes, she unhooked the corrugated hoses from Anna's tracheotomy tube and snapped off the ventilator.

"Don't!" Leila cried. "You can't—you aren't supposed to stop life support. Anna can't breathe without her ventilator."

Mitchell's eyes mirrored the ice coating the window panes. His voice, though soft, tore through Leila's heart like teeth.

"I know."

Burning rage reared in her head, surrounding Leila with a blood-red glow. Already, Anna's oxygen saturation started to drop. Crowing noises sounding like death rattles issued from her gray lips. Her wrinkled fingers clawed the air, groping for purchase that didn't exist. Something inside Leila died at the sight.

A pungent smell tugged at Leila's nostrils, warning her that a seizure was forthcoming. Lurching toward the bed, she shoved the nurse aside and fumbled for the ventilator's control switch.

A security guard yanked Leila by the collar, and she felt her feet rise off the floor. She had time to watch the medicine-stained linoleum rush underneath her. She had time to glimpse the cracks shaped like skulls in the tile, seconds before her shoulder slammed against the wall.

Horrible, burning pain flared through her shoulder, and colors danced around her eyes in sickening shapes. "You monsters!" she heard her voice shout. "Doesn't Anna have the right to live?"

Mitchell's voice, sounding like the crack of a harsh whip, seemed far away. "Silver Springs doesn't run charity wards."

"You...you..." The blood-red glow intensified, and a horrible wave of vertigo surged through Leila. When she looked toward the bed, head reeling, she saw Anna's graying face. Slow, gasping breaths escaped Anna's lips. The last thing that Leila saw, before fading into the blackness, was Anna's eyes rolling back, assuming utter blankness.

When Leila came to, she lay on a cot. Waves of throbbing pain muttered through her head and shoulder.

Charlotte sat in a chair wedged against the door. "Leila!" she cried, blue eyes bulging. "You gave everyone a scare."

"Where am I?" Leila asked, struggling to a sitting position.

"Dr. Keene brought you to her suite. She told Mitchell that you'd fainted." Charlotte's tanned face glistened with sweat. Her lips trembled, betraying alarm and, Leila suspected, disgust with Mitchell. "If he finds out you had a seizure, he'll make your life miserable."

Leila massaged her temples, trying to ease the throbbing. "Maybe I'd better quit. I can't stomach the way he withholds treatment just because someone's insurance expired."

"Neither can most of the staff," Charlotte said. "We should sign a petition or file a grievance with Human and Cybernetic Resources."

"It won't work, because legally, Mitchell's right. I've got to find another job, even if it means becoming a data processor."

"It won't come to that." Charlotte's plump hands eased Leila against the pillows. "When spring comes, you can look for something at another hospital. I'm sure Dr. Keene would be willing to help."

"Yeah, right." Leila rolled over and sobbed into the pillow. She couldn't care less about the other hospitals. As far as she was concerned, without Anna, winter would last forever.

Saturday night, Leila paced her living room, dressed in her blue bathrobe. Charlotte announced herself on the intercom. With an empty shrug, she padded to the door.

Charlotte stood at her patio, gazing at Leila through lifted brows. She ambled into the kitchen and sighed—a long, ghostly sigh that hinted at her own fear. "The carnival will start soon. Why haven't you dressed?"

Leila headed to a window and stared at the darkening sky. "I can't go."

Charlotte marched toward the window, lips tightened and arms folded across her chest. "Why not?"

"Because Mitchell and his friends will be there." Leila nodded, confirming this to herself. "They'll watch every move I make and hassle me."

"Let him try," Charlotte challenged Leila, stubbornness creeping into her voice. "They can't hurt you off-duty."

"Oh, can't they?"

Charlotte's set jaw and tight-lipped frown told Leila that she had no choice. She sighed. "Wait here while I change."

After rooting through her closet, Leila selected metallic purple slacks and a matching top. Head lowered and shoulders drooping, she shuffled to Charlotte's car.

Moments later, Charlotte parked on a grassy spot. They passed a brass eagle fountain and a maze of pavilions. Each one offered a tour through virtual reality. Shifting her eyes, Charlotte pointed to a neon red sign labeled *The Haunted Tunnel.* "We should check out that pavilion. Do you like ghost stories?"

Leila shrugged. Under other circumstances, she might enjoy surfing cyberspace with the Haunted Tunnel's spooks, but tonight, she longed for the carnival to end. "Yeah, sure," she mumbled, shuffling toward the ticket booth.

Moments later, Leila squeezed behind Charlotte into a gigantic white tent. She found herself sitting cross-legged on an air cushion, right in front of Mitchell and his black-suited friends. A bony, cold hand of dread wrapped around her throat. Even in the dark, she could feel his eyes drilling into the back of her neck, watching and waiting.

The stage screen turned neon blue, and moonlight flooded her surroundings with a pearly mist. Light pulsed from luminous figures emerging from the shadows, and columns of gnarled trees rose up like stalagmites, bearing corpse candles at the end of each glowing twig. Leila thought the whole thing reeked of overkill, and Mitchell's crowd ruined the effect even further with their scuffing remarks. But at one point, goose bumps rose on her shoulders. Looking up, she made out a flash of white moving through the darkened tent.

Moments later, she found herself enshrouded in darkness, except for the moon-silvered trees. Mitchell, the air cushions, and the tent walls ceased to exist. She tiptoed down a dirt-covered trail, her glow-in-the-dark sneakers casting rainbow patterns on the grass and twigs.

Any second, she'd smash into someone or bump into the tent's canvas wall. But the maze of twisted oaks seemed endless. She thought about her father and how they'd argued about her decision to go to respiratory school. "You're making a mistake," he'd said. "You've got a tender heart, and people who feel things have no business working in the medical field."

She'd tried not to hear the pain in his voice or notice his mournful eyes. In the end, he'd gone along with her, even financed her training. "Some people have to learn the hard way," she remembered him saying.

The night sounds impinged on her consciousness. Birds called to each other, their wings flaring and beating, scuttling from branch to branch. Flies and other insects buzzed around the berry trees, forming dark clouds over the fruit. Listening hard, Leila made out chomping sounds—caterpillars gnawing on the leaves.

Softly, almost hidden by the forest noises, slipper-clad feet whispered in the grass. The footsteps soothed Leila, reminding her of the evenings she used to read to Anna. Then she'd realized that she'd never left the tent, at least not physically. What started as a simulated tour had become real.

Leila mopped the sweat from her face and extended her hands, hoping to feel someone's shoulder. But her trembling fingers grazed tree bark. She told herself she was still in the tent, having the granddaddy of nightmares, maybe even a seizure, but she knew this wasn't true. Something about the sound drew her further into the forest, though the lights from her sneakers afforded barely enough illumination to see. The wet leaves and gravel, coated with a dense fog, greased her shoes, threatening to spill her into a back-breaking slide.

After the woods, she came across a dilapidated cemetery. A woman's groan issued from the tombstones. It sounded like Anna.

It's not possible, Leila tried to tell herself. *The dead don't come back to life.* Still, she kept heading toward the graves. Perhaps someone had gotten hurt, maybe a jogger. Perhaps the voice belonged to a robotic fruit-picker or gardener. Whatever it was, it called to Leila, and she felt compelled to answer.

A full moon overhead splashed silvery puddles on the grass and cracked stones. After rounding a curve, she slipped inside a trench, just underneath a maze of overhead vines. She did not feel coldness as her feet sank through wet sand. No trembling, sharp intake of breath, or cry escaped her as the sand swallowed her knees, her thighs, her hips. Somehow, she'd taken a trip through cyberspace, a detour leading to the cemetery, and now she only felt the absence of feeling. Her hatred and sadness had vanished, like leaves before a raging wind.

Leila's lungs did not starve for air, even when her head sank beneath the moon-silvered sand. The mud sucked her feet; the sand caressed her metallic clothes and crept up her pant legs. Someone was moving in her direction, cries that could be mistaken for no one else. Anna forged through the quicksand to greet her friend and caregiver.

Leila never felt Anna's hand grasp hers, though she knew they'd made contact. Nor did she feel her consciousness leave her body and enter that of her old friend.

Still, Leila's mind controlled Anna's movements as she clawed through the sand, and then staggered up the trench on two unsteady legs. Inhaling deeply, she savored the scents of berry trees, grass, and…Mitchell. A sweet aroma wafted from the pavilions, triggering images of ripping and devouring warm flesh, thoughts that had never occurred to Leila before. A crooked grin worked its way to her face.

Although the virtual reality tour had ended, the smell of liquor wafted from the carnival grounds. Leila guessed that Mitchell and his friends had gotten drunk and did other things that their wives didn't suspect. Her mind filled with fantasies of a certain doctor screaming in terror as her teeth ripped into his throat.

The creature that had once been Anna had become something inhuman, a revenant called from death. Attempting her first movements after so many months buried in quicksand, she plodded from the trench in slow, uneven steps. Anna could not know that she was little more than a skeleton coated with tufts of decayed flesh and clumps of tangled hair. But Leila knew—and she could just imagine the look on Mitchell's face when the patient he killed gripped his shoulder with her withered hand.

Through Anna's eyes, Leila saw the moon's silvery glow light up the tree tops. The stars overhead glittered brightly. The sharp scents of flowers and their bright colors threatened to overwhelm her senses. She could capture the calls of the chirping birds as if they took place in her inner ear. With it came a lingering sorrow that Mitchell had robbed so many people of the chance to appreciate such beauty.

The thought crossed her mind that if Mitchell died, another administrator would replace him. Perhaps a monster who'd stop life support just as soon as look as someone. Maybe she could reason with Mitchell or write a petition as Charlotte had suggested. But petitions had a way of ending up in the trash bin. Reasoning with Mitchell might work, though, if she got some help.

Merged in the same body, Leila and Anna took in the sights and sounds of the forest as they headed back to the trench. Leila knew that Charlotte would look for her, but that didn't seem important. Right now, she had to summon Mitchell's other casualties. Paused at the slate rocks lining the trench, she let loose a sighing moan. Grating noises followed, and moments later, bony hands reached through the sand. Skulls covered with matted hair bobbed through the mud. Skeletons coated with tatters of ragged flesh climbed from the trench in single file, their bones clattering against the stones.

Leila counted five adults and two children. Tufts of hairy flesh coated three of the grownups' chins. Their faces did not look familiar, and no one volunteered any names.

Mitchell had dumped them into the quicksand after terminating life support. That was all Leila needed to know. He'd cut treatment to save money, and Leila would see to it that he got his dividend. Death's dividend. Together, Leila and Anna led their skeletal companions through the woods. Maybe later, administrators at other hospitals could reap the dividends of cost containment. With a shriek sounding like hideous laughter, Leila plodded to the carnival grounds, ready to make the first payment.

Bad Seed

I heard the fireworks blast through the air, punctuated by the crowd's whistles and shouts. Their laughter drowned out the sound of my hushed sobbing. While the New Year's celebration exploded into rainbow colors, lighting the midnight sky, the frosty air chilled me to the bone. Though a sea of humanity swirled around me, no one looked my way. I was facing this new year alone.

Slowly, I turned away from the celebration, shuddering at the night that felt as cold and empty as my life. How I envied the crowd and their joyous smiles. More to the point, I envied those with relatives and friends who cared about them.

The crowd's gaeity had become more than I could bear. No matter how hard I'd tried to make friends, my thoughts remained my sole companions. The dark alley I wandered into provided a welcome silence. The gloom closed over me like a coffin lid.

I tried not to think about my poverty of friends. Sometimes I succeeded by keeping busy at my job as supervisor at Fairview Hospital's respiratory therapy department. During work hours, the loneliness whispered so softly I hardly knew it was there. At home, it gnawed a hole in my heart, especially during holidays. Watching people hug each other speared the memories through my consciousness, reminding me of the tragedy which had ruined my life.

During my last talk with my father, his tiny, hard eyes glittered like tarnished silver under the faint light in his living room. The faces on the football trophies lining his cabinet gave off more warmth than his shadowed features. He was delivering a harsh lecture. Telling me to leave home. Disowning me because of a car accident that had caused my fiancé, David Wood, to die.

He called me a bad seed because I inherited my mother's fondness for liquor. David died, he said, because I had too many beers before getting behind the wheel. Never mind that the car I broadsided had raced a red light. Never mind that David had refused to wear his seatbelt. Never mind that each day I relived the accident, watching David's head plow through the windshield, hearing the tinkling glass. I made a mistake, I remembered telling my father. Couldn't I have another chance?

My father's face turned crimson, and dark lines creased his granite chin. Meeting my gaze with his cold eyes, he pulled an envelope from his blazer pocket. It made soft wisps as he shoved it across his coffee table. The words on its contents blurred in the salty tears that flooded my eyes. A massive ache, warm and smothering, swelled up inside my chest.

The envelope contained a letter from the Woods' lawyer. They were suing my family for damages. According to David's father, I'd shown up at their home drunk the day of the accident, but David had borne the consequences. Head injuries had rendered him comatose, dependent on a respirator, while I'd gotten off with minor lacerations.

While I read the letter, my last visit with David came to mind. His eyes, fixed and dilated, focused at the ceiling. He did not respond to my voice. I recalled listening with helpless horror as the doctor pronounced him brain dead. I watched, eyes filled with tears, while the Woods had David disconnected from the respirator. Moments later, his heartbeat flickered to a stop.

David's father had called that night, threatening a lawsuit, Dad said. When my dad pointed out that David should have recognized my condition and taken over the wheel, his father wouldn't listen. Instead, he said two words before hanging up the phone: *bad seed.*

The sub-zero temperatures impinged on my consciousness, nudging me back to the present. The alley's stone wall frosted my cheek, whispering a rumor of the chill lodging in my heart. I imagined a jagged ice splinter wedging through my chest, draining the love I felt, leaving only a dead feeling. Sometimes I drank to ease the pain. It never worked. My loneliness became worse.

David's death had motivated my present calling, but mastering patient care skills wouldn't do. I had to *atone* for my crimes. That meant taking assignments in Fairview Hospital's long-term ventilator unit, where victims of car accidents languished for months. Not a muscle moved when I stuck these patients for blood. I never complained about working with these people. Instead, I thought about David, dead, his last breaths pumped by a machine.

Around my workers, I manufactured a brittle smile, and the stories I invented about my romantic escapades were limited only by my imagination. No one saw past my false front. No one cared to look, especially during my chart reviews. When I found errors, my harsh voice grated like fingernails on a blackboard. Sometimes my shouts drowned out the sound of my sorrow.

I gave one therapist, Gary, a written warning after I observed his Singer sewing machine method of drawing blood. He'd attempted the procedure without wearing gloves or swabbing the site with alcohol. The other therapists used to joke about Gary's incompetence, but I shadowed him during rounds, watching and waiting for him to screw up. After reading my memo, Gary called me a witch. I threatened to get him suspended for insubordination. He challenged me to go ahead. Gary ended up getting fired, and my father's voice whispered the words "bad seed" inside my head.

Brilliant red rouge covered up the memories. My grandfather clock ticked away like a time bomb while I stood before my mirror, sculpturing my face into that of a stranger's. Layers of hairspray froze my chestnut curls into place. I manicured and polished each fingernail. My hair clips and jewelry glittered like shields of armor. Though I created a flawless appearance, I still heard my father's voice calling me a bad seed. The memory faded.

Before I realized their intent, I felt my hands pulling at my leather gloves. The frosty air chilled my fingers as I yanked off my sapphire ring. David had given it to me as a pre-engagement gift. The gem glowed in the gloomy light afforded by the street lamps. At one time, that ring had meant everything to me. Now it had become nothing more than a hard stone, a symbol of everything that had gone wrong in my life. I tossed it into the snow-covered street. It made a faint plopping sound.

I turned away, ready to leave, when out of the depths of gloom floated a man's gravelly voice. "Susan," he called. "Susan, where are you?"

Whirling around, I searched the alley for the source of that voice. My eyes squinted, trying to see, but they only saw icy patches glinting in the half-light. My breath curled up before my eyes. I stepped into the shadows, heart thudding inside my chest.

Something cold and knobby brushed my leg, and I started. I covered my mouth, trying to stifle the screams building inside my chest. Looking down, I saw a man sprawled at my feet. He wore tattered hospital scrubs. No coat. White scabs and dirt crusted his bruised skin. Soon, he'd freeze to death.

I took off my overcoat and draped it over his inert form. My fingers felt ridges of bone beneath his scrubs. At first, I thought that he had already died, and that I'd imagined the voice. Instead, the man sat up, wrapping the coat around him. His arms and legs appeared bruised and blistered.

A profound sadness rolled through me, bringing tears to my eyes. His cracked skin stretched over his pointed chin and stick-like limbs. Bare bone protruded through the tears in his skin. His hair hung to his shoulders, clumped together with frozen mud. His swollen lips twisted into a smile that didn't touch his sunken eyes. For some reason, he looked familiar.

"Wait here," I told him. "I'll call an ambulance."

"No ambulance, Susan." His voice sounded like tearing parchment. "It's too late."

"Do I know you?"

Lame question, but I couldn't think of anything better. How did he know my name? Something moved under his eyelids, but I couldn't tell what.

He nodded. "We have unfinished business."

"You're hurting badly," I said. "I can't leave you here."

"My pain and suffering have ended. Now I'm alone." He paused. "Like you."

His anguished voice pulled at my heart, tugging also at the corners of my mind. Something shiny flashed before my eyes. When I looked down, he was fingering my ring. He stared at the ring as its sapphire flickered in the dim light. A wistful look crossed his face, and then he pitched the ring back into the street. His lips tightened, as if he'd tasted something sour.

"Alone," he said again.

No treatment could save this man, but I still felt the need to help him. Perhaps this need had something to do with David's death. Maybe I identified with another lonely soul. Whatever my reasons, I longed to do something for him.

To my surprise, the man rose to his feet without wobbling or moaning. I held him against my chest. Cold cobwebs of bone poked through the coat; he couldn't have weighed more than eighty pounds. The chill from his body seeped through my clothes, turning my skin to gooseflesh. I shivered.

My heart hammered away, each beat quivering through my muscles like pinpricks of electricity. He stiffened against my arms. His body had a rancid odor. The stench of advanced disease, perhaps forthcoming death.

"Alone," he repeated.

"I'm taking you home with me," I whispered into his scabbed ear. "I'll do my best to make you comfortable. If you like, I'll call someone from the clergy."

My companion looked up at me intently. His black pupils had swollen, covering most of his eyes. Like David's. He pressed closer to me, his elbow like a knife in my stomach. Alarms went off in my head.

"A lonely woman with a good heart," he said quietly.

"You think so?" Before I could stop myself, I burst into tears. My mascara ran, stinging my eyes. My sobs reeked with bitterness, tears I should've shed over David, but didn't. "Maybe you're right. The question is, do I have a soul?"

My companion laid his skeletal hand on my shoulders and stared into my eyes. His haunted face spoke of festering nightmares and the tragedies that had created them.

"You and I came from the same place," he said.

Without answering, I ushered him out of the alley and to a dimly lit lot, where I'd parked my Honda. The celebrants' shouting faded behind us.

At my townhouse, I led him to my kitchen, where I kept my first aid supplies. I draped an old blanket over his shoulders. After drawing up a pan of hot water, I set it on the linoleum floor. Gently, I lifted his fragile feet into the basin.

I soaked a rag with water. As I knelt before him, I expected to feel his sour breath against my hair, but the air remained still as death. This sent chills up my spine.

The shivers settled around my neck when I proceeded to wash his legs. Tufts of skin and fascia fell away from his calves, leaving behind naked bones. Within minutes, the water turned deep red. When I looked up, he was removing his scrub shirt. I screamed when the glow from the overhead light fell on his sunken chest. For a moment, my surroundings blurred. I squeezed my eyes shut, waiting for the dizziness to pass, but the image burned into my mind. I opened my eyes again.

The skin on his chest had withered and blistered, with ribs poking between the open sores. A gaping hole near his sternum revealed splintered bone and flesh crusted with dried blood. Streaks of blue and red laced his skin around his upper torso. I probed under his bony chin, knowing that I wouldn't find a pulse. The skin broke, oozing greenish pus.

"No, no," I wept, drawing back my fingers. I stood up and backed toward the sink. My mind whirled, trying to decide if I was going crazy. Maybe I was asleep, having the granddaddy of nightmares. "You can't be real."

"You brought me here," my companion said in a reasonable voice. "How can you deny my existence?"

"Dead people can't—they aren't supposed to come back to life." My voice rose and fell, hitching with sobs. "Who are you? *What* are you?"

"I think you already know, Susan," he said. "I'm not dead yet. I'm dying by inches."

He reached toward me, with his shirt in hand. Flakes of skin fell from his mottled arms like grisly rain. I looked at his shirt. A faded tag under its collar said, "Property of Fairview Hospital." I turned it over, imagining what the shirt looked like new, and …

The memory came back to me like a vision. The shirt had belonged to Gary, the therapist whom I'd gotten fired, the one who'd called me a witch. His savings had run out, and he ended up on the street, shot and beaten to death.

"No, Gary," I stammered. "Who did this to you?"

His eyes narrowed, and a tremble flickered over his lips. "I pulled the trigger because I saw how hopeless my life had become. Like you, I've lost someone dear to me. Like you, I've had to pay for my mistakes." His head tilted sideways. "Mistakes caused by liquor."

Sudden fire burned in my chest, melting my frozen heart. The terror I'd felt fled, and utter longing took its place. Love. Whatever his body had become, I saw the pain of unrequited love on his face. For the moment, I forgot that my visitor was a dead man. I forgot everything except the love blooming afresh in my bitter soul.

"What?" I gasped. "How did you know …?"

"You'd be surprised at what a person learns after death. I never knew, until my passing, that loneliness wears many disguises. For example, your anger toward people. Do you remember the day?"

The love I felt burned into my very heart, melting my thoughts and feelings. Images rose from the smoke, memories of the days I'd worked with Gary. Worked *on* Gary. His eyes held a blank look, like someone who'd wandered into a black hole. Did Gary drink because I'd broken his spirit? "I came down hard on you," I said at last, "because your work had gotten sloppy. What did liquor have to do with that?"

"I'd gotten wasted the night before, and a nurse complained that she smelled whiskey on my breath. I failed a breathalyzer test. Human Resources offered counseling, and I refused because I didn't want people at work knowing my business. So they fired me, and no other hospital would hire me." Gary affected a deep sigh. "My wife told me to get lost. My mother refused to help because I reminded her of my father, who'd lost jobs because of his drinking. She called me a bad seed."

From deep within the darkness of my closed eyes, I felt Gary's hand on my shoulder. I wept noiseless sobs, tears for Gary and myself. When I opened my eyes again, I gazed at his drawn face. I recognized his heartache, having seen it in my own mirror enough times.

"After my marriage went sour, it was like I went to a dark place, where no one could get to me."

"I've lived in that place," I said quietly.

"I know you have," he said. "I want to thank you for your honesty. Harsh as you were, you told me the truth when no one else would. I owe you for that."

Gary rose to his feet. "I must go now and rest."

"Don't leave," I begged tearfully. "We've left so much unsaid."

"No, we haven't," he said. "I couldn't rest until I made my peace with you. You've made every aching step worth it."

I had nothing more to say. Silence could describe my feelings; words could not. He turned and crossed the kitchen. After opening the door, he melted into the shadows on my porch. A heartbeat later, he was gone. His clacking footsteps became a memory.

I tried to picture Gary. I wanted his face to be etched forever in my mind. His papery skin and ragged hair. The bottomless pupils on a withered face. The self-inflicted wound on his chest, where the bullet had left an open hole, as if he'd sliced something from his body. I tried to imagine angel wings where only rotting flesh remained.

After some time, I got up and headed to the window, hoping to see Gary one last time. Outside, a full moon cast silver shadows on the snow-covered streets. Scattered stars surrounded the moon, glittering like jagged diamonds. Or like my shattered heart of ice. Somewhere the shouts of celebration drifted from the streets. The end of the old year. The start of the new.

Only this year, I loved.

The Lowly Workers

Hunched by scoliosis and herniated discs, Frank Mazer climbed a step stool to write at the highest level of the dry-erase board. His hair had aged deep silver, and his gray, businessman's suit concealed the brace that supported his spine. Underneath it, a lattice of thick scars covered his back. He managed Bancroft Hospital's respiratory therapy department. Sometimes he terrorized it, especially during meetings. A sly smile crossed his face as he pondered this.

On the dry erase board, he listed the topics for today's meeting. None of his workers made wisecracks. He had become infamous for summary firings. He could always figure out who had overstayed their break, who had lied about their reason for calling in sick, and who had fudged the figures on their flow sheets. His icy blue eyes, when focused on an errant worker, could turn the strongest heart to jelly.

"Your work has gotten sloppy," he began, pointing to the word "documentation," the top one on his list. "Don't look at me like that. You think I was born yesterday?"

He stared at the twenty therapists huddled around the white Formica table, inept people who suffered from the *no-one-will-notice* syndrome.

Jabbing his forefinger against the fingers on his opposite hand, he roll-called their offenses. "Some people don't list vital signs. Others don't chart treatments at all. Everyone continues the same therapies week after week, regardless of patient condition."

Anne, a freckle-faced women woman wearing a ponytail, raised her hand. "Mr. Mazer, most times, the doctors don't like it when we recommend different treatments."

"I realize that," he allowed. "Some physicians feel threatened when we question them."

He scratched his ruddy chin. Of course, he'd planned his strategy. The devil was in the details, as the old saw went.

"Wendell!" he shouted.

Wendell, who was drawing skulls on his assignment sheet, started. "Stop writing and listen. *Now!*"

The pen dropped. Wendell looked with dark, narrowed eyes at Mazer's back. "Sorry," he mumbled.

I'll make you sorry, Mazer thought, glancing at his television. He'd brought a video TV to the conference room before the meeting. Placing the TV next to the dry erase board, he angled it so that he could watch his workers' behavior in the light reflection there. He smiled whenever he caught them in their games. Looking ahead, he saw a ghostly, distorted Dee roll her eyes.

He would not comment. Not yet. Give her enough rope, and she'd hang herself.

"As professionals, we should know how to approach the physicians," he said. "Dee, can you offer Anne any suggestions?"

Dee frowned and twirled her stethoscope around her fingers. The conference room was hushed and sleepy in the late July heat. Most of the therapists had spent the day racing to cardiac arrests and other emergencies. Only Mazer's harsh voice kept them from nodding at his table.

"Don't keep us waiting, Dee," he prodded.

"Give the doctors your reason for suggesting different therapies," Dee said in an olive oil voice. "Like x-rays, breath sounds, things like that."

Dee's suggestion seemed like a conscientious gesture, but Mazer felt his skin prickle. Past experience had taught that her smooth voice emphasized the word "con" and left out "scientious."

"Talk to them in their own language," Dee added, draping her stethoscope around her neck. She rolled her eyes again and gave Mazer a lopsided smile. With a sick feeling, he concluded that Dee knew about his trick with the television.

Oh, well.

Mazer moved onto the subject of lateness, with no comments toward Dee. He decided to let his thin-lipped frown make its own observation. Any moment, she'd batter him with complaints, asking him to hire more people and buy new equipment.

Past arguments with Dee had left a sour taste in his mouth. He would've fired her long ago, but the hospital staff respected Dee. Besides, pages of documentation were required to dismiss an employee.

Her reflection in his mirror appeared shrunken and erratic, and Mazer had all but the barest corner of his eyes on his notes. He was waiting for her twenty-question routine.

Instead, Dee changed.

Mazer caught a fleeting glimpse, a horrifying flash of Dee's face turning into something gross. He spun around, only dimly aware of the stabbing pain in his back.

Dee leaned back in her chair and shrugged. Wisps of auburn hair dangled in her eyes. She poked at her stethoscope's earpiece, wiped it with an alcohol swab, and looked at Mazer.

"Dee." Mazer tried hard to find his lecture voice.

"What's the matter?" Dee's green eyes had a chilling, reptilian watchfulness, making Mazer feel like a field mouse gazing into the eyes of a cobra. Something wooden poked from her pink scrub top—a pendant of a man wearing a crown of feathers and horns. For some reason, the statuette looked familiar.

"Nothing." *I'm seeing things,* he thought, glancing through his notes. *I've been looking for reasons to fire her and found nothing, so my mind invented something. How nice.*

Hushed whispers buzzed around the room.

"Excuse me!" Mazer snapped, his face toward the group, but his eyes on Dee.

Dee looked back and smiled.

Mazer continued with his remaining topics. Afterwards, Dee gave him a cunning smirk on her way to the time clock. The look in her steely eyes said, *I know something you don't.*

The look wedged in his mind like a sliver of chicken stuck between his teeth—small, but feeling large as sheetrock.

At six, Mazer wolfed down a platter of meatloaf, potatoes, and spinach, still thinking about Dee. Reaching into his pocket, he pulled out a photo of a blonde woman—his ex-wife. The marriage had lasted eight months, and then one night she came home and informed him that she'd met someone. Mazer supposed that she'd used him as a meal ticket until she met someone more to her liking. Dee reminded him of his ex-wife—she had the same smirk, the same smug look in her eyes.

He patted his brace, a souvenir from his childhood beatings. His father, a barber, had used a razor strop for his work. At home, he hung his tool on the doorknob of his shed.

Mazer could still see his father's cold eyes and granite face when he got out his strop.

Whippings punctuated many of his younger days. Anything less than a B on his report card earned him a beating. If he left a mess in the kitchen or made too much noise, his father chased him with the razor strop. Sometimes, he used his fists.

Looking down, Mazer saw his hands gripping the table edge, knuckles turning white. The last beating had cracked three vertebrae, and he considered himself lucky to be walking. He told himself that his father's whippings had made him strong. At Bancroft Hospital, he had gotten commendations for cutting costs and weeding deadwood. He stroked his brace, thinking that he'd like to go after Dee with a razor strop.

He looked down at his meatloaf.

Wouldn't he?

Rubbing his arms and shivering, he got up and turned on another light.

That night, Mazer dreamed about Dee. Her pale face emerged from the shadows, and a crooked grin surfaced on her lips. Her face elongated, cheeks caving in, and her flesh became taut and leathery. Her eyes disappeared, swallowed by orbs of blackness. She radiated the stink of rotting tomatoes. Mazer opened his mouth to scream, but his tightening throat only allowed faint croaks. She was turning into something monstrous. Before he could figure out what she had become, his alarm clock jarred him back to reality.

Mazer struggled to his feet, rubbing his eyes. He'd only slept three hours. It was a fitful and uneasy sleep at that. He'd always had trouble sleeping, given his back pain, but last night was brutal. While searching for his work clothes, he kicked wastebaskets and slammed drawers. At the hospital, he went through every chart with a magnifying glass, hoping to find errors, but there were none. His staff passed him by without saying hello. He felt their eyes drilling into his back, watching and waiting.

Cut that out, he scolded himself. *You act more nervous than a student on his first day of clinical rotations.*

The day dragged on. By the change of shift, perspiration drenched Mazer's suit. He didn't bother with the evening or night shift therapists because he'd hired supervisors to oversee their work, but he'd foregone a day supervisor to save money. *Big mistake,* he thought, listening to his ragged breathing. He watched sourly as his day shift therapists scurried to the exit and out into the bright sunlight.

What did I see when Dee changed? Something bulbous and white. Something staring at me through bottomless pits. Something inhuman, a thing called from death…

"Mr. Mazer?"

His head jerked, and he bit back a scream.

It was Teresa, the supervisor from Environmental Services. She smiled sheepishly. "I didn't mean to scare you."

"What do you want?" Mazer demanded, more abruptly than he intended. He mopped the sweat from his moist forehead.

"Can you let me in the locker room? Someone called and said you were low on toilet paper and towels."

"I'll check." After banging his drawer shut, Mazer struggled to his feet. Hand rubbing his back brace, he shambled to the locker room down the hall. Snickers drifted from the break room as he passed.

Mazer sighed—a long skeletal sigh like wind blowing leaves. His therapists were laughing at him. He knew this as surely as he'd come to know the dread lurking in his heart. Maybe younger people didn't know the meaning of respect. Maybe Mazer didn't want to know why they laughed. The quiet contempt in their eyes sent chills up his spine.

He punched in the code to access the locker room. The room extended into an L, with lockers along both walls. At the rear, two bathrooms faced another row of lockers.

He inspected the towel containers and stalls. The towel containers were well stocked. Ditto for the toilet paper holders. Someone had called Teresa, knowing he would come, so they could get him alone in the washroom.

Mazer glimpsed his face in the mirror. The shivers settled around his neck. His gray eyes had a frightened, haunted look. Somehow, the image of Dee in his mirror had gotten inside him and festered like a cancerous ulcer.

The door opened, and he heard two men opening their lockers. One whispered something, and the other let out harsh laughter. Mazer started out of the bathroom, and then hesitated when he heard his name. He retreated toward the sink and pretended to check the towel containers.

"Mazer looked like he was about to …"

Gales of laughter.

"He figured it out all right …"

More laughter.

Mazer clenched the sink to keep his hands from shaking. Sweat dripped down his forehead, stinging the corner of his right eye. He knuckled it away.

Leaning sideways, he made out their shadows. Bright sunlight shining through the window was outlining two husky males. *Oh, Lord, they know I'm here*, he thought, listening to his chattering teeth.

Yes, they knew. The bastards had set up the ruse with the bathroom supplies.

A strange sense of peace settled over Mazer, easing his trembling. He promised himself to go through their notes and document every mistake he found. Something would turn up, and he'd fire them. Patient care would continue because he got twenty applicants for every job he posted.

Then the men's shadows grew long and narrow. Grotesque bumps protruded from their shoulders and hips. Skeletal arms pointed in Mazer's direction and a rancid odor permeated the air. Mazer cringed against the washstand, liquid fear running through his veins.

The laughter continued, only now, it sounded like pebbles had lodged in the young men's windpipes. The stench intensified, reminding Mazer of rotting meat. A yellow, wet smell.

He stared at the skeletal shadows and let out a mad cry of terror and agony. His surroundings blurred, and then he fainted. The laughter followed him into the grayness.

He dared not tell anyone the truth.

Mazer knew it, even as he opened his eyes. Teresa and Janine, a nurse, knelt at his side. Janine checked his blood pressure. Teresa glared at the two therapists by the lockers. "What are you staring at?" she hollered. "Don't you have work to do?"

The young men grinned at Mazer—crooked, wait-till-we-get-you grins—and left.

Right now, Mazer had to play along with them. He couldn't afford to have people thinking that Alzheimer's had sunk its claws into him. When the time was right, he'd expose their secret.

"I slipped on a wet spot." Hands clawing the tiles, he sat up, wincing at the spasms in his back.

"This is awful," Teresa said, shaking her head.

"Don't move," Janine told him. "I'll call the Medical Emergency Team."

"That won't be necessary." Mazer struggled to his feet, ignoring the shooting pains. "The brace protected me."

"You don't know that," Teresa said somberly. "You should go to Employee Health and fill out an incident report."

"I'm fine." Mazer smiled at her, then hobbled to the door. "I'll fill out an incident report. After that, I'm driving home."

Teresa gazed at Janine with widened eyes. Janine shrugged and said nothing.

The next day, Mazer summoned Dee for a disciplinary conference. He'd found three charting errors. Nothing major, but something he could use to build his case against her.

His back hurt—terrible, stinging pain that brought tears to his eyes. Every time he moved, muscles he hadn't known existed screamed in agony. He had a sneaking suspicion that Dee would try to take advantage of him… but he wouldn't let her. His back had ached constantly since his injury, but the financial rewards of his job had motivated him to continue working.

After closing the door behind them, Mazer motioned Dee to a chair before his desk. "Your documentation has gotten slipshod," he began. "You failed to note breath sounds or vital signs when you charted your breathing treatments. I won't tolerate carelessness, especially toward patients. Do you understand?"

Silence followed a moment, broken only by the tock-tocking of the wall clock. Mazer watched Dee, expecting a deep sigh or sagging shoulders. Instead, she sat up straight. A twisted grin played on her lips.

"What's so funny, Dee?" Mazer asked.

Dee shrugged and continued smiling.

"Do you find this conversation amusing?"

Dee fingered her pendant and studied it. She burst into giggles—noiseless laughter.

Up close and personal, Mazer recognized the statuette's feathered crown and horns. The face looked like Osiris, an Egyptian god. He'd studied about Osiris in his college history class. He'd read about the way Egyptians preserved bodies for the afterlife. Shuddering, he felt the silence close over him—except for the clock. It ticked away like a timed bomb.

"Many of us work here," Dee said, smiling. "Ten in our department."

Mazer leaned against his leather chair. "Your nonsense has got to stop," he said, mustering his authoritarian voice. "I expect you to act professionally. At all times. If we have this conversation again, you're out of here."

"Says who?" Dee's mouth broke into a wolfish grin. "Do you want to see the real me, Mr. Mazer?"

Mazer rubbed his arms, trying to soothe the goose bumps. "I've entered a written warning into your file. Next time I'll get you for insubordination. That, I believe, is punishable by suspension, followed by dismissal. You may go."

Mazer let out a deep breath. Any moment, Dee's face would crumble and overflow with tears.

Instead, Dee's grin widened. "Let's pretend I'm giving you a seminar. The real Dee used visual aids during her seminars. Visual aids can help the learning process, don't you think, Mr. Mazer?" Her smile curled up like dog-eared paper. "She's trapped inside my head."

"That's enough," Mazer said, rubbing his temples. The clock's ticking grated on his nerves. "I said you may go."

Dee changed. Her hair matted together. Her flesh melted, leaving behind a skeletal shape. Gleaming bone peeped through the holes in the taut leathery skin on her knuckles and chin.

She let out a gravelly laugh. Her shrunken lips revealed a mouth filled with jagged teeth. Her eyes disintegrated, leaving behind gaping black holes.

She got up, still laughing, and underneath it all, Mazer saw the battered remains of the real Dee, a gentle therapist held hostage by this mummified corpse, screaming in terror and pleading to be set free.

Mazer fled helter-skelter from his office, his cries echoing through the hall. Two passing therapists watched him with huge, uncomprehending eyes. Janine stepped off the elevator, almost colliding with him as he plunged outside through the double glass doors, a wild shaking figure silhouetted against the cloudy sky.

"Mr. Mazer!" Janine cried, pushing through the doors. "Mr. Mazer, come back."

Breath hitching with screams, Mazer raced down the concrete steps and across the parking lot. Horrible waves of dizziness rolled through him, causing him to pitch headlong into the street. Horns blared, and then a sixteen-wheeler truck careened from the corner, its driver chalk white with terror. His brakes screeched.

The truck skidded to a stop, just a foot from Mazer's brace-clad body. He shivered on the asphalt, gagging on the smell of gasoline. Crepe-soled footsteps impinged on his consciousness.

The respiratory therapists formed a C-shaped ring around him, like pallbearers staring into an open grave. Dee stood in front, her pale face somber, her green eyes shining like gemstones.

Mazer knew that if he continued looking at her, he'd scream again.

From the distance, he heard the truck driver's shaken rambling. "Crazy old coot...I damn near killed him..."

Janine stepped into the street. "The show's over," she told the onlookers. "Everyone not involved, get out of here."

The therapists shuffled back inside, and Mazer started to weep.

Mazer didn't return to work for two months. He told his boss, Dr. Kuhn, that he was taking a leave of absence because he hadn't been feeling himself. He considered resigning, but Kuhn told him this wouldn't be necessary. Mazer returned to work the middle of September, ready to face his workers.

During his first week, his staff regarded him with narrowed eyes. Dee continued her sly smiles, but he dared not reprimand her.

One day, while Mazer ate his lunch outside, Dee glided toward him. "You wouldn't believe how many of us work here," she said, lips curled into a sneer. "Neither would anyone else, if you told them."

Mazer clenched his fists inside his jacket pockets. "What makes you think I'd tell anyone?"

Dee smiled without answering him and headed back into the building.

Mazer brought the pistol to work in a briefcase. The gun had belonged to his late father, and Mazer had stored his father's weapons in his attic. Every three months, he oiled and cleaned the guns the way his father had taught him. He spent hours at this task, inspecting each weapon for dust and debris. The barrel had to be spotless. The one time it wasn't, he'd paid for his oversight with a particularly brutal beating, the one that left him with the cracked vertebrae. He broke into a sweat, reliving the painful memory as he worked, but clean them he did. All of them were good to go, an assortment of guns and clips of ammunition. After choosing a .45, Mazer loaded the gun the way his father had shown him.

During morning report, Dee stunk of the grave. Her death's head image lurked under the Shirley Temple curls and face. He did not know how the mummy, or whatever it was, had got inside her. Maybe the real Dee had gone insane, terrorized by this creature. After a moment of consideration, Mazer concluded that he was performing an act of mercy.

"It doesn't look too busy this week, so today, I'm doing a skill lab," he told his therapists. "The government regulations demand that we test our employees to ensure competency."

The therapists just looked at him. He could feel their vacuous stares penetrate his soul.

"I'll call you to the Learning Lab one at a time to test you," he said, nodding encouragement. "The one with the highest score will get a gift certificate."

They smiled their plastic grins and said nothing.

"Dee, I'll start with you."

Dee smirked at him, her eyes wide open and sparkling with hideous virility. "I'm ready."

Arms cradling his briefcase, Mazer ushered Dee to the Learning Lab, three doors away from the locker room. Ventilators and other respiratory equipment crowded the Lab. Windowless walls and burnt out light bulbs gave it the sinister look of an old storeroom that had become a warehouse for antiquated equipment. Paint sloughed off the brick walls, giving the room a gray look. Mazer had soundproofed the Lab after he had been taken on at the hospital, thinking that his new workers could practice on equipment without disturbing anyone.

"No one can hear us." He closed the door behind him and brandished his .45. "Either your games stop or I shoot."

Dee swaggered to a ventilator and propped her left elbow against its top panel. "Go ahead," she said, defiance rising in her eyes. "There are more of us where I came from, more than you can imagine."

Before he could answer, Dee's body twisted into her skeletal form. Mazer shot her between the eyes.

Dee sagged against the wall, blood spurting from a wound in her forehead. For a moment, she gazed at Mazer, lips twitching. Her head rolled back, and she slumped to the floor.

Mazer dropped to her side, groping for her pulse. He listened to his own raspy breaths, felt the color drain from his face. The crumpled figure didn't move. He felt a sluggish pulse, and then…nothing. She was human.

No, no, it's not possible, his mind screamed. *It's just part of their plan.*

Mazer went back to his conference room and called the others to his Lab, one by one. He shot five, and would have eliminated the entire day shift if Janine hadn't stopped by the Lab to show a student nurse the ventilators.

Janine's eyes widened like basketballs. One hand clutched at her mouth; the other grabbed her student. She let out a series of gut wrenching shrieks.

Mazer laid a hand on her shoulder. "I had no choice," he said, raising his voice above her cries. "My workers have turned into monsters."

Janine stared at the therapists sprawled on the floor and screamed. White-sleeved arms and sneaker-clad feet poked between ventilator legs. Blood pooled on the linoleum floor. The young student accompanying Janine covered her eyes, weeping punctuated by choking sobs.

"You're one of them," Mazer shouted, yanking the student by the arm. "Go ahead, show Janine how you turn into a mummy."

The student stared at him with terrified eyes and continued to weep.

"Come on, change, damn you!" Mazer waved his gun. "You filthy, rotten creature, change!"

Janine jumped on Mazer like a cat. The gun dropped. The agony of a thousand knives sliced through his spine, and his back gave way.

The news media clamored for a trial, the therapists' grieving families filed lawsuits, and Bancroft Hospital sat back in shock… but Mazer didn't go

94

to jail. The hospital's administration organized a committee to develop stricter safety measures and behavior guidelines. They gave the surviving day shift therapists a week off, and covered their slots with agency staff. Mazer went to Gravesboro Hill, where he received psychotherapeutic drugs and electroshock treatments. A year later, he began an experimental group therapy program.

Art Weisman headed Gravesboro's intensive psychiatric unit, where Mazer stayed.

Seated behind a one-way window, he faced a room furnished with a dry-erase board, Formica table, and twelve chairs—a simulation of Mazer's respiratory therapy department. Inside, ten nurses wearing scrubs and lab coats sat at the table, role-playing the change of shift and department meetings.

Mazer sat in his wheelchair, discussing absenteeism, work quotas, and other issues he faced as a manager. The nurses nodded, interrupting now and then to ask questions. Art observed the interaction and took notes. Two attendants disguised as nurses sat near Mazer, watching him for signs of aggression.

Neither Mazer nor the nurses knew they were being watched.

At first, Mazer seemed to respond well. He answered each question in a calm, businesslike voice, explaining why he couldn't hire more people or purchase extra supplies. He smiled, offering support, when a male nurse expressed concerns about job security.

While they talked, the young man pulled a wooden pendent from his scrub top—a wrinkled face wearing a crown of feathers and horns.

A frown creased Mazer's face, and he averted his eyes. "Take me out of here," he pleaded in a whimpering voice.

The aides took him away. Art regarded his nurses' eyes, wide as saucers and vacant. One smiled, and another wrinkled his nose. Two women nudged each other and giggled. All of them wore the same pendent.

That night, Mazer hung himself with a tattered bed sheet. After that, Art began to watch his nurses more and more, especially the ones wearing the pendants.

Root of all Evil

It was David's idea to call a family meeting that resulted in a violent death at Baker's Cemetery. In the end, he'd shoulder the blame, but he and his sister Colby nearly paid with their lives, too.

December 15. Marion's kitchen in Fishtown, Philadelphia. The house had belonged to their late father. Last year, he'd changed his will, leaving Colby the house. Instead, after his plane crashed two months ago, Marion ousted Colby, along with three suitcases full of clothing and medicines. Thankfully, her brother David and his wife opened their home to her. Now from where Colby sat, the living room looked obsessively neat – a cream-colored sofa and two chairs lined up around a marble coffee table. Not a speck of dust cluttered the slate fireplace or powder blue rug.

Huddling by the fireplace, Colby coughed and wheezed despite a Spartan regimen of therapies. Her asthma started acting up again during the fall. She gazed at the blue envelope, limp from the sweat in her clenched fist, wondering what to do. It contained her father's will. Despite his wishes, all of the money from his estate account had gone into Marion's mutual fund account. David had suggested a weekend visit so they could negotiate a settlement before Christmas.

Maybe she should have waited until spring instead of agreeing to a confrontation on a snowy night in December. Or maybe, judging from Marion's emaciated, pale face and circles under the eyes, she should let the matter drop and leave her sister alone.

Colby had David to thank for finding the damning evidence. A corporate lawyer, he knew his way around the computer labyrinth of bank deposits and withdrawals. Without his help, she might have never found out the truth. At least, not so soon.

Marion had made the job easy. Her voluminous handwriting appeared on all the withdrawal slips bearing their father's account number this past year.

Amazing, Colby thought. Dad had willed her 50% of his equity and cash, along with the house, hoping the funds would cover her burgeoning medical bills. He'd revised his will after the granddaddy of asthma attacks left Colby in the intensive care unit for a week.

Why did Marion take the money? she wondered. Marion's green wool coat, Neiman Marcus suit, and stiletto heels spoke of wealth, but her gaunt figure and hollowed pale cheeks whispered a rumor of incipient illness. A thirty-two year old CEO at Klyman Knitting Mills, Marion commanded a six-figure income. *It's not like she's destitute. Did she get cancer or something? If that's the case, why doesn't she just say so?*

But conversations between Marion and Colby seldom went beyond "hi" and "bye," let alone sensitive discussions about illness. When they did, Marion's voice reeked with contempt, peppering her comments with labels like "stupid" and "pathetic." *Sick or not, she took the money out of spite. I'll show her I'm not so dumb after all.*

Outside, the wind howled, punctuated by blasts of snow.

Colby took one last deep breath on her nebulizer. David sat on the couch by the slate fireplace, reading a newspaper. He kept glancing her way with skittish eyes.

During supper, he'd asked Marion if he could see their father's tax records. After a silence seeming long as death, Marion went to the basement for the files.

Moments later, Marion shuffled into the living room, lugging a cardboard box filled with file folders – their father's tax and bank statements. Panting for breath, she dumped the box on the marble coffee table. She cast a withering glance toward Colby, then flopped in a chair by the window. "It's getting dark," she said, gazing outside. "Listen to that wind. This will make great skiing weather."

The living room's bay window revealed mounds of snow on the lawn. Threadbare trees rose like shadowy columns surrounding the garage. The snow coating the trees made their skeletal branches flap in the wind. Years ago, before her mother died of pneumonia, Colby used to help her decorate those trees for Christmas. Christmas with her mother had provided fun, warmth, and never-ending light, but now only the trees remained. Ice crystals pounded the streets, sparkling like crushed diamonds. Despite the gloom, she made out Baker's Cemetery, seemingly removed from it all.

"Great time for cleaning up unfinished business, too." David steepled his fingers. "Like the matter of Dad's estate. Colby and I are trying to figure out what happened to it."

Marion shot a glance at David, eyes narrowing. "Dad's company had liabilities. Business obligations that don't concern either of you."

"Don't they?" Colby licked her lips, clenching and unclenching her fists. Projecting calmness was an uphill battle, given her history with Marion. "Dad's original statements showed a balance of two million dollars. David and I found the receipts proving that you transferred his money to your mutual fund account."

"You low lives!" Marion's face turned beet red. A vein in her temple throbbed. "You had no right to snoop through my accounts."

"We want to know why the money disappeared," Colby said, still hoping for a calm approach. "Why did you take it, Marion?"

"I don't have to explain myself to you," Marion snapped.

"Perhaps you'd rather explain it to a judge," David said in a measured, quiet voice. "Let's just say I know people who'd be glad to send you to jail."

"You wouldn't dare!" Marion's face turned parchment; her eyes bulged.

"Why, Marion?" Colby felt her voice rise in crescendo to a shrill pitch. "You never cared about Dad, and your job has you set for life."

"You want to talk about stealing?" Marion's voice cracked like a whip. "You've mooched off of Dad all these years, using your imaginary condition to avoid work."

"Don't go there, Marion," David warned, shaking his head.

"She already did," Colby said between clenched teeth. She turned toward Marion. "I suppose I imagined the weeks I spent in the hospital, too. The house belongs to me. It says so here in Dad's will. If you don't turn over the deed, I'll see you in court."

"I'll give you a deed," Marion said, shaking her fist. "You should be grateful I allow you two to visit. David, you're no better, encouraging her whims."

David thrust his newspaper on the coffee table and sighed. "Dammit, Marion, Colby's not your problem, and you know it."

"We'll have to go to court." Colby sighed, twirling her fingers through her thick curls. "I don't know what her problem is, but she hates me."

"No, Marion's angry with Dad," David said in a pained voice.

"Exactly my point." Colby gazed at the box of manila folders, still worrying her hair. "So why do you want his money, Marion? Never mind, I don't want to hear it." She stood up, ready to bolt.

"Calm down." David waved her back to her seat. "Marion will come around if we approach her in her language."

"Her language?" Colby arched her brows, taking in Marion's cachectic appearance. Her voice softened. "David, is she sick?"

"In a way," David said. "But that's neither here nor there. I promised Dad you'd get your share as he requested."

"That stupid man." Marion shook her head. "How could he leave that kind of money to someone who knows nothing about finances?"

"I get thirty-five percent for acting as her financial planner," David told Marion. "That leaves you fifteen percent."

"You bastard!" Marion stared at David with glittering, hate-filled eyes. "You started this whole thing, didn't you?"

"A promise is a promise." David's set jaw discouraged argument.

Putting her anger aside, Colby turned her gaze toward Marion. Marion's eyes held a vast emptiness, the look of a woman who'd become unhinged from the landmarks of her life. Colby had seen that look many times during Marion's temper flares. Mom had taken her to a psychiatrist, hoping that therapy would help. It never worked. She just became worse.

"You don't look well, Marion," she said at last. "Do you need the money for medical bills?"

"No." Marion smiled a weird, skeletal grin. "It's combat pay."

"Combat pay?" Colby echoed in a feeble voice.

"That's right," Marion said. "I've paid thousands of dollars in psychiatrist fees."

"That's true," David said. "Marion and Dad have a long history, and none of it good." Dragging his fingers through his moist, chestnut hair, David shifted his gaze toward Marion and then back to Colby. "Marion's only your half-sister."

"Half-sister?" Colby got up and looked at the portrait of Marion and herself alongside the front door. Marion's close-cropped blonde hair, blue eyes, and creamy complexion offered a contrast to Colby's dark auburn waves, green eyes, and freckled face. "Mom told me about that. She said Dad had Marion with his previous wife, but she didn't go into detail."

"It was a bad time for him," David told her. "His first wife – Jennifer – loved her booze and men. She took off with another man when Marion was four years old."

"He had a terrible accident after that, and then he met Mom." Colby studied David intently. His brown eyes registered determination mixed with sadness, the look of a man ready to complete his mission, no matter how unpleasant. "They were great together."

"They were." His gentle voice made her think that everything would turn out okay. "Her death broke his heart."

"One big happy family, right?" Marion's voice dripped with acid. "Dad never accepted me as his daughter. He thought my mother was carrying someone else's kid and that she was using him for a meal ticket."

"You're wrong," Colby said. "Dad never said any such thing."

100

"He didn't have to." For a moment, Marion's eyes brightened. She shuffled to the sofa and plopped in the cushions beside David. "Mom and Dad asked you and David about school, how you did on your tests. They laughed at your pranks. They laughed with me, too, but their eyes never smiled."

Colby walked toward to the portrait over the fireplace. In it, her father was holding a medal he'd received for making the most sales.

Reaching up, she traced her finger along the smooth lines of his chunky face and silver hair. She'd argued with him over clothes and curfews – he could be strict and overprotective. But he often took her fishing and taught her self-defense. During her asthma attacks, he and Mom took turns sitting up with her. He always lent his ears when she and David wanted to talk. Marion was...where was Marion?"

Upstairs in her room or out with her friends. Never with the family. *"Marion is a troubled girl," Mom said. "Forcing her to join us will only upset her."*

"How can I make her feel better?" Colby asked.

"You can't...unless she allows you," Mom replied in a cryptic voice.

Marion's cracking voice bumped her back to the present. "I overheard Mom and Dad call me their obligation," she said. "Obligation, a 64-cent word for feeling forced into doing something you hate."

"Your tantrums didn't endear you to them," Colby told her. "I never signed up for asthma; it just happened."

The room fell silent. For a long time, no one spoke.

When someone finally did, it was David. "Dad never meant to ignore you, Marion. It's just that Colby's asthma used to make him crazy. He was afraid of losing her."

"He was afraid all right." Marion shook her head.

"He was afraid for you, too, Marion," David told her. "He believed something bad happened to you before we were born, something you've buried for years."

"Like people," Colby murmured, thinking about Dad.

"Like people," David nodded with agreement. "Motherhood didn't suit Jennifer. She used to beat Marion, but never around Dad. He found the telltale bruises when he came home from work. When he confronted Jennifer, she cursed him like a drunken soldier. Do you remember that, Marion?"

"I'll show you what I remember." Shifting sideways, Marion hiked her silk blouse. A maze of scars etched across her back.

"Oh, my God!" Colby's voice came out a sob.

"Jennifer told Dad that she hated him for getting her pregnant," David told her somberly. "She threatened to get an abortion, but she didn't have the money. When Marion turned four, Jennifer left Dad for another man. Two weeks later, her body was found in a ditch; she'd been strangled. According to the police report, her lover did it."

Colby shook her head, dismayed. "How come no one told me this?"

"Dad and Mom wanted to protect you," David said. "Everyone who knew Jennifer despised her. No one gave her a funeral. Instead, two neighbors buried her in Baker's Cemetery, placed a headstone, and then pissed on her grave. Some send-off, huh?"

Colby nodded, listening.

"That night, someone out walking his dog noticed yellow flickering at Dad's house. When he got closer, he saw flames and smoke spreading everywhere. He called the fire trucks. Dad escaped by jumping out a second-story window." His voice saddened. "He wound up breaking his left hip and leg. Mom was his nurse."

Colby smiled. "That's how they met. Dad told me about that."

"People said that Jennifer left her mark on everything she hated. Dad's house burned to ashes. Only the bricks were left standing. Tom, her killer, never made it to trial. The next night, he sat up in his cell, screaming her name. When the prison guard found him, he was grabbing his neck, eyes bulging, as he stared out the window toward Baker's Cemetery."

"Jennifer's grave." Colby pressed her fist against her trembling lips.

David nodded. "Tom keeled over dead. The medical examiner ruled his death a heart attack." David then turned to Marion. "Tell the rest of your story."

Marion stiffened against the couch, her face bleached ivory in the subdued lamplight. "I can't do this."

"You must," David said firmly. "All the money in the world won't ease your heartache, but talking might help. After you finish, we can settle up the accounts."

Colby wiped the tears forming in her eyes and walked to the couch. The anger she'd felt earlier had dissipated, replaced by overwhelming grief. She longed to hug Marion and make everything better, but healing would not come easy for Marion. "I'm sorry I came down so hard on you earlier," she said instead, draping her arm across Marion's shoulders. "Talk to me."

"Since my mother died, I've had nightmares every night, especially during December," Marion said in a shaky voice. "In my dreams, she's hovering over me. Her face is bloated, worms crawling out of her nose and eyes. I can see the flesh hanging from her hands, smell her when she tries to strangle me. Her stink lingers in my room, even after I wake up."

Sobs crept into her voice. "I tried to tell Mom and Dad and their doctors, but no one took me seriously. I was so afraid to go out at night. Instead, I concentrated on my schoolwork, and tried antidepressants. Nothing helped."

Reaching into her purse, Marion scribbled something on a lined sheet and handed the paper to David. "Take this note to my accountant. He'll make sure you and Colby get your money." Rooting through her purse, she fished out keys and pressed them into Colby's hand. "The house is yours. Money or not, I'll still have to face that old witch in my dreams."

"It's no wonder," David said sadly. "Nothing grows on Jennifer's grave. It's just bare earth among the grass and weeds. No one found out what caused the fire. No sign of arson or—"

Colby raised her hand. "David, stop. We're upsetting her."

"She's got to face this," David persisted relentlessly. "Otherwise, she could have a mental breakdown."

Marion whirled toward David, her face reddened, her eyes flashing with indignation. "Face what? My past? My mother's extramarital affairs? My jealousy toward Colby?"

"No, you should visit your mother's grave. Talk to her, try to make peace, if peace can be made. Colby and I will go with you tonight. We'll take my car. I'll spring for the flowers for her grave."

Colby rolled her eyes. "Not tonight, David," she said gazing out the window. "It's still snowing, and the wind chill factor's almost zero."

"It has to be tonight because it's the anniversary of Jennifer's death," David said quietly. "I never believed in the supernatural, but when something quacks like a duck…"

"Leave me out of this, David." Colby rubbed her arms, shivering. "My asthma really hates the cold."

"Then wear a scarf around your mouth and chest," David said, his wistful eyes pleading. "Marion needs our support. You understand that, right?"

Colby balked, hands gripping her sweater, kneading it. Again, she took in Marion's pale-as-paper complexion and shadowed eyes. "I must be crazy for doing this, but…okay, count me in. Besides, Dad's first wife means nothing to me."

David reached for his coat. "I'll get those flowers now. Take another breathing treatment before we go."

"Good idea." Colby made a beeline for her nebulizer equipment. "I'll be ready in about fifteen minutes."

"Now, wait a minute." Marion stood up, favoring them with a censuring glare. "You've both decided for me, haven't you? What if I refuse to go?"

"I don't think you have a choice." David sighed. "Unless you want to keep having nightmares."

The ice crunched under David's car as he drove. The narrow streets barely allowed them enough room to pass. Something under the car popped, and then David skidded around a corner. His wheels screeched as he fought to regain control of his car.

The cemetery's wrought iron gate leaped up at them from the shadows, staring them down like an ugly monster. Skeletal fingers of terror inched up Colby's spine.

"My doctor warned me not to go out in this weather," she said, ignoring the phantom voice whispering that her fear had nothing to do with asthma. "I wish we could do this in the spring."

"So do I." David patted her shoulder. "So do I."

Snow stretched ahead of them in sheaths of white. Gusts of wind slapped at Colby's face, but she'd donned three sweaters under a woolen coat and matching hat. She tied her neck scarf loosely over her mouth. Thankfully, David had parked his car on the street, instead of in the cemetery lot. The thought of getting stuck and freezing here while waiting for a snow plow, especially near the grave of a restless soul, had left her with an unspoken terror.

Clad in knee-high, fur-lined boots, Marion stepped onto the white path between the tombstones. Her flashlight splashed yellow circles on rows of markers. Some were decorated with snow-covered flowers.

"Colby's right," she said, shivering. "We shouldn't have come here. Let's lay the flowers and go."

Colby carried six long-stemmed roses wrapped in cellophane, which David had bought at a supermarket. *Blood-red roses,* she thought sickly. Already, snowflakes large as hailstones had lodged between the petals. "Where's the grave?" she asked.

"Over there." David waved his flashlight toward an open expanse of woods, where the cemetery ended.

The snow came down so heavily that Colby couldn't make out any line between the ground and the sky. Ice crunched under her boots. Despite her scarf, she exhaled smoke with each breath. Her wheezing started again, announcing another invasion by her asthma.

What am I doing, playing Nature Girl in the snow? Then she reminded herself that she was doing the right thing. With a shrug, she took a blast from her inhaler.

Moments later, the rows of gravestones thinned out, leaving behind smooth alabaster mounds.

"There." David pointed again.

Colby stopped and looked. Just before the woods stood a solitary marker. Dark patches of earth surrounded the stone, as barren and empty as Jennifer's life. Even the snow didn't disturb it. The tombstone bore no cross, name, or floral design.

Maybe Jennifer had gotten lost in some black hole and couldn't find her way back to humanity. Maybe Colby didn't want to know what motivated Jennifer's actions. The shocked horror in Marion's eyes when she described her dreams spoke of a monstrosity bordering on the supernatural. Tears rolling down her face, Colby bent down to lay the roses, when David stopped her.

"No, Marion has to do it. She has to appease Jennifer's spirit."

Marion shook her head, as if she couldn't believe she was here and doing this. She took the flowers from Colby, and then laid them before the tombstone.

"So what's next?" Marion asked with a trace of sarcasm. "Will standing here freezing make my mother happy?"

Colby shook her head, rubbing her chest. She glanced toward the street, where its lamps glowed yellow and white, wishing they could say a prayer and be done with it.

"Tell Jennifer that you want to set everything right," David prodded Marion.

"You're asking me to talk to a dead woman?" Marion laughed. "I can't believe this. Okay…Mom, I'm sorry your boyfriend strangled you. I'm sorry everyone hated your foul mouth and rotten temper. You ugly witch!"

"Marion!" Colby gasped.

David's husky face bleached the color of chalk. "Take it back," he said urgently. "Now."

"No way! I'm still paying for what she did to me. The beatings, her affairs, the house fire. As if these weren't enough, she caused Dad's plane crash and Colby's asthma. I'm sorry. I just can't."

Blasts of wind rose from the shadows, whipping their coats.

"Jennifer didn't give me asthma. I inherited it from Mom. That's why the pneumonia killed her." Colby rubbed her chest again. "So much for soothing troubled spirits. I hope we don't all wake up with pneumonia or something worse tomorrow." She tried to smile, but it came out shaky and lopsided.

Marion ground her heels into the jumble of dark soil. "Go to hell!"

105

The ground shifted beneath their feet. Concrete shattered, and then the soil split. Something inside the chasm flashed white, exuding a foul odor, reminding Colby of fish that had gone bad. The wind sprayed drifts of snow over their feet.

"Damn!" Colby recoiled several paces.

The gravestone swayed before the wind danced it inside the hole. The chasm widened, allowing snow to drift inward with the crumbling soil. Slowly, skeletal hands dug through the snow, groping and seeking purchase. They latched around Marion's boots.

"Marion, take off your boots!" Colby hollered.

Too late. The boots were laced around Marion's calves. Naked bones, white and cold as the winter snow, yanked Marion by the ankles, knocking her off her feet. The flashlight dropped. By the time Marion reached for the ties, the skeletal figure had her by the knees.

"Help!" Marion thrashed uselessly against its grip. Her gloved fingers clawed for purchase, finding nothing but fine snow. "Don't just stand there, help me."

"David, do something," Colby sobbed. But David stood rooted by a tree, staring at the cold cobwebs of bone, snow-coated eye sockets and teeth. The skull and arms, followed by vertebrae and ribs, worked their way through the widening the hole to the stormy sky. David's quivering lips moved, but no words came. A lion in his courtroom, he was used to winning his battles by following a maze of rules and procedures. This courtroom knew neither rules nor procedure, and Colby feared that he would be no help at all.

Reaching for her flashlight, she hurled it at Jennifer. The flashlight whacked Jennifer's skull, but her arms pulled Marion relentlessly further down, and what was this? She was *biting* Marion, leaving ragged gashes on her face. Further down, the snow and soil obliterated the sound of Marion's cries. The whites of her eyes flashed at Colby seconds before the ground swallowed her. Colby panicked at the sight. She glanced around for a tree branch, rock, anything to use for a weapon, but the miles of powdery snow seemed endless.

Tears stung Colby's eyes. The snowflakes came down big as hailstones as she and David fled to the gate. Seated in David's car, doors locked, she shivered at the booming sound behind them. A glance in that direction told her the cause. Flames exploded around Jennifer's grave. David cranked the engine, glancing at the road, then at the cemetery.

The car would not start.

David keyed his engine again and again, cursing out loud. Sloshing footfalls echoed from behind them. Colby threw a glance over her shoulder, praying it was Marion. In the gloom, a long and narrow figure, with grotesque bumps protruding from the shoulders and hips, plodded from the grave. Judging by the frantic look on David's pale face, he must have seen it, too. She nudged his shoulder, and they ran, screaming, screaming, the ten blocks to the house. The footfalls grew louder and louder. Colby's lungs blew long, musical notes, and each note shuddered through her tightening chest.

Fists thudded at the door moments after Colby and David burst into the living room. Colby collapsed into a chair, groping for her nebulizer. David stood by the door, his hands cradling an axe. The thumping persisted. Cracking, and then a hairline fissure split down the door panels.

"Run!" David waved his hand, his voice laced with panic. "Hide in the closet."

The nebulizer dropped. Colby jumped from the chair, eyes on the crackling door. *The closet? Bad call, David. If she finds me in a closet, I'm good as dead.* At that thought, she gathered her nebulizer equipment and hastened to the kitchen, keeping her eyes on David.

Brandishing his axe, David yanked open the door. Gusts of wind rushed in, revealing only miles of snow-clad night.

"Our visitor's gone." David smiled, but his voice edged with tension. His eyes flitted like rabbits. "Get some sleep. I'll stand watch."

"How can I sleep, knowing that thing's roaming around outside?" Colby's eyes widened at the sight of the axe. "Let's hide at a hotel. We can take Marion's car."

David let out a long, skeletal sigh, sounding like wind blowing through snow drifts. "It would take an hour to get to the nearest hotel. Suppose we get stuck or in an accident along the way?" His voice cracked. "I should have never pushed Marion into visiting the grave."

"If it hadn't been you, one of her psychiatrists might have come up with the same idea." With a weary sigh, Colby gathered her respiratory supplies and shuffled to the stairs. "All right. I'll try to sleep."

Upstairs, Colby dumped her supplies in her old bedroom. She scanned the room for something that might work as a weapon and found it – a pointed umbrella by the vanity table. After changing into a flannel nightgown, she crawled into bed, tucking the umbrella against her chest. The feel of its cool metal and the sound of David's plodding footsteps took the edge off her shivering. Moments later, she drifted to sleep.

Stark fear speared through Colby when thumping at her window jarred her awake. She snatched up her umbrella, which had fallen on the floor.

Footsteps scratched across the roof, and something huge loomed outside behind her lace draperies. Another thump came, and the panes shivered.

Colby sat with her ear cocked to the window, the umbrella motionless in her hands. Though the thermostat in her room registered the temperature at 72 degrees, her skin turned to gooseflesh. Suddenly, she could hear so much. The whistling in her chest. The howling wind. The pattering ice on the roof.

She edged toward the foot of her bed, heart hammering inside her chest. The hallway was quiet as death.

What happened to David? Colby groped for her bed post, missed, groped again, and launched herself from the bed. "Damn you, Jennifer," she whispered. "What do you want with me?"

The bedroom window shattered, spraying shards of glass. Blasts of wind whipped the drapes aside, and then a snow-clad skeleton sprawled through – Jennifer, she realized with a sick feeling. Bloody gristle and tatters of scorched wool from Marion's coat clung to her bones. Her fetid stench assaulted Colby's nostrils, making her gag.

Of course, Jennifer wanted everyone related to Marion dead. Like David and herself. Jennifer made grunting sounds, her mouth opening and closing, showing pointed teeth. Colby stood where she was, frozen as Jennifer wobbled toward her, leaving snow-covered tracks on the floorboards, hands reaching.

Fleshless fingers touched Colby's throat. The shocked terror she felt fled, chased by fury at having her room invaded. Fists clenched, she drove the umbrella tip into Jennifer's ribs.

Jennifer toppled over the vanity table and landed on the floor. Her spine split apart, a curious sound, like cracking ice. Her cold, bony hands clutched at Colby's bedroom slipper. Colby had always worn her slippers to bed, never imagining that she would one day wear them to a fight with a dead woman. Wrenching her foot loose, she left Jennifer with only her slipper. She bolted toward the hallway.

Jennifer crawled after her, a monster determined, for what she wanted now didn't come in a liquor bottle. At least the top half of her did. Her teeth chewed at the slipper.

At the doorway, Colby whirled around and jammed the umbrella tip inside her mouth. Jennifer's bony fingers grabbed the umbrella and yanked. Colby maintained her grip on the handle. She tried hard to ignore Jennifer's sickening stench and the agony as her muscles were pulled like taffy. Stabbing pain and tightness tore through her chest. She darted a glance toward her bedside where she left the nebulizer, but Jennifer blocked her access to her medicine. Screams coming out in shrill whistles, she poked and prodded. She never heard footsteps until light flooded the hall.

"Holy shit!" David shouted, bursting from the stairs with his axe. He made three steps into the hallway, and then his foot snagged against the leg of a marble side table. Down he went, axe and all. The table toppled, socking his left arm and side.

Only dimly aware of his cries, Colby abandoned the umbrella. She grabbed the axe. Down went its blade, cracking Jennifer's skull in two. She chopped and chopped until her bones lay still.

Gasping for breath, Colby turned toward her brother. He was clutching his left arm. "Colby, behind you!" he cried, pointing toward her vanity table.

Jennifer's legs had somehow managed to stand and made it toward the doorway.

Hands raised, Colby brought down the axe in a whistling arc that split Jennifer's pelvis and wedged between the floorboards. The legs twitched for many minutes, then shuddered to a stop.

Her brother still needed help. *I can't lift that table,* she thought, and then David's reddening face and groans got her adrenaline cooking. She rushed to his side. Mustering her last reserves of strength, she hefted the table upright.

"Colby." David struggled to a sitting position, then flopped back with a groan. "God, it hurts to breathe."

"Don't move. I'll call 9-1-1." Colby draped a blanket over him. She made her way to her night table, gingerly stepping over the bone fragments. Sagging against her bed, she reached for her phone. She let out a sigh of relief when she got a dial tone.

After she finished talking, she looked over at David. "May Jennifer rest...in pieces." With that, she burst into sobs.

"Colby, I'm sorry about this. I promised Dad I would look out for you."

"We underestimated Jennifer. Please don't blame—" her voice exploded in a violent cough. "I'd better finish my treatment."

David gazed at her, his face a rictus of pain. "If the paramedics notice the mess in your room, not to mention the smell, they'll involve the police."

Colby nodded, wiping her eyes. She trotted her nebulizer equipment out to the hallway and closed the door behind her. "There. My overhead light shorted out. That's what I'll tell them if they ask. We'll have to fix the window and clean the mess after we come home from the hospital."

"The cemetery visit was my idea, so I'll hire someone to do the repairs and cleaning. Someone owes me enough favors so he won't ask questions." David struggled to a sitting position and this time made it. "Finish your treatment."

"In a minute." Blankets wrapped around her, Colby tiptoed downstairs and cracked open the front door. She then returned to her nebulizer and sat by her brother, watching him, and waited for the ambulance. The wind howled, whipping against the shattered window and drapes. The scattering of glass sounded like laughter, cursing, or perhaps whispers of dark promises for the new day whose dawn still waited to break.

Night Fighters

Todd was cruising through Malvern Hospital's emergency room when a young woman shuffled through its steel gray doors. Her badge said, "Liza Fabin, Nurse Practitioner." Dressed in green scrubs and a navy sweater, she looked in her mid-twenties, a target age for victims of the Ahmad Rouge terrorists. Her face wore an expression that Todd had come to know. She was fighting back tears.

Todd paused in mid-step and shuddered at the horrible wave of self-loathing rolling through him, though the feeling grew less urgent with each pickup. He kept thinking about his boss, Mahmud, a foul-smelling soldier who ran the terrorists' underground camp, and wondered what happened to the prisoners. Mahmud called them recruits, and said he needed them to work at his camp. His glittering eyes and skeletal grin discouraged Todd from asking for details.

The first time Todd drafted someone, he didn't sleep for a week. The second time hurt almost as much, but he reminded himself that the "recruits" provided a steady income, something he hadn't enjoyed for years. After a while, he quit wondering about the work camp and what it held in store for the recruits.

The young woman darted her eyes around the ward with increasing panic. White gauze peeped through her top's v-shaped collar. Gunshot wound, Todd presumed, and a nasty one at that. Badly hurt as she appeared to be, she had no business working around sick people. White blotches surrounded her eyes and covered her face. Her rancid odor whispered a rumor of infection.

Perhaps fear kept her going. He'd seen enough of it in his own mirror to recognize the look.

The woman glanced with pleading eyes toward the desk, where people in white were preparing medicines. No one looked her way. Her vacuous eyes and trembling lips told Todd that she'd gotten into serious trouble.

You look like you need a friend, he thought, approaching. *Here I am.*

Before he reached her, a man in combat fatigues ambled into the ward, whistling to himself. A government soldier, armed with an Uzi. Soldiers patrolled the floors at the hospitals and malls every day, but their presence didn't stop the Ahmad Rouge's guerrilla tactics. This trooper wouldn't hesitate to rescue a woman, putting Todd's life at risk.

Todd stepped back into the shadows. Pulling a sheet from his lab coat pocket, he pretended to glance at his phony list of patients. His eyes shifted between the trooper and the woman. A fly buzzed around her face. She slapped it away.

The secretary sitting at the computer waved down the soldier and said something to him. She was pretty, blonde, and the young man had dark hair and bulky arms. They huddled at her desk, making chit-chat—let's catch a movie, maybe a drink, blah, blah, blah, while Todd had a life-and-death mission. The secretary giggled at something the soldier said. How sweet.

Now was the time to make his move. The young woman leaned against a wall, weeping softly; someone would notice. Todd hated making a pickup with government soldiers nearby; but if he didn't meet his quota within the next twenty-four hours, two Ahmad Rouge guards would show up at his door and haul him to an underground camp. The Ahmad Rouge camps guaranteed death. He knew this as well as the dread lodging in his heart.

Todd walked up to the woman, trying hard not to gag on her foul odor. Surely, his business suit, professional demeanor, and gentle smile would invite her trust. He met her gaze, elbow leaning against the wall, and she lifted her eyes toward Todd. Fiery red curls surrounded her wan, frightened face. Her eyes, blue as sapphires, glistened in the lights.

"Excuse me, miss. . ." He touched her shoulder and fingered her badge. "Liza. Are you all right?"

"No, I'm not all right," she said, shaking her head. "My husband's missing."

"Who?"

"Ambrose. The Ahmad Rouge are kidnapping professionals like us, and I'm afraid those bastards got him." She began to sob loudly. A nurse charting at the desk looked their way.

"It's okay," Todd said, and she returned to her notes. He draped his arm across Liza's shoulders and glanced toward the computer.

The soldier had laid his Uzi on the desk, and he whispered something in the secretary's ear. Todd's trembling eased. At this point, a dozen Ahmad Rouge could swarm the emergency room, and the trooper wouldn't notice.

"He was supposed to meet me here hours ago," Liza wept. "It's not like Ambrose to show up late. What if the Ahmad Rouge. . ."

"You don't know that." Todd prodded Liza toward the exit. "Maybe he saw trouble coming and decided to lay low somewhere. Did you call the police?"

"I wouldn't trust the police. Some of them belong to the Ahmad Rouge."

"That's true." Todd heaved a deep sigh. "I'd be glad to help you look for him."

Liza looked up at him, eyes widening. "I'd appreciate your help, Doctor. . ."

"Just call me Todd," he said, grinning. "This war has been tough on everyone."

"You've got that right." She offered an empty smile that didn't touch her glazed eyes.

Todd glanced toward the desk to make sure that the soldier was still preoccupied. He was. "Have you tried calling Ambrose on his cell phone?"

She shook her head. "He never uses his phone unless it's a patient emergency. It's too easy for the Ahmad Rouge to intercept conversations. He had one close call when he stepped on a landmine. Now he'll only handle special cases. His looks frighten people, so he wears a disguise." A dreamy look crossed her gaunt face. "Did you know that his treatments worked wonders with leukemia? Before his accident, he used to run the cancer floor. Everyone knew him by his first name."

"Ambrose, the oncologist?" Todd smiled. "He's tied up with a patient."

"You two know each other?" Eyes widening and hand clasped over her mouth, Liza stepped toward a window and looked outside. "I'm surprised that he'd . . . never mind. When did he tell you this?"

"About an hour ago, we bumped into each other outside in the courtyard." Todd lowered his voice, not caring to cause a scene that people would recall later. "He apologized but said he was in a hurry. Patient emergency. I saw him over there."

Cracking the window, he pointed toward a maze of bushes and topiaries. At the far end of the garden was a brick restaurant with a neon sign, "The Commissary."

Liza arched her blonde eyebrows. "What was Ambrose doing *there?*" she cried in stunned surprise.

"Beats me." Todd's mind kept working fast. He needed more lines than a telephone directory to fool this woman. The clock ticked away, and he'd have to meet his quota or face the machine guns. Ambrose. Not Doctor or Dr. Fabin, but Ambrose. Liza had made that clear. Maybe Ambrose thought that the title "doctor" intimidated people. "I'm pretty sure he was the guy. Scrawny-looking man in a black suit."

"He wears brown," Liza said. "Always brown. He thinks that black depresses people."

"Maybe his suit was brown." Todd shrugged. "Like I said, he was in a hurry. Want me to drive you by the restaurant?"

Liza rolled her eyes. "Ambrose wouldn't go there. He shies away from crowds."

"Maybe I had the wrong guy." Todd sighed. "You've had enough, Liza. Last thing I want to do is cause you more grief." Turning on his heels, he started to the exit.

Liza did not move. He thought about going back and coaxing her, but with people nearby, discretion was the wiser course. By far. Maybe he could start over at another hospital. Pennsylvania General or—

"Todd, wait." Liza's crepe soles pattered behind him. "I told Ambrose I was hungry, and he knows I like my meat fresh. Maybe he thought he had to go to the restaurant to get it. I'm sorry I came off rude."

Todd turned around and smiled. "No need to be sorry. Let's see about finding your husband."

He led Liza to his van, a white and orange vehicle that looked like an ambulance. Its sun-filter windows obscured the inside view. He'd parked it in a lot reserved for physicians. Mahmud had given him identification cards and license plates bearing the necessary credentials, and few security officers questioned the doctors. More important, those lots had empty spaces, and the van provided a quick get-away.

Still, he'd do well to stay on his best behavior until Liza got in the van. After opening the door, he manufactured another grin. It was scary how he was getting so good at this. Liza gazed at him with her widened blue eyes, and then climbed into the front seat. "Make yourself comfortable," he said.

Liza smiled back, never suspecting that she faced death in a work camp. Very soon, judging by her emaciated appearance.

When Todd thought about it, he concluded that his troubles started with his interest in medicine. Every time he sat at his computer, he'd surf the Net for information about the latest laser procedure or surgical implant. He graduated from nursing school in 2020 and began working at Pine Run Hospital with dreams of saving lives.

Instead, unemployment soared to thirty percent after his hire, and six major hospitals, including Pine Run, ceased operations. In 2021, Ahmad Rouge terrorists invaded the United States, with New York and Pennsylvania getting most of the attacks. They began bombing official buildings with intent to overthrow the government, assassinating engineers, officials, and medical people. Army soldiers patrolled malls, schools, and hospitals, hoping to staunch the flight of bullets. It never worked. The Ahmad Rouge planted landmines, devices that appeared innocuous, but weren't. Todd went on job interviews, never knowing if he'd come home alive.

He could have avoided disaster if his interviewers had said no from the get-go. A prompt "no" would've discouraged him enough to try a different career. When a prospective boss smiled, offered encouragement, and set up follow-up interviews, you chased. Todd kept chasing for months until his assets dwindled to five dollars. He had no family or friends to help him. People in his class had called him the Lone Wolf.

Todd never forgot the day his landlord evicted him from the apartment. He crawled under a wooden crate, dazed, almost elated by the enormity of his situation. Even as he listened to the gunfire explode in the distance, he kept telling himself that he was down to his last five dollars—not five hundred, not fifty, but five one-dollar bills in his pocket. Every time he tried to think about it, he laughed until his sides hurt.

The laughter stopped a few nights later when two cops slapped him in handcuffs. Panhandling and loitering were illegal, they told him. One officer poked his gun in the back; the other escorted him to a truck filled with prisoners.

The officers dumped him into a closet-sized cell without heat. A tiny bulb overhead provided light. A rusty bucket in the corner became his toilet, since his cell did not come with running water. No cot or other mundane comforts. About once a day, someone brought him a tray of spoiled meat and muddy water. The guards beat him with heated rods. Every time he tried to sleep, rats skittering through the cell bit at his toes.

Within a week after his incarceration, Todd's dungarees swam around his bony frame. Dizziness overwhelmed him with the least exertion, warning that dehydration and shock were imminent. He curled up on the floor, waiting for Death's call.

Some time later, a burly officer wearing black marched into his cell. "Hadir wants to see you," he said flatly.

After hiking Todd by the armpits, the officer walked him down a dimly lit corridor reeking of mildew. Pain like rusty nails writhed through Todd's rat-bitten legs. His back ached terribly with each jarring movement, but the officer's stony face warned him to keep quiet.

At the exit, he shambled up a flight of steps that led to a paneled office. Inside, a bearded, husky man sat before a mahogany desk. His name tag said, "Baghel Hadir, President." He wore a black cassock and turban, the Ahmad Rouge's uniform.

"I'll do anything you want," Todd babbled at once. "I'll take any job, only please let me go."

"Shut up and sit down," Hadir ordered him.

Todd plopped into a chair, shivering.

"My men have taken over your prison. If I let you go, you'll run to the FBI. I could send you to my work camp, let you die in jail, or hire you as a spy. I doubt if you've got the guts, but anything is possible." Hadir rested his bearded face in his hands and grinned. "Suppose I send you to my factory to make bombs?"

"I'll do it." Todd swallowed hard, fighting an onslaught of tears. "I'll do anything to stay alive."

"No, Todd, you'd botch the job, then give me a bunch of shitty excuses. You're in the big leagues, and I play for keeps."

Tears flooded Todd's eyes, and he started to bawl.

"You belong to us now," Hadir said quietly. "If you don't cooperate, my men will turn you into a house plant. You'll lie in your own shit with tubes running out your nose and gut."

Todd's bony shoulders shook with harsh sobs.

"You and this fellow Mahmud might work well together, given your educational background." Hadir pushed a folded scrap of paper across his desk toward Todd. "Do what he asks, and he'll pay you well. Cross him, and I'll have you back here with my men ready to work on you. Now get lost."

Mahmud's address was written on the folded scrap. Todd went to see him and learned how to draft health care professionals for the work camp. Mahmud stipulated a quota: five recruits a month. That was when Todd began to cruise the hospitals.

Todd exited the parking lot and headed up the access road past the courtyard. Liza perched at the edge of her seat, hands folded around her knees, eyes darting like rabbits. At the traffic light, Todd went straight, avoiding The Commissary's drive-through gate, and kept going.

Liza's eyes bulged. "I thought you said. . ."

"Not here." Todd held a finger to his lips. "I'm going to the back of the restaurant. I saw him talking to someone by the dumpster."

Liza let out a sigh of relief. Todd couldn't help feeling sorry for her. He hated working for the Ahmad Rouge; really he did. But he'd rather that than jail or the camp. He'd never forget the feel of bugs crawling up his pant legs or the rats biting his ankles. If he failed to meet his quota, Hadir would have no compunction about eliminating him.

At the rear of the restaurant, he pulled up by the trash bin. The parking lot appeared deserted. He kept a stash of maps, tools, and a first aid kit inside a pail under the dashboard. While fumbling through his pail, he glanced at Liza. Her seat had steel backing covered with vinyl, with slits on both sides. Still rooting through his tools, he extended his left hand toward a red button under his steering wheel.

"Can I help you find something?" Liza asked. The tension edged back into her voice, but the quality of it had changed. Perhaps she realized she'd better worry about her own skin, and never mind Ambrose.

"I've got it." Todd pulled out an empty leather wallet and offered a sheepish grin. Past experience had taught him never to underestimate anyone. The second time out, an intern had kicked him in the groin. "I misplaced my driver's license. I can't drive without one."

"I suppose not," Liza said, easing against the cushions.

Still smiling, Todd pressed the red button. Steel belts popped through the cushion slits, clicking shut around Liza's hips. Then his troubles began. Liza bucked with superhuman strength, thrashing against the bands seeking purchase around her chest and shoulders. She twisted and turned, letting out gravelly cries.

Todd grabbed Liza's shoulder and shoved her against the seat. Her flailing hands, cold as marble, seized his wrists, and she bit his right arm. The pain of a thousand knives flared through his muscles. He socked her in the jaw with a hammer. Its impact made a sickening crunch, but Liza slumped back, dazed. The steel bands snapped shut, securing her arms and shoulders. Todd checked her ties, and then inspected his wounds with a flashlight.

His arm throbbed terribly. A gash with rat-bitten edges formed a crater in his forearm, blood streaming from the wound. He'd need stitches for sure, antibiotics, and probably a tetanus shot. Human bites were the worst, and this one was brutal.

After wrapping gauze around his arm, he headed to the exit gate, past The Commissary. He turned left. Mahmud's underground campsite lay beneath a maze of shacks surrounded by woods, just outside the city. If he used secondary roads, he'd get there in an hour.

"You'll regret this," Liza said, as they rode through a pitch dark street surrounded by woods.

She was crying again, muffled sobs. The smell he noticed earlier had gotten nauseatingly strong, the stink of spoiled fish. The white blotches around her eyes shifted, and insects buzzed around her face. Did Liza have a contagious disease? The burning pain in his arm warned Todd it was too late to worry about that now.

"Ambrose will get you for this," Liza added.

With a deep sigh, Todd slowed to a stop. At the light, he turned left down an unmarked road surrounded by marshy fields.

Liza strained at the bands and wept silently.

"Cut out the waterworks," Todd snapped, blotting the blood seeping from under the gauze. "It won't do any good."

Liza continued squirming against her ties, making a groaning noise that sent chills up Todd's spine. Already, her chair back had loosened from its sockets. Mahmud had built that seat for prisoners, and no one, not even a two-hundred pound athlete, could move once restrained. *Shit,* he thought, *if she's this strong half dead, I'd hate to see her when she's healthy.*

Liza squirmed at her ties again, and this time Todd heard splintering sounds. She couldn't weigh more than a hundred pounds. How could she break through steel?

She's panicking, a phantom voice whispered. *That's how.*

But none of his other recruits had been able to it, and most of them had become far more terrified than Liza by this stage.

He pulled over to the shoulder. Reaching into his pail, he brought out a hypodermic needle that Mahmud had provided for emergencies. "Use this sparingly," he'd warned. "Too much can kill your guy before we get work out of him."

"See this?" Todd held the silver tip before Liza's eyes. "It contains a muscle relaxant. Once this drug takes effect, you won't be able to move or breathe. Do you want that?"

Liza shook her head vehemently. Strong or not, she feared for her life, he was glad to see.

"Smart choice." Todd mopped the sweat from his forehead. How he hated having to bully someone into submission. Then the shadowy voice reminded him that nurse practitioners like Liza had denied him work, and he stopped worrying. "Quit yanking your ties, and I'll put this away. Okay?"

Liza nodded, lips quivering, face chalky with terror.

After wiping his head again, Todd pulled onto the road. He drove a little faster, having gotten off the main highway. Liza's behavior didn't seem natural, and he wanted to unload her on Mahmud and scram.

"What you do won't matter," Liza said quietly. "Ambrose will find me, and when he does, he'll make you pay."

"Yeah, right." Todd shrugged. "I'm real scared."

"Ambrose can smell me from miles away."

Todd believed it. His experiences with others taught that fear had a pungent odor, but this woman smelled like a mixture of sweat, spoiled meat, and rotting tomatoes. Something was seriously the matter with her, but soon that would become Mahmud's problem. As the old saying went, let the buyer beware.

Todd cracked his window. On his left, moonlight splashed silvery puddles on miles of dense forest.

"Ambrose can run faster than your van," Liza said, smiling. "All dead people do. They travel fast."

"Oh, yeah?" Todd hooted with laughter. "I'll bet he flies after he's had enough uppers."

"Ambrose—"

"Enough about Ambrose already," Todd snapped.

Five miles later, Todd came to a stop sign. He bore left up a gravel road, past an open corn field. This path led to Route 85, an S-shaped street that would take him to Mahmud's work camp.

He glanced toward the corn field. Rows of plants stretched ahead, their leaves glistening like silver in the moonlight, and then the moonlight faded.

He heard a clattering outside, like someone dragging chains along the road.

"Ambrose!" Liza cried.

"Be quiet, lady!" Todd shouted, his voice more shrill than he liked. "It's just a couple of rocks."

Skeletal fingers of terror inched up his spine. Liza grinned, showing grayish gums and jagged teeth. The bugs formed dark clouds around her eyes. He tried to tell himself that none of this was happening, that he was in bed having the granddaddy of nightmares. But his saner mind went on autopilot, clicking along as if he'd taken speed.

He knows I like my meat fresh.

Before his accident, he used to run the cancer floor. Did he go on disability?

His looks frighten people, so he wears a disguise.

Something hard thumped the roof of the van.

"Ambrose!" Liza cried, and Todd could not see the road. A human skull followed by skeletal hands glided across his windshield. Even in the gloom, he could see tufts of gray flesh clinging to the bones.

His looks frighten people.

Todd screamed and slammed on the brakes, hoping to dislodge the creature's grip from his roof. It didn't' work. He couldn't see the road, and worse, the groaning started again, the sound of the steel bands protesting, followed by a snap. Liza lunged forward, digging her fingernails into his cheek.

"Ambrose, that creep tied me up," she called to the windshield in her gravelly voice. "He works for the Ahmad Rouge."

I didn't sign up for this, lady, Todd thought, reaching for his syringe again. *When the Ahmad Rouge tells you to jump, you obey.*

A bony hand smashed through the window. The syringe dropped. Todd watched, quivering, as Ambrose tore away the van's driver-side door, leaving jagged hinges. The full moon illuminated a skeletal male wearing a three-piece suit. It was brown, just as Liza had told him.

Ambrose yanked Todd from the van, his fingers digging into the meat of his shoulders. His eyes were empty olive pits. He reeked of things long dead, exploded by the gases of their own decay.

"Someone with a rare blood disease needed my help. The job took longer than expected because staffing was short. You terrorists have taken out my best workers, including Liza." His death's head grin widened. "Some of us didn't stay dead. We decided to become night fighters and go after scoundrels like you. You should have left us alone."

He threw Todd to the ground, and then ripped open his shirt. Only dimly aware of the cold cobwebs of bone squeezing his throat, he heard Ambrose ask sweetly if Liza still wanted fresh meat; he heard Liza say yes, the creep had frightened her with a hammer, and now the craving had become unbearable. He saw a flash of silver before it disappeared under his chin. 100,000 kilowatts of sheer agony flared through his shoulders as Ambrose ripped away skin, fascia, and the muscle underneath. Gray dots rose before Todd's eyes. The last thing he heard, before floating into the darkness, were the sounds of tearing flesh and Liza chewing and swallowing while Ambrose brushed her hair with kisses.

Garden of Souls

The crystal vase beckoned to Dianne, its curves reflecting rainbows from the sunlight streaming through the curtained window. Standing on tiptoe, she reached toward the cabinet shelf that held the glass antiques. Capital mistake. The vase tottered on its edge and slipped through her trembling fingers before crash-landing on the floor.

Stomping feet exploded from the hall and her fiancé, Victor, burst into the living room. His tanned face turned deep red, and his blue eyes narrowed into tiny slits. "Dianne!" he cried. "What are you doing?"

Dianne swallowed hard. "I was just—"

"Idiot!" He let loose a disgusted sigh. "That vase was worth thousands of dollars."

Dianne cowered against the velvet drapes, dragging her fingers through her chestnut curls. The glass fragments on the floor glimmered like a queen's ransom of diamonds. She gazed at her purple cotton tent dress, a sharp contrast to Victor's tweed suit, silk shirt, and Rolex watch. Next, he'd complain about her clothes and diet.

"I can't take you out in that rag," he continued, as if following a cue. "Why do I bother? When we do go out, you order fat burgers and cheese fries."

Daddykins chewed him out and he's taking it out on me. Again. Dianne continued worrying her hair. Unless she spoke up, he'd start harping on her weight, too. Since she graduated nursing school, she'd gained about 25 pounds. "What I eat is none of your business."

"It is if I'm going to buy you decent clothes."

"I never asked anyone to buy me clothes. The dresses and diets you yammer about cost money I don't have."

"Because you spend it on gory novels. That trash has to go, Dianne."

"I stopped reading horror literature months ago." Dianne fingered the key in her dress pocket. The key belonged to a hidden suitcase filled with Stephen King novels and cheese-flavored snacks. She averted her eyes, hoping he wouldn't notice the smile playing on her lips.

"It's not funny, you dumb bitch," Victor shouted through clenched teeth. "That vase belonged to my grandmother." Yanking Dianne by the arm, he marched her outside to his bright red Lexus. "I'm taking you home."

The cool vinyl seat sent a prickly sensation through her skin, but the snug seatbelt took the edge off her shivering. Dianne always buckled up before getting into a car with Victor, especially during his foul moods. His moods worsened after fights with his dad. Next, he'd take his temper on the road, and there was no telling what would happen.

Victor treated the expressway like a serpentine course, snaking around a sixteen-wheeler and almost slamming into a Jeep. Every few minutes, he rolled down his window and cursed out a driver. His fists clenched the wheel, knuckles turning white. She could smell his anger, bitter and acrid, oozing from his soul.

The ride bumped Dianne out of the present and back to the graduation party at school last April.

The liquor flowed freely. She'd gotten a strong buzz by the time Victor ushered her off the dance floor. Laughed when he called her a stupid drunk. He sped down Route 22, the street where she lived now, his tires the hiss of angry serpents. The laughter died in her throat when a van ahead of them swerved into the shadows. Seconds later, screeching tires were followed by a smash. On their right, light billowed from the ravine, punctuated by a blast.

"Victor, stop!" she cried.

"What for?" Victor asked tonelessly.

"I think the car ahead of us got in an accident. I heard something crunch in the ravine."

"No, you didn't, silly," Victor said, laughing. "That guy turned at the next intersection. The noise you heard was just thunder. We're getting a storm."

Dianne gazed out the window but only made out faint outlines of trees and highway. Maybe the van made the turn too fast, but there was no mistaking the light coming from the ravine. "It sounded like an accident," she said, shaking her head. "We should stop and check. Better yet, call the police."

"There's no accident. It's the booze talking." Irritation edged into Victor's voice. "Be quiet and sleep it off."

His stony face discouraged further argument. Still, the blast sent chills up her spine. Maybe the liquor sent her imagination into overdrive. That night, Dianne made a promise to stop drinking.

"Moo." Victor's voice penetrated her thoughts.

Dianne's head snapped sideways. She found herself facing the Cottage Green Apartments, her home in Northeast Philadelphia.

"I said, move it!" Victor shoved her toward the car door. "I've had enough of your nonsense."

Before Dianne could react, Victor's cell phone rang. He made no move to answer. The phone continued to ring in his jacket pocket. "Answer it," she said, nudging his shoulder. "Maybe it's important."

"It's Dad," Victor said ponderously. "Every time I leave the bank, he finds an excuse to hassle me."

"Then I'll answer it." Dianne two-fingered the phone from his pocket. "Hello?"

"Where's Victor?" barked an older man's voice.

"He can't come to the phone. Can I take a message?"

"I don't believe this." A long, deep sigh followed. "That gutless wonder's hiding behind a skirt. Okay, tell Victor this. His incompetence today cost the bank a million dollars."

"Maybe you'd better tell him." Dianne handed the phone to Victor. She eased herself out of the car, watching him intently. The anger in his eyes fled, chased by his father's scolding.

It wasn't the first time Victor crumbled under his father's tongue-lashings. When Dianne applied for a school loan for $23,000, Victor had seen to it that she got the money. His smile and willingness to help invited her trust. Later, he paid for his generosity with a harsh lecture from Dad. The first time he made love to her, he showed her the crisscross scars on his back, souvenirs of childhood beatings. Dianne hoped that loving Victor and getting him to talk about those scars would enable him to heal.

The squealing tires of his Lexus warned that healing would not come easy for Victor. He sped onto Route 22 in a cloud of blue smoke. Dianne prayed that he'd get to the bank alive. Head lowered and shoulders drooping, she shuffled to her apartment.

While she lay awake that night, buzzing voices murmured from outside, like wind scattering leaves. She heard them every night since she moved to Cottage Green in June, but it seemed louder tonight, almost like wailing.

There would be no sleep tonight. Instead, she donned a sweater over her nightgown and put on a scarf and slippers. Grabbing a flashlight, she slipped out of her apartment and headed down the steps to the exit. Outside, a stiff October wind whipped her cheeks, whispering a rumor of frost. Hugging herself against the cold, she tiptoed down the walkway toward the dimly lit street.

Her light cut yellow swords over a plethora of weeds along the road. Their leaves sprouted up her legs like prickly tongues. Seconds later, her flashlight went out. She hadn't thought to check the batteries, but she had a full moon. The moon overhead splashed silver on the lawn and asphalt. Beyond the guard rail, a humped rib cage of trees sloped toward a valley with railroad tracks. The perfumed scent of lilac wafted from the ravine's wildflowers. No, that couldn't be. Lilacs blossomed in April or thereabouts, not October. She inhaled deeply. October or not, it was definitely lilac.

Perfume and whispers mingled, beckoning to Dianne, and she crept across the street. At the guard rail, she hesitated. Its metal had warped as if someone—or something—had smashed into it. She'd noticed it before but several of her neighbors reported having fender benders there, so she thought nothing of it. A dog howled in the distance, its cries punctuated by the buzzing voice.

The sound seemed louder, harsher, like thousands of voices trying to speak, and yet the sweet, floral scent tempted her to explore. Liquid fear and cold surged through Dianne's bones, turning her skin to gooseflesh. Why hadn't she put on regular clothes? What if the dog attacked her? But the barking didn't frighten her; the voices did. They sounded like tiny screams.

She glanced over her shoulder toward the apartment complex. Studded with porch lights, the building glowed like a shiny mass against the sky, a friendly giant willing to protect her. Victor was not here now to belittle her stupidity about the flashlight. He'd never have to find out that she investigated a noise, only to falter and flee. Her cowardice would remain another of her secrets.

The sound would continue; she knew that as well as she'd come to know the dread inspired by Victor's changeable moods. She had hoped that the whispers would lull her to sleep. Instead, they taunted her, daring her to investigate. She'd go as far as the first grove of trees. If the source of the sound didn't show itself, she'd return to her apartment and explore some other time.

As her eyes adjusted to the gloom, Dianne made out thick clumps of weeds and bushes behind the trees. Perhaps the noise came from chirping crickets or squirrels. Whatever it was, the murmur came from some place inside the ground and didn't fade at her approach.

The voices seemed loudest around a twenty-foot-square soil patch in the valley. According to her neighbors, nothing had grown there for some time. This past summer, the sun baked and cracked it into fissures. Another smell crept in with the lilac—death amid life, a rotting disease begging for a cure, lest it spread. But it didn't. Clusters of shrubs, grass, and weeds formed a perfect square around the barren soil.

After rubbing her arms to soothe the goose bumps, Dianne edged her way toward the valley. The ground sloped at a forty-five degree angle. She braced herself against tree limbs as she descended. Closer to the square patch, she felt—or thought she felt—a slight vibration. Perhaps an animal had gotten trapped inside that hideous patch. Whatever it was, the vibration called to Dianne, and she felt compelled to answer. As the ground leveled off, she stepped onto the bare patch. The dewy soil soaked her slippers, chilling her to the bone.

Seconds later, the dirt shifted underneath her. Dianne jumped backwards and laid her hand over the moving soil. In the next instant, something sharp slashed her palm. She screamed.

The dog howled again, as if echoing her cry. Stunned, Dianne held her hand to the moonlight. Blood spurted from a jagged cut stretching from thumb to wrist. Another scream came and died in her throat. Something climbed through the soil, but before her mind could register what it was, she bolted up the ravine.

By the time Dianne reached the sidewalk, her surroundings started to blur. Rustling foot falls crunched behind her. She wrapped her scarf around her injured hand to stop the bleeding. It didn't work. Blood soaked through the cotton, dribbling on the pavement and apartment stairs. "Help!" she cried, lurching up the stairwell in a sidestroke motion. "Oh, dear God, someone help me!"

A door by the landing cracked open, and a husky woman with salt-and-pepper hair stepped into the hall. Mrs. Robinson, a neighbor. "Dianne!" she cried. "What happened?"

"I don't know." Dianne tightened her makeshift bandage. The sting of razor blades twisted through her hand. "My hand's cut real bad. Do you have any compresses or towels you could spare? If I can stop the bleeding, I'll drive to Memorial Hospital."

"You can't drive like that." Mrs. Robinson waved Dianne into her apartment. "Please sit. I'll drive you there myself after we stop the bleeding."

Mrs. Robinson pressed a folded compress into Dianne's hand and then wrapped it with an elastic bandage. "You've got a wicked cut. You'll need a tetanus shot and stitches."

"I know." Dianne swallowed hard, fighting an onslaught of tears. She glanced at the wall clock. It was almost midnight. The blood leaking on her gown and the linoleum floor was bad, her pain worse. "I'm sorry for bothering you so late...and about this mess."

"No need to be sorry. What matters is that you're okay." Mrs. Robinson squinted as she inspected Dianne's hand. For the moment, the bleeding had stopped. She glanced toward the phone. "Want me to call Victor?"

"No!" the word came out more sharply than Dianne had intended. Noticing Mrs. Robinson's arched eyebrows, she lowered her voice. "What I mean is...I don't want to worry him. I appreciate your kindness."

"How did this happen?"

Dianne lowered her eyes. "Well..."

"Get dressed. You can tell me on the way to the hospital."

"It sounds ridiculous." Dianne gazed at the road stretching ahead. "Since I moved here, I've been hearing this weird murmur at night."

Mrs. Robinson braked gently for a traffic light. Even a gentle stop jarred her cut. "From the ravine out front?"

"Why, yes."

"Harry, the fellow who rented your apartment before you, heard it too. After he made a federal case over it, three fools sat up with him one night. They heard it coming from the soil patch."

Dianne sagged against her seat. "Then I'm not hearing things."

Mrs. Robinson stopped for another light, and then turned left up Cherry Street, the road leading to the hospital. "The sound's real, but I never paid Harry much attention. He's got something wrong with his upper story. He got so spooked that he moved out a couple of nights after that."

"I can see why." She laid her hand across her lap, hoping that keeping it straight would ease the stinging. *What did you see in that moving patch?* a phantom voice inside whispered. *A blackened skeleton? A skull with sharp teeth? What about the lilac smell?* "Something climbed out of that patch and bit me. Maybe it was an animal. Maybe some animal bit me. Whatever it was had sharp teeth. I had no business poking around in the bushes in my nightgown."

"You're right about that," Mrs. Robinson said gravely. "You could have fallen and gotten badly hurt...or worse."

"I realize that. And I appreciate you taking me to the hospital. I would've never made it there myself." Dianne shifted in her seat, wincing at the throbbing in her hand. Straining her eyes, she made out Memorial Hospital's neon lights. "What do you think is causing the noise?"

"It's just the wind blowing the tree branches and leaves. But Harry ..." Mrs. Robinson heaved a sigh. "Oh, he's got to be crazy."

"What did Harry say caused that sound?"

Her neighbor's car whined up a sharp incline, then putt-putt-putted to a stop in the Emergency Room parking lot. She leaned against the steering wheel. "Harry claimed that something was missing from that barren patch, and that it has to do with the O'Malleys' car accident."

"The O'Malley family?" Dianne's eyes widened. "That name sounds familiar."

"It's been in the papers. Someone ran their van off the road last spring. The police never caught the culprit. Humph. The way they drag their feet, he'll get away with it. Harry claims that the family's ghosts are looking for retribution."

"How?"

Mrs. Robinson shrugged. "Beats me. He hightailed out of here without any explanation. Said he kept a notebook somewhere." The older woman opened her car door, and then leaned against the cushions. She toyed with her keys, and after a pause, said, "I don't mean to frighten you, but I saw Harry running through the valley the night before he left."

"Near the empty plot?"

"That's right. He'd cut his hands bad."

Dianne would have given anything for a day or two in bed. The skin around her cuts rubbed raw, as if something with pointed teeth gnawed at them. At work, she squeaked by with using the two-fingered method of changing dressings. A newly hired surgical nurse, she had not accrued any sick time. Requests for time off drew raised eyebrows from her boss and coworkers. Had she told anyone about the severity of her cuts, they would not allow her to work until the stitches healed. Given her $23,000 school loan, she dared not jeopardize her income. She soldiered through the week, crawling into bed each night, exhausted.

By the weekend, the sound was annoying her again. Friday night, Victor called and said he was coming over Saturday. "I'm sorry for yelling at you," he said in a contrite voice. "It's a dog-eat-dog out there. If you want to survive, you've got to look your best."

"I suppose you're right." Dianne's fist tightened around the receiver. Where was she going to get money to buy silks and cashmeres? Both her parents were on Social Security. Maybe if she went through her closet, she'd find something that would pass muster.

Standing before a full-length mirror, Dianne assessed her features: ruddy face and hazel eyes. Not bad. Her navy blue, V-neck tunic concealed the bulges from her hips and stomach. *These tunics hide a lot,* she thought, smiling ruefully. *If Victor had his way, he'd toss all of my clothes, and make me live on carrots and juice. He acts like his father; he even calls me the same names his father calls him. How will he treat our children? He's not going to change. I'd better ease out of this relationship, as carefully as if I were handling a timed bomb.*

Careful meant keeping the Saturday date. Dianne rooted through the back of her closet, hoping to find an outfit that Victor could tolerate. She kicked shoes aside until her foot brushed against cardboard. Bracing herself against the door, she dragged an old shoe box across the carpeted floor.

"What the hell?" Dianne gazed at its contents—newspaper accounts and scribbled notes relating to the O'Malley accident. Left behind by Harry, she assumed, in his haste to vacate the apartment.

After fortifying herself with a bag of Doritos, she sat cross-legged by the closet, munching and reading under the glare of the overhead light bulb. She had to admire Harry for his thorough research.

Last April, Joe and Susan O'Malley drove down Route 22 in a van with their two boys, Walter and Kevin, and Joe's mother, Alma. As the story went, the O'Malleys went through a hard year because of Alma's emphysema, so they decided to spend a week in Atlantic City. Their doctor, as quoted by one reporter, made arrangements to have Alma's oxygen delivered to their beach house.

The O'Malleys never made it to the shore. According to one witness, someone in a red car was hurtling down Route 22 at eighty miles an hour. The red car almost rear-ended the O'Malleys' van. Joe, the driver, swerved to avoid a collision, and instead, skidded down the ravine. The van flipped over, and the engine caught fire. All of the passengers wore seatbelts. The airbags deployed, but the precautions didn't work. A liquid oxygen tank strapped to Alma's shoulder, along with the fire, caused the car to explode.

The smoke smothered Alma within minutes. The boys and parents fared much worse. Broken bones had immobilized them, and the fire burned them alive. Crackling flames and crumbling metal drowned out the sound of their screams. The fire spread to the surrounding trees, and the O'Malleys' remains seemed to have burned to ashes.

Tom O'Malley, Joe's brother, visited the site every day to gather information about the accident. He listened stoically while the witness who'd seen the accident described the way the red car's driver sped away without looking back.

Young Tom grieved his mother, brother, sister-in-law, and two nephews. Yet, he did not flinch when he visited the burnt patch where the van had exploded. He probed the soil, allegedly finding human skulls, but no one confirmed this. His wife's thoughts on his digging were anyone's guess.

Though reporters interviewed Mary O'Malley, none of her comments reached to the newspapers.

"April 20," Dianne whispered. "We had plenty of lilacs then." A skeletal finger of terror crawled up her spine. Victor drove a bright red car like the one described in the newspapers. Didn't she hear a crash that night on the way home from the party? Didn't Victor often have near-misses on the road?

"No." She shook her head. "It's not possible. Victor may be a jerk, but he's not a killer."

But the damning evidence pointed to a hit-and-run driver. Not necessarily a killer, but someone irresponsible and angry. Like Victor. The O'Malleys wouldn't rest until he confessed, and they would continue to lure people with the ghostly floral scent. How could she get him to listen to her, let alone go to the police? Suddenly, she knew what she had to do.

Saturday, after donning a woolen ivory suit, Dianne visited the soil patch again. She took a side street that snaked from Route 22, leading to the valley. Better that than creeping down the slope, infecting her injury, and risk ruining her clothes. The outfit cost two overtime shifts at work, but with what she'd planned for Victor, she wanted to look her best. When she rolled down her window, the perfumed lilac scent called to her. Her eyes wandered to the empty patch, dull black amid the plethora of weeds and wildflowers. It did not expose any skulls, but she heard them sobbing through the earth.

Rumbling sounded from Route 22. Victor's car screeched to a halt. After a moment, it sped up again. Moments later, he came up the side street. The Lexus squealed to a stop. Victor stepped out of his car and stood facing her from the opposite side of the soil patch, his eyes narrowing. For a moment, Dianne felt as if she were gazing into a black hole.

"What are you doing down here?" Victor asked in a puzzled voice. He sniffed. "That's weird. It smells like lilacs down here."

"It does, doesn't it? That's why I felt like going for a walk." Dianne averted her eyes. Tremors edged into her voice. "No, that's not it. We have to talk."

Victor's stony, gaunt face told her how thin he was getting. He looked like a man suffering from a wasting disease. But Dianne's mind focused so vividly on the blank patch that her teeth chattered. There Victor stood, within twenty yards of that spot of yawning emptiness. Those skulls smelled their killer.

"I read about the O'Malleys," she said in a measured, quiet voice. "Their van smashed over the guard rail and exploded right here on April 20, the night of my school party. The witness described a car like yours, Victor.

The timing and location are the same. More important, I'm a witness, too. I heard the crash and explosion."

Dianne watched Victor intently for hardened eyes, reddening face, or clenched fists. Signs that he was about to lose his temper. "We should have stopped," she continued, her voice rising and falling. "But we didn't." It would sound lame to apologize to O'Malley's brother.

"You can't let this go, Victor. Do the right thing. Tell the police what happened. I'll go with you for support."

Silence followed a moment, and then Victor burst into gales of laughter. "That's great," he said, wiping tears from his eyes. Then his voice faltered, and his blue eyes widened. "Dianne, the beer caused you to hallucinate. That's when we agreed that you should stop drinking."

"What's this 'we' business?" Dianne looked him in the eye without flinching. "I made my own decision about quitting booze." Stepping back, she watched as Victor came within fighting distance of the skulls. Victor, gaunt and hard, overwhelmed with anger; the skulls patient, with the draw of the earth behind them, and scenting their killer like radar.

Dianne saw it as plainly as if she'd seen two large gangs prepare for war—the ground shifting, the blackened heads of the skulls poking through like emissaries. Would the bodies rise from the ground like a scene in *Night of the Living Dead?*

"Now Dianne," Victor said, his voice reeking with false cheer, and then his voice slurred. He missed his words, and his lips trembled. His face loosened around the bones of his cheek. "You've got an overactive imagination," he pressed on in his pompous voice. "It's time that…that—"

He broke off abruptly and looked about him. His face turned crimson, and a vein throbbed on the side of his neck. "What's that?" he cried in a voice charged with terror. "Those horrible things! Why are they making that noise?"

He pointed to the moving patch. Before Dianne could answer, he scrambled from the street. The skulls came up through the soil, their ghastly grins turned toward Victor. He paused before the barren patch, eyes bulging.

After what could have been moments or hours, he turned his gaze toward Dianne. Perhaps he thought he'd escape punishment if someone took his place. Maybe Dianne didn't want to know what motivated his actions. The gleam in his eyes hinted he was trying to score a power play.

"Dianne," he called in a sweet voice. "Come here."

His voice was the cry of a desperate man. Part of Dianne longed to run. Another part longed to go to him, hug him, and assure him that they could work this out. Instead, she moved nearer to the edge and screamed.

Her throat tightened, allowing only faint croaks, drowned by the gravelly cries of the skulls.

Victor whirled around, throwing up his arms. His mouth formed an open O of terror. It didn't surprise Dianne when the skulls bobbed through the patch, followed by shoulders and arms, cold cobwebs of soot-covered bones and tendons.

At the edge of the patch, Victor wobbled, and then lurched away, but not quickly enough. Skeletal hands caught him by the ankles. Victor screamed, arms flailing, trying to yank his feet loose. He couldn't. His eyes, big as saucers, betrayed utter terror.

Dianne ducked behind a tree, longing to help, afraid to try. Three more skeletons bobbed up through the patch. The five figures huddled around Victor, blocking any would-be attempts to free him. Dianne's gaze settled on a fallen tree limb, something that might work as a weapon. She started to reach for the limb, then one of the figures turned toward her. Its mouth twisted to work a jaw long shut.

"Do not interfere if you know what's good for you."

The message came through loud and clear. She bolted for her car, rolled up her window, and locked all the doors. The O'Malleys blocked her exit, not that she was in any condition to drive. They were busy thrashing Victor, exacting their own brand of punishment. Any passerby tempted to intervene would think twice when they got a look at his assailants.

Dianne shuddered behind the wheel, squeezing her eyes shut, not caring to watch. Horrible waves of dizziness swam through her body. Despite the closed windows, a wet, putrefied stench lingered in her nostrils moments before the grayness engulfed her.

When Dianne came to, Victor and the O'Malleys were gone.

The next evening after work, Dianne found a well-stuffed envelope in her mailbox from Victor Kuntz, Senior. Victor's dad. With shaky fingers, she tore open the envelope in her kitchen. A slip fell out and fluttered to the floor. With trembling fingers, she snatched it up. It was a check for $10,000, made out to her. Lips quivering, she retrieved the letter.

> *Dear Dianne,*
> *Last night, Victor informed me he caused the O'Malley accident, and that you saw what happened. This must have been terrible for you. Please accept this check as compensation for your suffering.*

> *In return, I ask that you don't discuss Victor or the accident with anyone. His car caught fire with him in it last night. He didn't survive. Making this public now will only cause grief for my family.*
> *Yours truly,*
> *Victor Kuntz, Sr.*

"Oh, my God!" Dianne burst into tears. Much as she had come to dislike Victor, she never wanted anything to happen to him. Underneath it all, she feared that the O'Malleys would come after her next. She doubted it—she was only a passenger, and Victor had ignored her pleas to stop. So she was ninety percent sure that the O'Malleys would leave her be, but ninety percent wasn't good enough. She would always remember to look over her shoulder. If not, her hand gash and the scar that would follow served as forcible reminders.

The empty soil patch fared much better. Before Dianne moved the following summer, it filled with rambling wildflowers, strong, well-fed, and teeming with life.

One Last Favor

The Uprising: Tara Gray's auburn curls glistened in the sunlight as she stepped over the dead bodies. Each movement was a high-wire act, threatening a nasty spill over someone's arm or leg. Skeletal corpses littered the five blocks between her home and work. Despite the food she and her coworkers donated to the poor, the ranks of people dead from malnutrition swelled. Many had lain on the sidewalks for days, their wasted bodies baking in the intense summer heat. Green insects buzzed around their bony faces. The air reeked of fly-blown meat.

I can't look at this, Tara thought, gagging on the odor. *Maybe I can focus on the sidewalk or the buildings. Not that the architecture's offering anything better.*

Indeed, they didn't, for the government had condemned most of the buildings years ago. The structures looked as if someone battered them with a wrecking ball. Fallen bricks jutted from the sides of the buildings, ready to topple on an unsuspecting passerby. The cracked, uneven slabs of maroon-splattered concrete sidewalk threatened a backbreaking fall to the unwary. *This town is death waiting to happen.*

"Tara!"

Tara paused. The plaintive voice came from her right, where a tanned man clad in black cutoff trousers lay sprawled on the concrete steps of a dilapidated building. He wore a silver chain with the word "Joy" inscribed on the pendant. Up until now, he had been a primary recipient of her lunchtime shares. She'd gotten him to laugh a couple of times.

At the sight of his face, Tara gasped. Something—or someone—had ripped open the left side of his cheek. Bone fragments jutted through the bloody gash. The man held a dirty rag over his wound.

"Kraven!" she croaked, rushing to his side. She knelt beside him, cradling his injured head in her arms. "Who did this to you?"

"Last night, I went begging for food. At one of the homes, the owner sent his Dobermans after me. I think they busted my ribs." Kraven coughed and spit fresh blood on the pavement.

"Oh, my God!" Tara cried. "Can you stand? If you lean on my shoulder, I'll walk you to the hospital."

"No, Tara."

"Then I'll ask someone to come here and get you with a stretcher."

"I'm not going to any hospital," Kraven said flatly.

"Kraven, your injuries are serious." *So is your malnutrition,* she added silently as she gazed at his protruding ribs. "You're coming with me if I have to carry you myself."

"And listen to Desatnick's condescending voice?" Kraven asked sharply. "I'm not dealing with that pompous ass. Why don't you take your charity somewhere else?"

Tara began to weep. "Kraven, I thought we were buddies. I can't leave you here to die."

Kraven' voice softened. "Tara, I won't last long enough to get to your hospital anyway. At least I'm going out with my head held high."

"I wish you'd come to me yesterday. I could've smuggled food from the kitchen. Would it have wounded your pride that much to ask for help?"

Kraven sighed. "Tara, you've done too much for me. You're a caring person and a beautiful woman. In another place and another time…" His voice trailed off as he stared into space.

His brown eyes blazed into embers of hate. "Those government bastards are going to pay!"

"Pay for what? How?" Tara gazed at him, her eyes widening.

"You'll see." A crooked grin surfaced on his battered face.

Moments later, his head slumped against her arms. His mouth froze in a smile while his lifeless eyes stared at the sky.

As Tara held Kraven's head and whispered a prayer, tears streamed down her freckled face. So many people had dropped dead from starvation that the government workers couldn't bury them fast enough. The plethora of corpses on the street had made driving impossible. Welcome to government bureaucracy.

People wasted natural resources without any thought for tomorrow. That was a capital mistake. Now, here in Pennsylvania in the year 2060, tomorrow had come. Congress had done away with public welfare programs in 2020. Now they had begun rationing food, not that destitute people could afford food tickets. The pretzel stands and food trucks of the 1900's had ceased operations long ago. In Philadelphia and its suburbs, only Hartland Clinic offered food to the poor.

Tara gazed at the battered, wasted corpses, contemplated *Gone with the Wind,* her favorite read from English Literature in college, and said to herself, "I can't deal with this now. I'll think about it tomorrow when I'm off duty. Tomorrow's another day. Maybe I can find another way to help these people."

But the privations had long ago precluded an easy fix. People lined up for a mile to get soup from Hartland's kitchen, a charity orchestrated by Dr. Atkins' mother. Most hadn't eaten for days. Tara tried to help these people—really, she did—but their frail bodies couldn't hold on any longer. If evidence of this was needed, one only had to look at the protruding ribs, sunken eyes and gaunt cheeks.

Hartland Clinic, a dome-shaped building, loomed ahead. At the emergency room intake desk, Tara clocked in and began screening patients who had come to see Drs. Desatnick and Atkins. The ones she approved went to individual cubicles, where robotic nurses examined them.

Dr. Myles Desatnick, who stood by the desk typing something on his handheld computer, glanced up at Tara. "You're late," he observed with a smile that didn't touch his cold, gray eyes.

"I'm sorry," Tara mumbled, eyes on her keyboard.

"Being sorry isn't enough," Desatnick said harshly. "This is the second time this week."

Domineering bastard. Just like my father. Tara looked up at Desatnick. "Well, fiddle-dee-dee! What's five minutes when someone is badly hurt? A man outside was mauled by dogs, Dad—I mean, Doctor. I was trying to talk him into coming here for treatment."

"Obviously, he didn't listen to you." Desatnick's toneless voice told Tara he personally didn't give a damn.

"He listened, but his injuries were too severe. He was almost dead when I found him."

Before Desatnick could pursue the subject any further, Chris Atkins entered. "Damn, it's hot out there," he said, wiping the sweat from his pale face. "Tara, would you mind taking water out to the people in line?"

"No problem." Tara smiled at Chris, grateful for an opportunity to get away from Myles Desatnick. She filled two gallon jugs with water and raced outside.

At the sight of water, wasted men, women, and children swarmed around her like flies. The walking skeletons thrust out cupped hands and battered tin cups in front of her.

135

"Please hurry," an elderly woman begged.

The speaker leaned on a cane and lurched with shuffling steps. Her cracked lips and shriveled pale skin spoke of dehydration. "I'm moving as fast as I can," Tara said, choking back a sob.

About an hour later, loud singing echoed down the street. No, not singing. Chanting.

HIC ENHIC EN SPIRITUM
SED NON INCORPORE
EVOKARE LEMURES DE MORTUIS
DECRETUM ESPUGNARE
DE ANGELUS BAALBERITH
EN INFERNO INREMEABLIS

Although Tara knew some Latin, the chant didn't sound like any of the rote prayers her mother had taught her. According to her studies, "Baalberith" was a demon. A bald man wearing a black velour robe sprinkled water on the dead, chanting as he went. Four others surrounded him, carrying lit candles.

The woman who'd pleaded for Tara to hurry turned away from her. "Justice at last!" she cried.

"Is that man praying for your dead?" Tara asked.

The woman looked back at her with hard eyes. "No, he's making sure that the evil the government did comes home to roost!" With that, she limped away. Her companions followed, along with the remaining crowd.

"Wait," Tara called after them. "There's plenty more water. Please stay."

The crowd walked away without answering her.

Tara dropped her jugs and raced back to the emergency room. "Dr. Desatnick, we've got trouble outside," she said as she burst through the doors.

Desatnick shrugged. "So what else is new?"

"What's going on, Tara?" Chris asked kindly.

"Some man wearing a black robe is chanting in Latin. Everyone left the grounds and followed him. They're talking about justice and getting even. I think this guy's stirring up a riot."

"Let him," Desatnick said. "We've got security officers and guns. It only takes a few shots to maintain peace and quiet."

Tara shook her head. "Not this time. That priest, or whatever he is, seems to have a hold over them."

136

"We'd better alert Security," Chris said.

"Don't buy into her hysteria," Desatnick said, with a dismissive wave of his hand. He turned toward Tara. "So you heard an old man rant and rave. That doesn't mean anything. Charity time's over. Get back to your desk and do some real work."

Tara's face reddened. She dragged a set of trembling fingers through her curls. "Dad, there's no reason to—"

"Damn it, Tara, I'm not your father!"

"Fiddle-dee-dee, Pops," Chris said, laughing. "Way to go, Tara."

"Don't encourage her." Desatnick cast a withering glance toward Chris, and then turned back to Tara. "I don't understand this. Why do you—"

Crash! Bang!

A mob of people crowded the entrance and thumped the glass doors. Wasted figures, looking many days dead. The glass shattered, raining on the linoleum floor. Marching in, the figures smashed into the robot nurses. A foul stench blew in with them, reminding Tara of fish that had gone bad. Where were the security officers who patrolled the entrances? Gone, no doubt, killed or run off by these walking corpses.

Up close, their faces looked like something from a nightmare. Pus leaked out of one man's eye socket. Insects swarmed their bodies. Maggots covered their gray, bloated faces. Cold cobwebs of bone peeped through the tears in the skin and tattered clothes. Tara stood, watching, her feet frozen to the floor. Grabbing her by the shoulder, Chris pulled her underneath the desk. She watched the massacre unfold through a corner porthole in the desk panel.

A mob of figures headed for the patient cubicles. In the next instant, the sound of bloodcurdling screams and tearing flesh assaulted her ears. Tara recognized the sound, having assisted with surgeries.

Desatnick pulled out his gun and fired. His bullet flashed through an elderly man's chest. Despite the bullet size, he did not bleed.

No blood? Tara gasped at the sound, huddled against Chris's shoulder. *Doesn't he have any?*

The man dug his finger into the hole and withdrew the bullet, loosening green pus. "Shit," he muttered in a gravelly voice.

He leaped at Desatnick. Before Desatnick could fire again, the figure snatched his gun and tossed it aside. Its bony hands wrapped around his throat and squeezed. Tara and Chris hugged each other, screaming. *They're dead, dammit,* she kept thinking. *What are they doing here?*

Maybe they picked up some virus that turned them into zombies. Just like in the *Night of the Living Dead* documentary she'd watched in her Literature class. They reeked like carrion. They were dead, after all. Dead people weren't supposed to come back to life. *Apparently, someone forgot to tell them that.*

The crunching of bones and smacking of lips were punctuated by ear-splitting shrieks. Something wet rolled into Tara's knees. A glance at the floor gave her the source. Geysers of blood from Desatnick's wounds sprayed the floor and flowed under the desk.

If Scarlett was here, she'd fight. Tara nudged the doctor's shoulder. "Chris," she whispered through panting lips, "if we stay here, we're good as dead."

Chris nodded with agreement; his shoulders trembling, green eyes wide and fearful. "You've got that right. But we need weapons. There's a fire extinguisher on the left wall, by the cubicles."

Tara pressed her face against the desk panel, scanning the wall for a potential weapon. There it was, an extinguisher hanging by the first cubicle. "I see it," she whispered. "Lucky for us, Desatnick insisted on keeping these things in every room. We've got oxygen tanks in the storeroom, too. Think we can grab some protection and run while these zombies are busy with Desatnick and his patients?"

"I think we can if we go out the back, through the kitchen. That's where I'm heading."

Tara eased from under the desk, followed by Chris. She snatched the extinguisher while Chris made a beeline for the storeroom. She sprinted to the hall, hugging the extinguisher under her arms, Chris ahead of her.

Minutes later, strong, skeletal hands clutched her by the shoulders. Tara wrenched free, ripping the collar from her uniform. She walloped her assailant on the head. His skull cracked open, spilling fluid resembling Cream of Wheat.

Tara spurted ahead, hoping to catch up with Chris, but he was gone. Clattering footfalls sounded behind her as three of the creatures chased her down the hall. Whirling around, she aimed the nozzle at her assailants. Gray smoke swirled, providing an effective screen between Tara and her attackers.

She ducked inside a soiled utility room. The door had a combination lock, but such devices wouldn't stop the walking dead. Where could she hide? If there were live humans around, these monsters would smell them.

The laundry chute. No doubt their brains had rotted, and they'd never think to search the laundry room. Tara keyed in the combination and crawled inside the chute. Hands gripping the door rim, she dangled her feet.

The drop had to be twenty feet. Pounding at the utility room door. Those creatures smelled her. Any second, they'd break in and see her fingers on the rim of the chute door.

She let go, screaming all the way down. She landed on a mountain of dirty linen.

Landing on that soft pile spared her from broken bones. She scurried away from the chute and nestled between bags of soiled clothes. Surely the dirty linen smell would camouflage her scent. She'd have to remain intact if she wanted to escape.

Later, she would search for Chris Atkins and see if she could team up with him. He had become a good work buddy, someone she could trust with her life. For now, her best chance for survival lay in sitting tight and waiting until the beasts had either satisfied their hunger or given up to hunt somewhere else.

A tall, wasted man dropped from the chute. She'd underestimated them. Hadn't she told herself that combinations wouldn't stop the dead? This one landed in the same laundry pile she had. Something had eaten away half of his gray-complexioned face. He slithered toward her, his hands outstretched.

"Go away!" Tara screamed. *What was this creep doing here? A dirty linen room was the last place to be hunting prey.*

Her visitor stared at her through glassy, clouded over eyes. His crooked grin revealed needle-sharp teeth. "I'm the one who gives orders, woman," he cackled in a guttural voice.

A zombie who can talk, she thought crazily. But there was no mistaking the menace he exuded. His silver necklace looked familiar. Kraven Loyola, her buddy, had worn that chain. This creature had the same stringy black hair that he did. The man who'd gotten first dibs at her donations was threatening her life.

I don't deserve this, she thought, her eyes flashing with indignation. Her freckled face turned beet red. *I did my best to help these people.* "How dare you?" she shouted. "What have I done to deserve this? How often did I forego lunch so you could eat? How often did I come by with water so you wouldn't go thirsty? Is taking my life your way of thanking me?"

Much good that did. Zombies didn't understand gratitude or fairness, and she had no way to destroy this one. Tara cringed against the linens, waiting for the inevitable agony.

Instead, Kraven folded his stick-like limbs across his chest and bowed. "Tara, you're right," he said evenly.

She found that hard to believe. Perhaps he was trying to disarm her before moving in for the kill. "Does this mean you'll let me go?" she asked in a small voice.

Kraven sat next to her on the laundry pile. The odor of his infected wounds made her gag. She tried to recoil, but he stopped her. His hands, emaciated from lack of food, cradled her cheeks.

"Don't hurt me," she pleaded, tears rolling down her face.

"I'm not going to hurt you." Kraven stroked her cheeks and ran his fingers through her thick curls. "Your hair is soft. You always were a beautiful woman. You still are."

How dare that monster touch me? Watch your mouth, Tara. His sick attraction to you might improve your chances of getting out alive. "I tried to help you, Kraven, because I saw a kind, sensitive man under your rough exterior. I'm not your enemy."

"I know that. And I appreciate what you did for me. Now it's my turn to help you."

"Will you close your eyes while I escape?" Tara folded her hands, her eyes meeting his gaze. "You know, pretend to your companions you didn't see me?"

"I won't lie to my people, but I can persuade them to spare your life."

"Thank you." Tara breathed a sigh of relief.

"Before I speak with my friends," Kraven continued, "I want one last favor from you. We need a leader to represent us."

"A leader?" Tara echoed feebly. "Dead people can't...they aren't supposed to come back to life. I can't begin to understand your people, let alone lead them. Why...how?"

"We're revenants, people who come back from the dead to complete unfinished business with the living," Kraven told her. "The leaders of this country have starved and killed us. They only care about people who have jobs. A friend who practices black magic contacted Baalberith, a dark angel. Baalberith provided him a spell with which to raise the dead. If we feed on our oppressors, Baalberith will enable us to live forever. The craving demands human meat, so we take it out on those who hurt us. Sometimes the innocent die along with the guilty."

You beast. Tara opened her mouth to shout, but her inner voice stayed her tongue. *Watch yourself, Tara, he's holding the cards.* "So you're getting even with the people who put you out of work and on the street," she said, humoring him. "I don't agree with your methods, but I can relate to your feelings of oppression."

"The hell you say!" Kraven frowned. "You look well-nourished to me."

"The hell I don't say." Tara's voice tightened as she contemplated her childhood. "I experienced emotional starvation when I lived at home with my father."

She drew in a deep breath. "My father was an Army general. At home, he treated me and my mother like he was still on the battlefield. My mother suffered an emotional breakdown and died of a drug overdose. He used to call her awful names. I tried to hug him once, and he stiffened. He never told me he loved me."

Kraven scratched his bony chin. "I'm sorry to hear about your mother," he said, his voice softening. "I sensed something was bothering you, but I couldn't put my finger on it."

"I haven't spoken with my dad once in the last five years. Dr. Desatnick acts like him. He's even stout and has salt and pepper hair like my father."

"I believe it. I've seen you around Desatnick. When he comes by, your eyes jump like a frightened rabbit. Don't worry. My good buddies eliminated him."

"That's the point I'm trying to make. Killing people isn't right, especially if they work at Hartland. All of us, including Desatnick, tried to help you."

Kraven shrugged. "As I explained, sometimes the innocent die."

"Not necessarily. I hated my father for the way he treated me, but I turned over my anger when I became a nurse. Working with sick people was therapeutic. If you could use your powers to help the poor who are still alive, you'd feel better, too."

Kraven hooted with laughter. "Oh, we're helping them plenty by killing and turning them. Our society is getting stronger, but we need someone to act as our ambassador. That's where your favor comes in. I want an offspring who will do the job."

"Offspring?" None of this made sense. "I don't have any children. How would I provide you with this offspring?"

Kraven offered her a malevolent grin while loosening the ties on his pants. "Let me put it to you this way. Our reproductive organs remain functional for several weeks after we rise."

With that, he pushed Tara flat on the linens and ripped open her powder blue uniform. His cadaverous body loomed over hers. Screams came and died in her throat. Then the grayness washed over her.

Chris sprinted to the kitchen, throwing glances over his shoulders. When last he saw Tara, she was clobbering a zombie with a tank, and then disappeared. In the kitchen, he squatted underneath the oven, hoping that the smell of cooked meat and vegetables would override his scent. After what felt like hours, the screaming and plodding footsteps faded. He cracked the door leading to the hall. Silence. What the hell happened to Tara?

The garage. He had to make it to the hospital garage. His car was parked there, and he planned to drive to his parents' home as soon as it became safe. Not safe. Doable. Safety had become a pipe dream. The walking dead and sprawled bodies had turned the streets into a serpentine steering course, especially the one where his parents lived. Someone had bashed in the windows of all the homes. At his parents' three-story townhouse, something had trampled on the rose garden in front. The door was ajar. The lights were out. No surprise there.

Muddy footprints besmirched their front sidewalk. They led inside, where the smell of death greeted him. The chairs lay askew and the glass coffee tables shattered. He followed the tracks into the hallway.

"Mom? Dad?" he called.

No answer.

Heart pounding, Chris followed the trail and almost stumbled over his father's briefcase. His father, a lawyer, had on a three-piece suit, now shredded to tatters. He lay in a large pool of drying blood.

"Oh, Dad, I'm so sorry," he whispered.

His father's vacant eyes stared at him, mouth frozen in a widened circle of horror.

Something scraped upstairs, faint, but there. Chris went to the study and retrieved his father's gun from the safe. After making sure it was loaded, he followed the tracks to the stairs.

"Mom?" he called, forcing one foot before the other.

From one of the bedrooms came a cold, gravelly giggle that made Chris's skin break into goose bumps. The fetid stench became sickeningly strong.

He kept moving, praying that his mother was all right. He thought about Tara, wondering if she'd escaped. At the landing, he paused, gazing at the wall, one hand in his pocket, the other on his gun.

That scraping again.

Chris turned left, and there laid his mother who had opened the soup kitchen at the hospital. Her legs were splayed the way his father's were. Something had bent her head at an unnatural angle.

He walked toward her.

Blood splattered the walls in irregular shapes. Bites and gashes peppered her face, arms, and legs. Their teeth and brute strength had torn away her fingers. Her wedding rings lay in the blood flowing from her stumps. Suddenly he saw his mother, really saw her, and Chris Atkins began to scream. His shrieks echoed through the house where now only death walked.

Click! Chris jumped. A bedroom door was opening.

He looked up and started, another scream building in his throat. Here was a creature from the hospital, its face and hands smeared with blood and gristle. Its teeth pulled back in a death's head grin. Brandishing a hammer, it lunged at Chris.

Chris pulled back, and the creature overbalanced and stumbled. He kicked its feet out from underneath it. The thing fell on its back. Chris shot it in the forehead.

"Hungry," the thing whispered. Its face contorted and writhed. Its arms reached. "Hungry, hungry, hungry…"

Another blast. The creature lay still.

After its movement had ceased, Chris shuffled down the stairs, head lowered. None of the phones worked, but he had his cell phone. He was calling the police. He got through on the first dial, and they put him on hold. The circuits were overloaded with emergency calls.

Tara woke up alone in her own bedroom. Beads of sweat trickled down her face when she sat up. What a nightmare!

She clicked on a lamp. No light. No humming sounds came from her refrigerator. The power blackout, the odor of spoiled meat, and the stickiness between her legs convinced her that this was real. Kraven must've brought her here. No doubt a search through her purse would've given him her address and access to her key. Then again, little things like barcodes and combination locks wouldn't deter the walking dead.

Grabbing a flashlight, Tara rushed to the bathroom. She huddled underneath the shower for an hour, washing away the stink of death, and cleaning the cuts she'd sustained during her chase. Most of all, she needed to purge the feeling of dirtiness. She might as well face it; the pig raped her.

As the steamy water danced on her flesh, Tara let out a sigh. She'd gotten off lucky, and not just because she survived the massacre. Kraven never asked her about birth control, nor did he remove the hormone patch she wore behind her left ear. No ambassador was forthcoming to represent these monsters.

Hands groping through the living room, she felt for her laptop. Sharp pain followed as she stubbed her toe against a chair, and there was her laptop on the coffee table. It had a seven-hour life on its battery. The Net was still up, to her surprise, with a plethora of news clips about the revenant invasion. The headline "Walking Dead Butcher Doctor's Parents" caught her eye.

"Dr. Christopher Atkins escaped the massacre at Hartland Clinic only to find a killing field at his parents' home," the article said. With numb fingers, Tara pulled up gruesome images of the bodies as she read. When she saw his mother's body, her mutilated hands, she gasped.

"Oh, my God," she whispered, burying her face in her hands. "That man looked out for me. I've got to let him know I'm okay."

Better yet, the first chance she got, she'd change her locks. Then she'd search for Chris. If he or anyone else survived the slaughter, she would form a battle plan to stop these predators. Maybe one day, she'd put this nightmare behind her.

When Tara missed her period a couple of weeks later, she knew that would be impossible. By then the revenant army had invaded other cities.

Ten years later: No more bodies littered the squeaky clean streets when Tara walked the five blocks to Hartland Clinic. These days she worked out at a gym and learned how to shoot a gun. Every so often, a soldier patrolled the street. People weren't dying from malnutrition any more. The growing society of the dead had destroyed many towns during the last four years, putting paid to the problem of overpopulation. The resulting destruction, including torn power lines, along with the recent laws banning the sale of burning wax candles, forced survivors to pony up the money for generators.

High-rise condominiums replaced the dilapidated tenements. A playground with a tennis court and a swimming pool covered an entire block. Sometimes one or two officers sat at a picnic table, watching the grounds. Not today.

A fetid odor drifted from the trash bin by the pool. Slowly, a dead person crept out of the bin and shuffled toward Tara. Lips quivering, she retrieved her gun and assumed a fighter's stance. She aimed and fired. The creature's head exploded in a wash of green pus and brains. It dropped to the pavement. Later, officers would come by and clean up the mess. According to the police, only headshots felled these things. She practiced with her gun until she got it right, and then some.

Hartland Clinic reopened a year after the dead assaulted Philadelphia. Chris and she emailed each other regularly, but it took a lot of begging from him before she agreed to work there again. Otherwise, positions opened and remained unfilled. Carolyn Barrett, an internist, had taken over Desatnick's position.

After years of psychotherapy, Tara talked about the rape with Chris and other trusted friends. Last year, she began meeting Chris for workouts at the gym, and later, dinner, but told her coworkers she was taking a class. Despite battles with the walking dead, the rumor mill ran, necessitating discretion. On nights without any interference from the revenants, Chris and Tara finished up the evening at his or her apartment. Chris was good for her, and oh, so gentle. Even so, she'd never forget the horror of watching the monsters eat Desatnick alive, or the revulsion of forced sex on a pile of dirty linen. Worst was her daughter's kidnapping.

Scenes from the past flashed through Tara's mind each day she entered the dome-shaped concrete hospital. One minute, three of the predators chased her down the hall. Next minute she was in Dr. Ashley's office, listening to him say, "Tara, you're six weeks pregnant."

Prosaic methods of birth control hadn't worked with a dead rapist.

On her way to the patient floors, Tara stopped by the operating suite to pick up soiled instruments. She started to go in, but the glass door was locked. She knocked. Inside, a blonde husky woman in a lab jacket carried a tray of instruments. It was Dr. Barrett. The door opened. Dr. Barrett handed Tara the tray and started some idle chit-chat. How are you, how's the weather, blah, blah, blah. Tara smiled and excused herself. She didn't feel like chitchatting because she'd nearly bought it in that operating room. Images played through her mind – the failed abortion, the near-fatal arrhythmia on her heart monitor, the week in the Intensive Care Unit, not knowing whether she'd live or die. She broke out into a sweat.

To Tara's relief, the child looked like an ordinary infant girl. Stunning, too, for her baby had red curly hair and blue eyes. She remembered holding the baby and thinking about her grandmother's saying about an ill wind that blows no good. Hours later, shouts and the thudding of sneakers impinged on her sleep. Someone had kidnapped one of the babies from the nursery.

Her baby girl.

She spent the next six years on a fruitless search for her child. She'd walk through fire to hold her daughter again.

I can't think about this now, she told herself. *Tomorrow's another day. If the child's meant to be found, I'll find her.* She marched to the second floor and proceeded to sterilize the instruments that Dr. Barrett had given her.

A stocky woman with shoulder-length blonde hair sat before a computer terminal, talking on the phone. Kelly, the nurse manager. Her green eyes flitted from chair to chair, and she kept tugging at her hair with shaky hand.

"Good morning, Kelly," Tara said after her boss had hung up. "Are you all right?"

"I'm working on it," Kelly said with a smile that didn't touch her fearful eyes and trembling hands. "Dr. Atkins is swamped in the emergency room. I told him I'd send you there to help. Do you mind?"

"Not at all." Tara smiled. She'd take the emergency room with a trusted friend and lover over the operating suite. Chris lived through some of the same horrors she did. Judging from the way he groaned in his sleep sometimes, he suffered similar nightmares, too. "I'll go after I put these in the autoclave."

"Watch yourself. Some weird kid came around here this morning, looking for you." Kelly pulled a revolver from her drawer.

Seeing that, Tara stroked her fanny pack, which held her own pistol. The feel of hard metal took the edge off her shivering. "The dead seem active this morning," she nodded with agreement. "I picked off a zombie on the way here."

"Doesn't surprise me." Kelly's features blanched slightly. "You should hire a security guard to walk you to work."

"Kelly, it's either the security guard or maintenance fees for my generator. I can't afford both. Since I'm good at headshots, I'm voting for electricity." She smiled, averting her eyes, not caring to add that Chris sometimes drove her to work.

This morning she had patients to assess, real live people, and IVs to start. Chris gave his orders in a soft voice. When no one was looking, he whispered jokes about their next "class," and Tara giggled. He was one of the few people who could coax a laugh out of her. No matter the danger, patient care came first. Hartland Clinic was just another hospital. Before Tara knew it, her shift was over.

Just as she prepared to leave, a small hand tugged at her blue uniform. A frail little girl with scarlet-red ringlets gazed up at her. She wore a pearl gray satin dress with puffed sleeves and she was carrying a burlap sack. Tara regarded the child's ghastly complexion and gaunt appearance with widened eyes.

"Are you lost?" she asked, trying hard for a smile. "What's your name?"

"Lilith," the little girl replied. "You have red hair like me."

"That's right, I do. Where are your mom and dad?"

"My dad brought me here. I never met my mom, but he said I could have her for my birthday. He said she works here, but she's never here when

I come. I've been coming here every week so I can meet her. Dad said her name's Tara Gray."

"Oh, Lord!" Tara gasped, and then tried to cover it up by adding, "I see."

But the child was on to her. "Are you afraid of me?"

"Of course not." Tara manufactured another smile, but it felt frozen. "It's just that…well, you look like you're feeling sick. My name's Tara. What's your daddy's name?"

"I'm not allowed to tell. He said you'd know."

This kid looks bad. Smells funny, too. Maybe her father realized she was sick, and dumped her here. Tara darted a glance toward the desk where Chris sat, then turned back to the child. "Lilith, it's not safe for you go anywhere alone. May we contact your father?"

Lilith shook her head.

Tara shot another questioning look toward Chris.

He shrugged. "She shows up on different floors every week, looking for a mother. Unless it's a dire emergency, we can't treat her without her father's consent."

Tara sighed. "Did anyone *think* to call the police?"

Chris nodded. "More than once. By the time the officers got here, the kid had taken off."

Tara shifted her gaze toward the little girl again. "How old are you?"

"I turned ten last month. Can I come to your house?"

That would put her birthday at May. If my kid were here, she'd celebrate a May birthday. Yet, this felt wrong, deadly wrong. Kelly had warned her about strange characters, and she knew nothing about the child. But the kid was traveling alone and too young to own a handgun. Tara walked over to Chris, giving him another pleading look.

Chris heaved a sigh. On the job, he looked ancient and gaunt, his scrub top hanging loose as a necklace. "If you can keep her hanging around here long enough, I'll contact Social Services and get clearance to assess the child tonight or tomorrow. I've been through hell ever since I lost my mom and dad, so I'm having a hard time walking away from this, too. All the same…" He spoke in a dim voice, placing his hands over Tara's. "We have to cover ourselves. Don't bring her to your house, honey."

Since when does he call me honey at work? He looks terrified. Tara arched her brows. "Why not?"

"That kid gives everyone the creeps. She doesn't make eye contact or anything."

"Maybe because she's afraid. I don't feel comfortable with this either, but I can't leave any kid alone, not after what happened to my own child. Besides, you'll know where to find her when you get clearance from Social Services. "

"That's true." Chris's voice softened. "Be careful, Tara. If things get ugly, call me. Better yet, call the police."

"I'll do that."

Chris turned toward his readout screen. "I'll call you later tonight," he said, looking back up at her. "Be ready to answer by the third ring. If you don't, I plan to show up with the police."

"I appreciate you looking out for me." Tara smiled and patted his hand, then turned to the child. "Lilith, it's dangerous for you to travel alone. I'm bringing you to my house until we make other arrangements. We'll walk. I only live five blocks from the hospital, on Raven Hill Road."

"Okay." Arm curled around Tara's, Lilith followed her out the exit.

"We'll be coming up on a park where people swim and play tennis," Tara said, pointing ahead. "Do you play any sports?"

"No, Dad said our kind wouldn't be welcome."

"Anyone can go to the park. Look…" Tara pointed toward the pool. "Some people your age are taking swimming lessons."

As they passed, three girls in the pool looked their way. Tara recognized one of them as Gloria, Dr. Barrett's daughter. A security officer accompanied each child. All of the girls burst into snickers, chanting: "Here comes Scarecrow! Here comes Scarecrow!"

A cold glint crossed Lilith's blue eyes. She clenched her bony fists. "I hate this park. Those girls always call me names."

"Ignore them," Tara said, stroking her hair. "If they see you getting upset, they'll tease you more."

"Hey, lady!" the instructor called from the pool. "Watch yourself. She's a zombie."

Tara bit her lips, drawing blood. She hugged her arms, trying to ward off a chill she felt despite the summer heat.

Lilith gave no sign of noticing. "They'll be sorry. Dad knows they call me names. He said he'd teach those creeps a lesson."

Tara shuddered. *If her dad's an abuser, God help those kids.*

Lilith stared at the high-rise apartments on Tara's street, where marble patios lined the front of the white brick buildings. "These are beautiful houses," she cried.

"They're condominiums," Tara told her. "The fancy ones have the marble patios. I couldn't afford marble, but I've got a generator and comfortable furniture. I live at the end apartment on the tenth floor."

"White walls," Lilith murmured when they entered Tara's two-bedroom apartment. "Dad told me you love white."

"I do." Tara pointed to a bright red leather chair. "Have a seat. Can I get you something to eat?"

Lilith shook her head. "Dad says the food you eat is bad for us."

"What does your father feed you?"

"I'm not allowed to tell."

Whatever. Tara sighed, filling a glass carafe for coffee. She shuddered to think of when Lilith had last gotten a decent meal. No doubt, she eked out her survival by scavenging food from trash bins. "Are you allowed to tell me what your dad looks like?"

Lilith scratched her head thoughtfully. "I guess so because he never said I couldn't. Daddy looks like a stick man. He wears a silver chain. Our neighbors look like walking sticks, too. Everyone smells."

We need a human to act as our ambassador. The chills crept up Tara's back and settled at the crest of her neck. She closed the spigot and looked at Lilith. "Is your dad Kraven Loyola?"

Lilith nodded, smiling. "He said you were my mom."

"If Kraven's your father, that'd be right. Someone took you out of the nursery when you were born." Tara swallowed hard. A tear cruised down her cheek. She longed to throw her arms around Lilith, but the situation felt an ocean from right. If Lilith grew up with Kraven, he probably fed her human meat, and along the way, she caught a blood-borne disease. Worse, he may have "turned" her. So far, though, she'd done such a good job convincing herself that Lilith was human that she had no choice but to humor the child until Chris came through with his social worker. "I'm glad I found you."

Lilith grinned, revealing pointed teeth. A whole mouthful of them, with maroon stains. "Dad gives me extra special presents. Do you know what I asked for?"

"A doll?"

"No, you. Can I live here?"

Tara's teeth chattered. The coffee pot dropped, spraying water on the kitchen floor. She blotted it with a towel, concentrating on her chore, and trying hard not to notice those teeth. Lilith just sat there, watching her. Tara continued wiping. "Have you talked to your father about this?" she asked.

149

"Uh-huh." Lilith nodded. "He said it's okay since he knows where you live."

Not good. Changing locks wasn't enough; she should have moved. No question about it; Kraven turned their kid into part monster. Her teeth…no wonder the kids call her names. "You can stay, but tomorrow, I'm taking you to a doctor." The smile she tried to muster felt frozen. "You can sleep in the spare bedroom. I'll loan you a nightgown. I'm making stewed beef for supper. Would you like some? You look starved."

Lilith shrugged, grinning. "I'll try it if it's got raw meat on a bone."

"I told you I don't eat this!" Lilith shouted when Tara placed the steaming hot stew before her. "Your food's bad for me."

"You haven't tasted it."

"It smells like shit!" Lilith shoved the plate off the table. Beef cubes and brown gravy sprayed the wall as the plate shattered on the linoleum floor.

"That wasn't necessary!" Tara shouted. "We don't live like animals here. You make a mess, you clean it up."

"I'm not cleaning up any damn mess." Lilith glared at her, teeth bared, defiance rising in her blue eyes. "Daddy said your people act worse than animals. Our government starved his family to death."

"Well, fiddle-dee-dee! I shared a lot of lunches with your father," Tara said. "I'll clean this up, but you're going to bed. I want you to do some thinking. You've got a serious problem."

"Dad says you're the one with a problem," Lilith said as she got up.

Tara sighed. Kraven had turned her little girl. Forget the doctor; Lilith needed ten specialists. There had to be some way to undo the spell. She wasn't prepared to destroy her kid, at least not yet. Tomorrow, she promised herself to take Lilith to the hospital if she had to drag her, kicking and screaming. Better yet, given Lilith's sharp teeth, shoot her up with a tranquilizer. With that in mind, Tara finished cleaning the floor.

Afterwards, she dialed Chris's number and got his answering machine. "Chris," she said into the recorder. "Things aren't going well. Call me when you get this message."

She hesitated, hoping Chris would pick up. He didn't. Perhaps he was tied up in some emergency, and couldn't get to his phone. Sharp teeth and a harsh temper made a deadly combination. She'd never make it to the hospital with Lilith by herself. Besides, without a social worker involved, no doctor would touch Lilith. *I can't think about this now,* she thought, shaking her head. *Maybe tomorrow, after I get some sleep. Tomorrow's another day.*

With a deep sigh, Tara showered and changed into her pajamas. After considering the maroon stains on Lilith's teeth, she placed her gun and a flashlight under her pillow and locked her bedroom door. Not good enough. She pulled her chest of draws in front of the door and turned on her nightlight.

Despite her precautions, she wouldn't rest easy. Thankfully, her bedroom had its own bathroom. No reason to venture through a dark hallway to take a leak in the middle of the night. She hugged her pillow, imagining Chris's sinewy arms around her. Despite her romantic feelings before sleep claimed her, skeletal revenants chased her in her dreams. During her wakeful moments, she listened for the patter of little feet, or small hands tampering with the lock.

Silence.

Eventually, her body relented, and she sank into a deep sleep.

Sometime later, the sensation of warm fluid trickling down her leg woke Tara. She sat upright and felt a lump between her calves. *This can't be real*, she thought.

Moonlight from outside threw shadows on the plaster walls. Her bedroom smelled like something had crawled inside it and died. The stink and sensation of balmy liquid bathing her feet warned that this was real.

Tara snapped on her crystal lamp. To her chagrin, her door was wide open, and her chest of drawers pushed aside. She threw back her covers, revealing a human head between her calves. Its mouth froze in a widened O of terror, with its black tongue hanging over the lips. Blood from the neck cavity soaked her pajama pants and bed sheets. Stringy blonde hair matted with blood surrounded its mottled face. Despite the damage, Tara recognized Dr. Barrett's features.

Dad said he'd teach those creeps a lesson. And teach them he did. Tara screamed.

Quickly, she snatched her gun and flashlight, and tucked them into her pajama pockets. She bolted from her room, leaving crimson footprints on the ivory carpet. This grisly surprise had Kraven's name all over it. No doubt he was sharing the doctor's body parts with Lilith. Teeth chattering, she paused outside Lilith's bedroom door.

Crunching noises. She placed her ear against the door. It sounded like someone chewing on a chicken breast. *Yeah, right.*

Her heartbeat thudded as she turned the knob and cracked the door. Lilith's room was draped in darkness. Tara's light washed over the walls, bureaus, and Lilith's bed. When it settled on the floor by the bed, pure terror surged through Tara.

Lilith sat cross-legged on the parquet floor. Blood trickled down her chin and dripped on the pink nightgown that Tara had loaned her. A severed women's arm lay on her lap.

"Lilith!" Tara shouted. "What are you *dooo-i-i-i-ng?*"

"I told you I'd eat if I got hungry," Lilith said in a what's-the-big-deal voice. She snapped on the lamp, illuminating her gruesome snack. "Dad brought me real food. Dr. Barrett smelled yummy, and we made her spoiled brat sorry. He left something for you, too. It's part of my birthday present."

"I don't know what you're talking about." Tara mustered a harsh voice and stared Lilith in the eye. "What you're doing is wrong. I do not allow consumption of human flesh in my home."

"Why not?" Lilith asked innocently.

"Because it's wrong. Monsters feed on humans, and that makes them dangerous. Kraven may think it's okay, but that doesn't make it right."

"We have to get back at the people who starved Daddy's family and friends. Daddy calls them the autobrats."

"You mean autocrats," Tara corrected her. "Kraven's had a hard life. Unfortunately, his experiences have warped—"

Bony hands seized Tara by the shoulders. She froze as they slowly turned her around.

Her old friend Kraven had returned.

Ten years hadn't improved his looks. Half of his face was covered by shriveled gray flesh. On the other half, an open gash stretched from eyeball to chin, with flecks of pink and gray flesh. Insects buzzed around him. He smiled, showing his teeth, all of them pointed and coated with blood. Like Lilith's. Saliva dripped from his lips onto his silver chain and red satin shirt.

Tara stared at his shirt and his gabardine black pants. *Fancy clothes. Probably got them from Dr. Barrett's significant other. I'll be damned if I let him see me afraid.*

Kraven clenched his fists. "Stop poisoning my daughter's mind. If you've got problems with her behavior, come to me."

"Fiddle-dee-dee! No one poisoned her mind except you. First you rape me—"

"Silence!" Kraven raked his fingers along the wall, scraping paint. To Tara, it sounded like the screaming of tortured people. "I haven't had dinner yet, and I'm hungry."

Tara's mouth snapped shut. The gun remained satcheled in her pocket. Kraven's eyes were on her, and she'd do well to remember that before fumbling for her gun. At one time, she used to enjoy chatting with this man. But that nice man was gone, destroyed by his greed for flesh. If she'd gone public about her romance with Chris, he'd be as dead as Dr. Barrett.

"That's better." A malignant grin curled on Kraven's lips. "Drop the holier-than-thou attitude, Tara. You tried to have an abortion. Some of my friends disguised themselves as hospital workers. They bugged Dr. Ashley's office and recorded all your conversation."

"That's impossible! They couldn't have gotten away with it because of their smell and rotting flesh."

"The newly turned revenants hadn't been dead long enough for decay to set in. These people knew how to set up spy bugs."

Kraven grabbed her shoulders. "One of the newly turned happened to be a pharmacist. He put a little something into your IV to distract your doctor."

"How did all of you get past the security guards and surveillance cameras?" Tara recoiled from his grasp. Her hand inched toward her gun, but curiosity about Kraven overrode her terror.

Kraven shrugged. "The guards made an easy dinner for us. As for your simplistic cameras, a little knowledge with surveillance devices works wonders."

"I suppose so," Tara said with defiance. "Your friend almost killed me."

"Dad, can I have Mom?" Lilith piped up eagerly. "You promised."

"In a little bit," Kraven told her. "Why don't you finish your snack somewhere else while I get her ready?"

"I want to stay and watch."

"Do as I tell you." Kraven raised his voice a notch.

Dribbling blood on the carpet, Lilith scampered off with her gruesome dinner.

My carpet. All my overtime pay gone down the sewer. Tara gagged on his rancid odor. She then jarred to attention at the harsh ring of her portable phone. Chris was returning her call, no doubt. She'd left the phone in the kitchen; she remembered that now. But it was coming from some place much closer.

"Looking for this?" Grinning, Kraven held up her phone, flashing and ringing in his hand. "My, my, Tara, you should be more careful with your things. No one's coming here to help you."

With that, he hurled the phone. It smashed through the window, leaving a jagged hole in the glass in the night. Watching it fly, he laughed. While his eyes trained toward the window, Tara withdrew her gun and pulled the trigger. Gunfire roared, exploding Kraven's head in a spray of maggots and decayed flesh. His body slumped to the floor.

Tara, what are you doing? A voice inside quivered. *You were trained to heal.* But she couldn't heal someone who was already dead. The Kraven she knew died ten years ago, replaced by a revenant, a monster.

Patter of feet. Thuds on the door. "Mom! Dad!" Lilith screamed. "What are you doing?"

The knob rattled but did not give. Kraven must have locked it in his bid to keep would-be rescuers from interfering. Still, Tara was going to have to deal with Lilith. Dead or not, Kraven was still her father.

"What did you do to Dad, Mom?" More rattling, followed by thumps.

Quickly, Tara pushed the dresser in front of the door. All those workouts in the gym were paying off. Breath coming out in pants, she shook Kraven. No movement. She rooted through his pockets for a plastic card. Somehow, he'd gotten a copy of her bar-coded card she used to exit and enter her apartment. As she searched, her fingers slid over an envelope. She two-fingered the envelope from Kraven's pocket.

With trembling fingers, she ripped it open and held the contents to the lamp. Ignoring the thuds at the door, she continued reading.

RAISING THE DEAD

Light four candles at nightfall and cast them to the four directions (North, South, East and West). Then place a glass of water at the base of each candle. Place human bone, hair, or fingernails in a copper bowl and ignite. Place the bowl in the center of the four candles, thereby completing the pentagram of negative space. Lay a solid line of moist earth in a complete circle around the candles. On the outside of that circle, lay another circle of common salt.

NOW BEGIN THE INCANTATION BELOW AND SPEAK LOUDLY AND CLEARLY

HIC ENHIC EN SPIRITUM
SED NON INCORPORE
EVOKARE LEMURES DE MORTUIS
DECRETUM ESPUGNARE
DE ANGELUS BAALBERITH
EN INFERNO INREMEABLIS

NOW VERY, VERY LOUD AND FAST

WA WA TA NA SLAM
WA WA TA NA SLAM
WA WA TA NA SLAM
WA WA TA NA SLAM
WA WA TA NA SLAM

EXTINGUISH CANDLES

"They must've used this incantation to raise the dead on the street," she concluded aloud. "So that's what that man in black was doing."

Tara's eyes dropped to the sack by Lilith's bed. She'd never gotten around to asking Lilith about that bag. *I'll bet she's got candles and other contraband in there.*

The door splintered. Lilith screeched at the top of her voice. The dresser wouldn't keep her at bay forever. Tara gazed forlornly toward the window, ten floors above ground, and no fire escape. Chris did promise to show up if she didn't answer. *Oh, Chris, please hurry,* she thought. *Don't know if I've got the guts to shoot a kid, even if she is dead.*

Just as she reached for the sack, the door split in pieces. The dresser toppled. Tara leaped back. Not quickly enough. The molding from the dresser slammed on her right ankle. Cracking sounds like twigs followed, and white agony flared through her foot and ankle. The gun dropped. Screaming, Tara toppled to the floor besides Kraven.

Lilith barreled through the door. Plopping on top of Tara's lap, she straddled her hips and shrieked. Those teeth. All those sharp teeth. Hands braced against Lilith's shoulders, she mustered all the strength she could to keep Lilith from getting within biting distance.

"You monster!" Lilith hollered. "You took away my daddy. He warned me that you'd think you were too good for the likes of us."

She thrust toward Tara's face, but Tara fought her. It was getting harder. Her pajama seams ripped. Sharp points of her sweat-drenched hair pricked her face. For a frail-looking kid, Lilith was damned strong. She'd never realized that revenant children were as strong as adults. Sweat spilled down Tara's forehead, her limbs trembled, her foot pain worse. The dresser kept her pinned by the ankle.

Lilith's fingers went for her eyes, and Tara swiveled her head to the right. This weakened her hold on Lilith. In the next instant, Lilith went for her shoulder, mouth gaping. Tara smashed the side of her hand into the bottom of Lilith's jaw. Lilith flew backwards, gripping her head and neck.

The gun. She groped on her right, and felt it on the floor, a trusty weapon ready to save her. Too slow. Lilith was coming at her again. This revenant, a thing called from death, was not her child. The blow Tara delivered might fell a human, but Lilith appeared immune to human assaults. As it was, she needed both hands to restrain Lilith.

"Quit fighting me," Lilith hollered. "You're my present. Dad promised I could have you."

"I'm not your damned present. And you're not my child."

A door opened. Her front door. Hushed voices. Footsteps. *Did Lilith hear them? Evidently not. She's too busy salivating!* "I was hoping that a doctor could reverse what Kraven did to you. Guess I was wrong."

"No one can undo the spell. He said I was too young to turn, but one of the others got hungry and killed me. So Dad had to bring me back. That's how come I eat meat on a bone, and why people smell so good."

Blood red tears rolled down her face, and she let out a screech. "You killed my daddy. I'll get you."

She went for Tara's throat. Tara shoved her shoulders, but blaring novas of white hot agony blazed through her foot and ankle. Her shoulders and arms ached. If only she could get her foot free. If only—

Head up, eyes rolled back and mouth gaping, Lilith angled for her throat. A dart whickered through the air, slamming Lilith in the back. She slumped on Tara, a limp form.

"Tara!" Chris stepped over the battered door and dresser, tranquilizer gun in his hand, followed by two officers. One tall and lanky, the other with crooked scars on his face. "My God! What the hell happened here?"

Rushing forward, the two officers lifted the dresser off of Tara's foot. That relieved her pain, but not by much. At least she could move. She pedaled away from Kraven, pushing with her good foot. "Zombies, revenants…whatever you want to call them," she managed between panting breaths. "They turned my kid, and they were coming after me. Lilith…the child…she tried to…tried to…"

"Easy, Tara," Chris said. "I've got to splint that foot."

"We saw what happened," the tall officer nodded. His nametag identified him as Richard Bogart. "Sorry it took so long to get here. The elevator wasn't working."

"Kraven probably broke it. Like he did my phone. Like he trashed my condo." Tara looked at Chris, who splinted her foot with cardboard and towels. "I found this spell." She held up the paper. "There must be something that can reverse what they did to Lilith."

Chris and the two officers exchanged looks. Finally, the scar-faced officer spoke up. "We already know about that. That's why our government banned wax candles. Our priority is getting you out of here and to the hospital. But first..."

The officer pointed his gun at the sleeping child.

"Officer, don't," Chris said, holding up his hand. "Wait until we get Tara out of here. She doesn't need to see that. It's still her kid."

"Damn right." Tara's voice hitched with unshed tears. "I made this mess by allowing her in my house. So I have to clean it up. Chris, does she have a pulse?"

Chris palpated Lilith's throat and shook his head. "No pulse."

Tara looked at Lilith, who lay still, appearing dead or asleep. To her right, Kraven, lying prone; beige fluid spilled from a bullet hole in his head. The smell pouring off both of them was awful. "Stand back, guys," she said, holding her nose. "Dear God, forgive me."

The men stepped back, and she placed the barrel against Lilith's head. Another bull roar as blood and brains spattered. She looked at Chris, a tear trickling down her cheek. "I'm sorry."

"This wasn't your fault," Chris said, taking her hand. "Shit happens. I'm not letting you go through this alone."

"Tara, there's an ambulance downstairs," Bogart said in a let's-move-on voice. "They've got ten floors to get the stretcher here, or you could try hopping on one foot with two of us helping you."

"I'll hop," she told her rescuers. "The sooner I'm out of here, the better."

Scarface ran ahead, speaking into his walkie-talkie. Chris and Bogart got on either side of Tara. Arms laced around her shoulders and back, the two men hoisted her to her one good foot. Slowly, they made their way out of her apartment. Down the hall, past the defunct elevators. Each hop jarred her foot. Her eyes moistened. The hall spun around her. "I'd better sit," she said through clenched teeth. "We're going to have to wait for your cavalry to bring the stretcher."

"No need to be sorry." Chris lowered her to the floor and hugged her. "I got your message, but the ambulance had just brought Gloria to the hospital. The things got her mother and father. They would have gotten Gloria, too, if the police hadn't arrived. That was when I knew things were bad here."

Liquid fear ran through Tara's veins, making her shiver. There were more like Lilith and Kraven out there. Dead, yet alive. And dangerous.

Shuffling footsteps. A moaning voice.

"Shit!" Bogart glared at his partner. "How many of those things got in here?"

"Hell if I know—"

A figure came running out, eyes dead white and burn-scarred cheeks, brandishing a knife. Tara's surroundings blurred. Her head swam. Through the blur, she made out Bogart cocking his gun. A blast followed, and she screamed as she fainted.

Two months after paramedics had carried her down ten flights of steps, Tara budgeted her time between Hartland Clinic and her new home, a condominium she and Chris purchased together. She was still wearing an air cast and getting by on crutches. Kelly promised Tara she'd hold her position. According to the doctors, the injury would leave her with a limp, but she *would* walk, and eventually return to work. *When?* Tara wondered. *No one has any answers.*

During Chris's long hours with his patients at the hospital, Tara surfed the Net too much, keeping abreast of the latest casualties wrought by the dead walkers. Sleep eluded her most nights, and during the little that she got, her nightmares were brutal.

After dinner together at a café one night, Chris drove her to their apartment. She dreaded the walk from the elevator. The corridor looked five miles long, with thick carpeting, not easy to navigate with crutches. Tara began loping to the apartment, teeth clenched, purse satcheled in her elbow, hands gripping the crutches. *Clickety-clack, clickety-clack,* like the sound of skeletal feet.

Her right foot throbbed. The doctors had stopped giving her heavy pain medicine. More than anything, she longed to return to patient care. Each time she went to the hospital, she asked her caregivers how soon she could resume working.

Everyone she asked gave her blank looks and noncommittal answers. *Clickety-clack, clickety-clack.*

Now for a delicate operation – getting her plastic key card from her purse without dropping anything. "I've got it," Chris offered, putting his arm around her.

"My therapists want me to get used to using the crutches and opening the door. In case you're at work."

"Good point."

"Okay then." With a deep sigh, she leaned her crutches against a wall. As she turned, her good foot caught against a snag in the rug. She stumbled and dropped her purse.

"Dammit!" Her crutches went flying.

Tara leaned against the wall and fought the tears rolling down her cheeks. "I hate this," she told Chris. "Scarlett would never cry in a hall."

"That may be true," Chris said, reaching for his own key. "But if that prima donna had to fight those angry revenants, she'd never survive."

"You've got that right," Tara said, laughing through the tears.

The door clicked open, and the laughter died in her throat. The apartment was awfully dark, and it stank. Tara recognized the smell – rotting tomatoes and dried blood.

A figure leaped up from behind the sofa, and in the light from the hall, Tara made out Lilith's skeletal face. Lilith brandished a kitchen knife. "You killed my father," she shrieked through a mouth full of razor sharp teeth. "Both of you shall die."

Tara turned to run, lost her balance, and fell to the floor. "Chris!" she hollered. Where did he go? She crawled to the door. Something pulled at her right leg and gave way. She thought she'd made it until she turned to see her leg a bleeding stump. Lilith leaped on top of her, knocking her flat.

"Die!" she screamed.

Tara sat on the floor, rubbing her head. Chris really had unlocked the door. He'd stepped out to reset the lock, and she'd pulled the drapes before they left the apartment. Although she fell, the figure was just Spook, Chris's German shepherd dog. The dog looked at her with wide brown eyes and whimpered. He was a cute thing, chestnut-brown coat with a white underbelly and white streaking his head and back.

Chris was beside her seconds later, holding her and kissing her head. "Honey, are you hurt?"

"I'm okay." She rubbed her side. "I landed on my hip. Nothing's broken."

"You're going to need an x-ray." Tension edged into his voice. "You saw Lilith again. Was that why you were rubbing your head?"

Tara nodded. "It's not the first flashback I had, and it won't be the last." She gazed at him with pleading eyes. "My foot's okay. Can we hold off on the x-ray until tomorrow? If I'm hurting, I'll get one."

"Sure." The tension faded from his voice like air let out of a balloon. "Fortunately, Spook is good at sniffing out revenants and zombies. Right now, he needs to be let out. I was going to ask you to come along, but now…"

"Chris, I'm okay." She managed a weak grin. "Hey, Spook! Want to go for a walk?"

What am I doing? She shifted her gaze between Chris and the dog. *I've never walked with Spook before. I must be a glutton for punishment.*

After getting to her feet, Tara went to the kitchen for aspirin, followed by Spook. That didn't change what she was about to do – attempt to keep up with an energetic dog on crutches.

Except...

She wanted to do it because she owed Spook the effort. Spook remained at her side since the day she left the hospital. When she woke up at night, screaming after a nightmare, Spook was at her bedside, guarding her against any monsters that might intrude. He stood at the ready while she did her exercises and lay next to her foot when she cried out in pain.

More to the point, she didn't want to be alone. A smart part of her believed that the smart revenants could break into their apartment any time. Tara tucked biscuits in her pocket and turned at the sound of footsteps behind her. Kraven and Lilith were shuffling from the kitchen, skeletal hands outstretched.

She squeezed her eyes shut, opened them, and saw the same old nothing. *I'll think about it tomorrow.* "Let's go, Spook," she said, heading to the door. "I think I'm going to be okay."

"Are you sure about this?" Chris gave her a doubtful look.

"I have to get used to being alone. Just not tonight, okay? Besides..." She grinned at the dog. "You're going to have a battle getting Spook to leave me. So I have to be okay."

They went to the condominium's dog park, an enclosed area where people allowed their dogs to roam without a leash. Every so often, she fed Spook a biscuit. At the park, she rested on a bench in a well lit area while Chris unhooked Spook's leash and let him go.

"Chris, I'm sorry I scared you earlier," Tara said when he joined her. "I'm trying to fight the flashbacks. I can't help thinking that if some kind of spell raised these people from the dead, there must be something to send them back to hell."

"Sometimes I think that, too," Chris said, regarding her with saddened eyes. "Unfortunately, our government officials are too busy sitting around with their thumbs up their asses to do anything about it."

"Maybe they just need to think outside the box." Tara raised her right forefinger. "I'm talking magic, not bombs or explosives. Kraven and his followers used some kind of spell to make the dead rise. There must be a way to undo that spell, and I intend to find it."

"Perhaps a combination of science and magic could undo his spell. If it's possible, Tara, I will help you find a way. But first, you've got to give your body time to heal."

"Time." Tara sighed. "I don't do patience well."

"Can you do trust?" Chris took her hand and caressed her cheek. "I'm not letting you fight those beings alone. I love you, Tara. Every day, I thank God I got to you in time."

"I love you, too." She gazed at him, badly wanting to put the nightmares behind her. It wouldn't happen any time soon, at least in a country overrun by the dead.

Chris retrieved a wooden ring box from his jacket pocket. After opening it, he withdrew a wad of tissue paper and handed her a diamond ring with sapphires. "This ring belonged to my mother," he told her. "I want you to have it. Tara, will you marry me?"

Tara gasped. She allowed him to slip the ring on her finger. Its diamond and two sapphires glittered amidst swirls of white and yellow gold. The ring exuded a faint aroma of soap, but that was okay. Very much okay. She would have given anything for a family. And Chris—he'd been oh, so patient with her recovery, never raising his voice. Sometimes he laughed at things she said. Not a hint of her father or Dr. Desatnick. "Yes," she shouted with glee. "I'd love to marry you."

She threw her arms around him and hugged him. He bent down to kiss her, and as he did so, he dropped the box. It clattered to the pavement.

Chris bent over to retrieve it, but the box landed out of his reach. Tara retrieved it and grimaced at the acrid odor. The inner cushion had popped out, followed by a stone that rattled by her foot. Not a stone, but a finger bone coated with debris. Perhaps one of his mother's missing fingers. *Clickety-clack.*

I'll think about it tomorrow. Tara squeezed her eyes shut. She opened them again, but the smell was still there. Chris's face had gone ashen. He was hurriedly stuffing the box into his pocket. "Chris...what happened here?" she asked.

He lowered his eyes, dragging his fingers through his hair. "I found the ring near my mother, so I had it cleaned. I never thought to check the box. I'm so sorry, Tara."

"Don't be. Your mother was a kind woman, and the revenants are shrewd." Tara embraced him again. "Are you okay?"

He nodded, still trembling. "I'm okay because we're going to fix it."

"Of course, we will." Tara held the ring up to the lamplight and mustered her best smile. It looked beautiful, but she got to thinking about

Chris's mother and how she'd died. Perhaps the revenants were sending her and Chris a message. One they'd need to answer soon. She smiled at Chris and took his hand. They'd answer it together.

About the Contributors

Barbara Custer:

Since her high school days, Barbara has enjoyed a good scary flick whether it involved traditional monsters or invading aliens. She fantasized about composing such tales, but the writing didn't begin until 1990, when a college professor encouraged her to try writing as a way to grieve over her mother's death. A Stephen King fan, she began with horror fiction, and it enabled her to turn over her grief. Most of her protagonists grieve over deceased parents. Her horror and science fiction short stories have appeared in numerous small press magazines. She later moved on to science fiction and dark fantasy novels to appeal to a wider audience.

Night to Dawn published some of her work before the former editor retired. She's been editing the magazine since 2004.

Her first novel, *Twilight Healer,* has gone through three printings. Author Tom Johnson collaborated with Barbara on an anthology, *Blood Moons and Nightscapes.* The anthology ran for three years. Last year, Tom and Barbara collaborated on *Alien Worlds* and *Starship Invasions,* also short stories collections. By the end of this year, she plans to release *Steel Rose,* a book featuring a young woman whose search for a cure leads her to a romance with a Kryszka alien and a battle against zombies.

In most of her tales, Barbara brings her background as a respiratory therapist to the printed page, blending it with supernatural horror. With "Death's Dividend" and "One Last Favor," the political elephant appears in the room that is the health care crisis. Her medical training provided the technology and grist for the written pages in these tales. Alas, she fears that the political elephant will turn into the monster it becomes in these stories if Congress doesn't address it now.

In 2008, she began publishing books through the Night to Dawn imprint. Novels by Tom Johnson, Neil Benson, Rod Marsden, and others have gone to print through NTD and many of them enjoyed four-star reviews or better on Amazon. Tom followed up his share of the tales with *Pulp Echoes,* an anthology of pulp tales, and *Cold War Heroes,* which details the day to day life of a soldier. Barbara's on Facebook, Linkedin, Twitter, and The Writers Coffeehouse forums. Look for the photos with all the Mylar balloons, and you will find her.

Barbara lives in Pennsylvania. When she's not working on my projects, she's shopping for Mylar balloons or enjoying a great fright flick.

To contact Barbara, e-mail her at barbaracuster@hotmail.com and put Night to Dawn on the subject line.

Website address: www.bloodredshadow.com

Facebook: www.facebook.com/barbara.custer

 **Teresa Tunaley**: Originating from the UK but now residing in the Canary Islands for the last 10 years, freelance artist Teresa Tunaley finds more time to devote to her love of art and painting. For more than 30 years she has been doodling with pencils and dabbling with watercolors. More recently she has been painting traditionally in oil and creating large canvasses full of color and life. Sometimes she uses a more modern technique using software such as Photoshop, Corel Draw and Paint Shop Pro to produce her creations for online publications.

During her art career, she has produced countless illustrations, book covers and paintings. Along with published stories and poetry, she can be credited with award winning cover art and illustrations for author stories. Her work can be seen online and in print across the UK, US, Canada and Europe.

May 2011, she opened a new Exhibition in Puerto del Santiago (Tenerife, Spain) entitled Tutto per la vita (All for the life). She has over 30 works on show and is hoping to be selected to participate in the Capitals annual Art Festival. Should she win, there will be invitations to exhibit her work in a whirlwind trip across Spain and Italy.

Touching and spectacular "has been the inauguration; Tutto Per la vita" Some thirty of their works appeared, giving you a journey to Spain, Africa, America, Japan and Thailandia. The work was intense with feeling, in full color and textures, where figures, landscapes and moments will leave the visitor with a memory of a magical trip."

Jose Francisco Morales
Comisario de la Exposicion (Tenerife)
http://www.artesigloxxi.org

I like to think that I am very versatile in my choice of subject matter - my new surroundings provide the inspiration for me to paint on a daily basis and the fact that others may enjoy my work gives me the confidence to continue.

Website: www.artstopper.com

www.ingramcontent.com/pod-product-compliance
Lightning Source LLC
Chambersburg PA
CBHW031913190626
46814CB00003BA/1295